BEFORE TAKEOFF

BEFORE TAKEOFF

ADI ALSAID

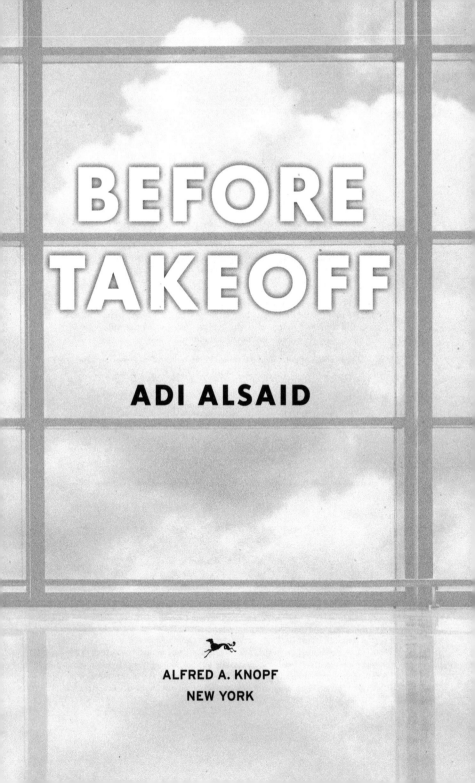

ALFRED A. KNOPF

NEW YORK

THIS IS A BORZOI BOOK PUBLISHED BY ALFRED A. KNOPF

This is a work of fiction. Names, characters, places, and incidents either are the product of the author's imagination or are used fictitiously. Any resemblance to actual persons, living or dead, events, or locales is entirely coincidental.

Text copyright © 2022 by Adi Alsaid
Jacket images: figures in airport © Jasmin Merdan/Getty Images; palm tree in sand © Roine Magnusson/Getty Images; snow © Philippe Marion/Getty Images; cracked window © fongfong2/Getty Images. Chair and luggage carousel used under license from Shutterstock.com

Visit us on the Web! GetUnderlined.com

Educators and librarians, for a variety of teaching tools, visit us at RHTeachersLibrarians.com

Library of Congress Cataloging-in-Publication Data is available upon request.
ISBN 978-0-593-37576-1 (trade) — ISBN 978-0-593-37578-5 (ebook) —
ISBN 978-0-593-56833-0 (int'l ed.)

The text of this book is set in 11-point Adobe Text Pro.
Interior design by Cathy Bobak

Printed in the United States of America
10 9 8 7 6 5 4 3 2 1
First Edition

Random House Children's Books supports the First Amendment and celebrates the right to read.

This one, I think, is for me.

ONE

\\\\\\\

IN CONCOURSE B OF HARTSFIELD-JACKSON ATLANTA International Airport, in between a bookstore that consistently miscategorizes its books and a franchise restaurant whose staff consistently ranks as the happiest in the annual airport-wide employee survey, there's a blinking green light that will soon cause all hell to break loose. It's on a wall with no signage to indicate what it could possibly be.

The only person who seems to notice it is James Herrera.

He's got his big headphones on, listening to music that drowns out the sounds of the airport. We would list all these sounds, except the music is loud for us too, and we're as interested in the blinking light as our new friend James is. There seems to be no particular rhythm to the light, although at the moment it kind of syncs up with the music in a cool way. James looks for the cracks of a hidden door, or a camera keeping its eye on the light. A woman walking by accidentally bumps

James's leg with her rolling suitcase, then turns to give him a mean look.

James shakes his head, hooking his thumbs through the straps of his backpack. He scans the passersby, waiting for the authority figure who will tell him to move along, maybe blame him for putting the light there. James is brown-skinned and sixteen, and he's used to hearing the bizarre accusations the world throws his way. Used to it the way you get used to a toothache, or someone's stench on the bus.

Families walk by all in a row, oblivious to their slow-moving obstruction of the hallway. Lethargic but annoyed airport employees driving carts yell for people to get out of the way. Cute girls, backpackers he feels a pang of jealousy toward, suits on their phones.

Back at gate B36, his family waits for their flight, fast-food leftovers at their feet, eyes on the monitor announcing their delay, daring it to push back takeoff again, complaints already on the tips of their tongues. James stares at the light, thinks about returning to school, junior year continuing on, leading inexorably toward the future, a familiar flutter of fear in his chest. Only a matter of time, the flutter says, until it's your turn. Can't escape bad luck forever.

"What do you think it is?" the girl we haven't yet met says. We can hear this, but James can't, though he does pick up on the presence of someone else nearby, either watching him or watching the light. He feels her at the edge of his periphery, and his senses immediately call out: Girl! He turns a little to confirm, but real cool about it, obviously.

Then he notices she's talking, and he pulls his headphones down so they loop around his neck. "Sorry," he says, and then tries to explain further, but his voice trails off, like it knows he has no idea what to say and it will have no part of the interaction.

"What do you think it is?" she says again, this time audibly to all parties involved. There's a hint of a foreign accent that James can't place. Which, come on, James, it's been a sentence. Give it a second.

James just shrugs, hating himself for not being instantly funny or smooth.

"It's an American thing, no? See something, say something. Should we be saying something?"

James looks at their surroundings, presumably to find someone to say something to, because what if it really is a thing that could cause harm? But also to get a better look at the girl. Except he forgets—miraculously—the first part and focuses on the second. Dark hair, light brown eyes, nose ring, lips that would make you not pay attention for a whole semester if she was sitting anywhere near you in the classroom. And, of course, the girl notices that he's not looking around for anyone, just flat out staring at her.

"Shit, I'm sorry," he says, when he notices her noticing.

"Sorry about what?"

"I, like, looked at you. Too long. I don't know why I couldn't just stand here and look at the green light and shoot the shit with you about it without having to look at you. I'm sorry. It sucks I did that."

The girl smirks and looks at him curiously. We know this, but James doesn't, because his embarrassment has caused him to look away. "I don't mind. People look at each other, it's a thing we do."

James nods, feels the urge to say something intelligent in response, resists the desire to look at her again. Behind them, a collective groan emanates from gate B17 as the airline representative announces that the 5:30 p.m. flight to Kansas City will now be departing at 9:00 p.m. The green light blinks on, then off.

James and the girl stare silently for a while. A flutter—a different one this time—in James's chest tells him this is a moment he will always remember. Or maybe that he still gets nervous around girls. The cheerful voice of a waitress at the nearby restaurant cuts through the din of the airport. She offers a businesswoman the chance to make her margarita a double for an extra dollar fifty.

"It's gotta be a camera, right?" James says. "Some sort of security thing?"

The girl chuckles. "I wonder how much footage they have of people just staring at it, wondering what the hell it is." She takes a step closer, reaching her hand out to it. She's got her sleeves rolled up to her forearm, and he notices her arm. Not any specific thing about it (delicate wrist, barely noticeable hairs, a single freckle like the stray mark of a pen), just the fact that it's there. That she's got skin and muscle and bone, and all of it is very close to him.

"Don't touch it, man! What if you're not supposed to?"

"Oh please," she says, but her hand slows its approach, lingering just far enough away so that the glow of the light reaches back out and brushes her fingers. The light, too, seems somehow excited by her proximity. It starts blinking almost imperceptibly faster, matching its rhythm to James's accelerating heartbeat.

She looks over at James, raising an eyebrow, grinning. James can't handle that look on her face, and he starts to come up with an escape plan. This is the last thing in the world he wants, escape. But his brain is overwhelmed by the stimulation and demands some distance from this girl and her skin and the way she looks at him. He turns away, biting his bottom lip, clutching at his shoulder straps. "I should probably go back to my gate," he says softly, practically a stage whisper for our benefit.

The girl's hand pulls back from the light. Disappointed, the light stops blinking for a second, then returns to its regular rhythm. Does she look hurt? James can't tell. His brain wants him to just move on, pull the headphones back over his head, not look like a moron.

Then she smiles. "I'll walk with you. Where are you headed?"

"Um, B36," he says, motioning toward the end of the hall.

"No, I mean where are you flying to?"

"Oh, right. Chicago."

They start walking away from the light. Late-afternoon sun glints in the windows, casting the airport in a golden hue that makes people squint. "Is that where you live?"

"Yeah. Sorry, I should have said that. We're going back home. We were visiting family in Tampa for Christmas. Which is a stupid place to be for Christmas, but my parents hate the snow."

"You like the snow?"

"Better than rain. We go to Florida for the sunshine, supposedly, but it fuckin' rains all week. At least you can play in snow. It's pretty to look at. Rain, you just sit indoors. Watching *Family Feud* and shit."

"Sure. But when it's cold, you sit indoors anyway. It could look nice out, but as soon as you want to escape and enjoy the beautiful day, you're miserable with cold and you just want to go back inside."

"I guess. But still, fuck the rain," he says. His brain goes: Dude, are you arguing about weather with this random attractive girl who, for some reason, is actually talking to you? You've imagined an exact scenario like this at least a hundred times, and it never goes to an argument—it goes to you being smooth and shit. And the other side of his brain goes: Yo, we don't know how to be smooth and shit. Plus, I really hate rain. "Where are you from?"

The girl sighs, puts her hands in her pockets. He realizes she's not carrying anything with her, no bags, which feels weird at an airport, even though he's guessing she left her stuff with her parents or whatever while she took a walk. He could have done that too, but his little sister is a nosy brat and likes to snoop. Sure, he doesn't really have anything for her to snoop on, but that's beside the point. "I hate that question."

"How come?"

"Because I have a French dad and a Thai mom but was born in Switzerland, then moved to Jakarta, then Buenos Aires, and now I'm in Canada. So if I say only one of those places, I feel like I'm lying, or people want more of an explanation because I look the way I do and have this accent that morphs unless I'm focusing on how I'm talking. Then I have to give this whole spiel anyway. And I swear to God if you laugh and say, 'So, you're from everywhere!' I will punch you in the neck. I'm not from everywhere. I'm from a few places."

"I wasn't going to," James says, though she just saved him from doing exactly that. "That's cool, though, about your accent. It just changes? Like it's alive?"

She laughs, then adjusts her nose ring. "That's a good way to think about it, I guess. It drives me nuts sometimes. I hate it when people think I'm automatically interesting because of it. Plenty of dickheads and bores have accents."

James considers this and sees how it could get old. They're at gate B25 already, quickly approaching his family and the lone empty seat that's waiting for him. His brain is still not quite sure how to handle this conversation, but it's starting to become a little more convinced that they should stick to it instead of just running away. The green light, for now, has been forgotten. "So, where are you flying to?" he asks.

"Toronto, then Quebec. It's been a long day. We keep getting rerouted. We were in France, visiting my grandparents." She walks with her head down for a few steps, glances away from James. "It's probably the last time I'll see them," she says, then turns to look back at him. Their eyes meet and James doesn't know how people go around making eye contact with people that they're attracted to. "Sorry, I shouldn't just say that to you. We don't know each other."

"I'm cool with it. If, you know, you just need to talk." Here, more evidence: tragedy befalls everyone, and James will not avoid it forever.

She smiles in that cute way where, like, only part of her mouth is smiling. And who knows why that's cute but it works. "No, it's okay. Too intense. We don't know each other's names yet. I'll tell you about my tragically moribund grandparents some other time."

James nods, stomach fluttering at the implication that they'll see each other again, despite the obviousness that they won't. He spots his family's gate up ahead and wishes he hadn't led them in this direction. Should have taken a detour somewhere, though the terminal is just one long hallway, unless you take the escalators down to get to the other concourses. "I think that's something cool about air travel: how it makes people more prone to confessions. I overhear people on flights doing that all the time, saying way more than you usually would to a stranger. Like you know you'll never see them again and you might as well talk about real shit."

"See, I've never had that experience. Airports always feel more isolating to me, not the opposite. Usually when I travel, I'm with family and can't find an excuse to step away and meet any fellow travelers. Or if I'm on my own, I end up being shy, eating quietly at the food court or by my gate. I look around and feel this immense curiosity about the people near me, a desire to know everything about them, talk to them, find out about the shape of their lives. But I don't know how to start, and so I end up frozen, feeling lonelier, further away from them. I fantasize romantically about people in airports more than anywhere else, but I haven't had a single profound conversation with anyone."

"Until now," James says, surprising himself.

The dude working at the coffee shop they just passed—who's been eavesdropping on the pair since they entered earshot—resists the urge to say, "Ooooh!" and pump a fist in the air. He loves these moments from his job and wishes they came more frequently. People being good to each other, real connection happening, moments that are gems.

"True, until now."

They look at each other and smile—James briefly, so as not

to come across like he knows what he just said was smooth, the girl with a bite of her bottom lip, like she knows he's trying to hold back. They're at the gate now; James's family are slumped in their chairs, faces slack with boredom and despair. James fiddles with the cord of his headphones a bit, then notices the monitor at the gate says his flight is delayed another forty minutes.

"I'm James, by the way," he says, still fiddling with the cord. He wonders if he should stretch a hand out or something, but this girl's so worldly, and handshakes seem like such a weird, impersonal thing to him, formal and distinctly American. He thinks about how his grandparents greet everyone with a kiss on the cheek, how he's never felt fully comfortable doing that.

"Michelle," she says.

And then the airport goes dark.

TWO

\\\\\\\

THERE ARE A COUPLE OF SCREAMERS, LIKE FROM A horror movie. Most of them are not in the B gates, so their shrieks don't make it to Michelle and James. Our two heroes stand in the hallway made eerie by the lack of electricity. Only the weak golden rays of the fading sun illuminate the terminal (and not far behind them, the blinking green light casts its iota of luminescence). Their hands accidentally graze against each other, and they both pull away.

Others are frozen in place, waiting with bated breath for what will come next. Some do not notice at all, busy as they are with their personal screens, their e-books, their tossing attempts at little naps in between flights. Plenty of people clutch at their armrests, or at their belongings, feeling fear without being able to say exactly why a little darkness scares them.

The lights flicker on again. Monitors come back to life, and one by one each flight gets delayed another hour, like falling dominoes. One person yells out, asks if they're under attack, not bothering to direct the question to anyone, just lobbing it at the air in hopes that someone will respond and tell them what to do.

"That was weird," James says, his voice on the verge of breaking. Wasn't me, he prepares to say. His fingers clutch his backpack straps, knuckles tight. What does this little blip mean for him, for his life? A silly question, maybe, but one that's been tugging at him all the time, even before getting to the airport, even before Florida. Since the fire, since the night with Marcus, since a million little clues that have added up to the one thing he knows is true: the world can change in an instant.

People are sitting up straighter, ears perked, like prey on alert. A few make their way to the check-in counters, and you can see the airline personnel starting to hate their lives. The line is ten deep in a matter of seconds.

A man jogs past James and Michelle, a laptop bag slung diagonally across his chest bouncing with every step he takes. James looks over at his family, and they seem to have barely noticed the commotion. His mom's reading, his dad's doing a crossword, Ava is sitting by an outlet with her phone plugged in. He lets this sight calm him down. It's strange to him how often others look relaxed when his insides are churning with panic.

"Looks like my flight's not going anywhere anytime soon," James says.

No PA announcements offer an explanation for the power outage, and though there's a gentle murmur of excitement and confusion in the air, things seem to be back to normal. He usually hates the lack of control associated with a flight delay, but right now it feels like the universe is granting him an extra hour to keep being nervous around Michelle.

"Wanna get some coffee?" Michelle answers.

Oh, the ways heartbeats can respond to a sentence. James avoids eye contact, not wanting to reveal that he's incapable of being chill. "Sure," he says. "Let me go tell my folks."

He steps over to his parents, who look up from their airport pastimes with a mix of bored resignation and silent pleas that what James will say will rescue them from this hell of inconveniences.

"I'm gonna keep walking around a bit, since we're delayed," he says.

"Take your sister with you," his mom says.

He's about to protest, but Ava beats him to it. "No thanks, I'm good."

Their mom gives Ava a playful kick. "Lazy." Then she looks back at James, and he quietly prays that she notices Michelle standing behind him, that she'll tease him, making it somehow more real. "Keep your eye on the flight boards. I don't want them to say 'final call' and sit here wondering where you are."

"C'mon, you know how I am. I'll be in line before you even notice they're boarding."

"Have fun," his dad says, his tone implying that there is no such thing as fun inside this building.

James and Michelle turn back around the way they came, toward the light and the bookstore, which is home not just to misshelved books but also a café. They walk quietly, and James wonders if the magical ability to talk slunk away during the power outage, never to return. At the counter, he orders something sweet and blended. Michelle orders a simple black coffee. He lets her lead them toward a table at the edge of the bookstore, facing out at the terminal.

They're within view of some departure monitors, and James double-checks for his flight. "Shit, the whole airport is delayed," he says, wondering if that carries a larger significance. His mind starts going toward extremes: a tornado, an attack, a fire.

"Kinda cool," Michelle says, popping the cap off her coffee and stirring in two packets of sugar. "I hope it lasts all night. Like one big slumber party. We'll eat junk food and watch movies, stay up past our bedtimes and whisper about our crushes and our fears."

James tucks his hands into the pockets of his sweatshirt, focuses on Michelle to keep his worries at bay. "That'd be dope. I miss slumber parties. Although my friends never really talked about our crushes. We'd play video games and have pizza, then keep ourselves awake making stupid jokes."

"You never talked about love with your friends?"

"Not really."

Michelle rolls her eyes. "Typical men. But you probably thought about it, right? Girls, boys, whatever."

James chuckles. "Yeah, man. All the time."

Michelle arches an eyebrow at him. "Do you call everyone 'man'?"

"Shit, you caught on," James responds, blushing. "I say it a lot, to everyone. Trying to break the habit."

"I don't really care. Defaults to the male too much for my liking, but better than you addressing me as 'woman.'"

He unloops the headphones from his neck, folds them away, and puts them in his backpack. Maybe that slight act is enough of a distraction to keep his brain from overthinking, maybe it's something else, but James feels the need to go on. "I remember the first girl I had a crush on: Sandra. I'd start making fun of her to my friends just so I could talk about her. I even remember being at a slumber party at my friend's house, all of us in sleeping bags in his living room. We'd watched some horror movie and played video games and then we did that whole thing where we pretended we were going to sleep but kept talking and laughing until my friend's parents had to come down and tell us to shut up. And guys started falling asleep until it was just me and my best friend, Marcus, whisper-laughing. Every break in the conversation, I just wanted to bring her up, you know. I wanted us to talk about her all the time. But I couldn't figure out how the hell to do it without breaking the vibe of the night. I didn't know what Marcus would say, and since *none* of my friends ever talked about girls, I figured I wouldn't either.

"That's one of the things I remember most about slumber parties, actually. Middle of the night, someone else's living room, belly full of junk food, wanting to talk about a girl I was into but not knowing how. Not the worst worry in the world." James realizes he's hunched over, leaning toward the table like he's huddled over a fire for its warmth. He tries to relax back into his chair, improve his posture. He takes a sip from his frapped coffee. "People always talk about how you experience love for the first time when you're this age, but when I think back to those nights and how much I thought about girls even when I was a little kid, I think that those people have no idea when love starts."

"You think that was love, though? Being a kid, having a crush on some poor girl you and your friends made fun of?"

"Shit, yeah," James says. His eyes are on the red font on the departure monitors, a column of DELAYED flashing down the screen. People keep stopping in front and shaking their heads, grumbling. "It's a different love than maybe we experience now, being sixteen, or whatever—I don't know how old you are. And it's different, I'm sure, than the kind of love we'll experience when we're in college and twenty and thirty, full-on grown-up shit with marriage and all that. But it was the kind of love a nine-year-old is capable of, and just because it's not the kind of love an adult is capable of doesn't mean it wasn't love. Just because I couldn't explain what love was at the time doesn't mean I didn't know what it was."

James braves a look at the girl he's just unloaded this tirade on, wondering if she's regretting the cup of coffee. One eyebrow's raised, one leg up on the empty chair next to her. She's chewing on the stirrer she used to mix sugar into her coffee. "Did you ever tell the girl? Sandra?"

"Hell no!" James says with a laugh. "I was terrified of talking to girls back then." Still am, he thinks, but he doesn't want to jinx this roll he's on.

"So nothing ever came of it? No kiss? Nothing?"

James shrugs, takes another long pull from the straw. "Nah. But whatever, you know. I was nine. You ever have any romantic success when you were nine?"

Michelle scratches her nose, doesn't bother answering the question. She looks away from James, drinking her coffee slowly. Her eyes land on a middle-aged white guy on a cell phone, big belly protruding from an open blazer. This is Joseph Flint, but we'll meet him again later. He's irate, cheeks red, spittle on his lips, the way old, angry white dudes typically look to James. Like they can't believe the world isn't bending to please them.

"I don't fucking know, Janet," he half yells, pulling back and controlling himself when he realizes everyone can hear him. "Call the other airlines, see if there's anyone that can get me to Detroit tonight."

James watches the guy run a hand through his thinning hair, hang up the phone, then walk over to the bar at the neighboring restaurant.

"Why do you think people get so angry at airports?" Michelle asks. "Everyone seems so pissed all the time."

James shrugs, glances at the monitor to see what time it is. He's afraid his flight might get un-delayed, or that maybe time is passing by too quickly. That the hour in bonus time with this girl that the power outage has provided him has already vanished, and soon she'll be a thing of the past, relegated to some romantic memory, one he won't even be able to bring up to his friends because there'd be nothing really to share.

"Adults at airports always look like kids to me," Michelle continues. "Always looking lost, asking for help, not knowing what's expected of them. Maybe that's why they're so quick to be angry or annoyed or frustrated. Most of the time, they're in control of their lives, but at airports, they don't really have that."

"You think adults are really in control of their lives?"

"You don't?"

James pops the cap off his cup and uses his straw to scoop up some whipped cream. "Nah. It's a trick. I think ninety percent of them don't know what the fuck they're doing. The other ten are just pretending."

"How about that guy?" Michelle asks, pointing at a guy in his twenties who's walking slowly while reading a thick hardcover book. He has a pant leg tucked into a sock, as if he's getting ready to go biking. James and Michelle don't know that this guy, Roger Sterlinger, has intense social anxiety, often soothed by riding his twelve-speed mountain bike. On travel days, he indeed pretends he is simply getting ready to go biking, for the comfort the self-deception provides.

James laughs. "That guy's cool. Not pretending to be in control, that's for sure. Doing his own thing. I respect that."

They watch him make his way down the hall, surprisingly

good at avoiding others while he continues to read, blocking out the world around him. Outside, the Georgia sun has dipped below the horizon, lighting up the tiniest slivers of clouds in its retreat. Runway markers and wingtip lights stand out in the settling dark, but James notices the lack of movement. The few lone planes not docked at their gates are frozen in their taxiing queue as they wait for the airport to sort shit out, listless faces visible in their windows.

"Eighteen," Michelle says. James looks up at her, feels his attraction to her is plastered all over his face, and has to look away again. "You asked how old I am."

"Cool." James drags out the word, honestly impressed. The age has always felt magical to him, always far off no matter how much he approaches it. The truth is that he's terrified of eighteen and the changes it'll bring. It's not like his parents are gonna boot him out or anything, but it still feels like, at eighteen, he'll have to face the world on his own. The world and all its worries—climate change, political divides, wealth gaps, natural disasters, rent, taxes; he's not sure how anyone can handle it. It feels absurd at times. "What's it feel like?"

"The exact same as sixteen," Michelle says, and laughs. "Maybe like I'm a little closer to having to pretend like I know what I'm doing."

"Are you still in high school?"

"Yeah, graduating in June." James starts to ask a question, but Michelle interrupts. "I have to warn you, if the word 'plans' is in your next sentence, I will pour the rest of my coffee on your head."

James reaches over and lifts her coffee cup, peeking inside, then making a face that says, Eh, it's not that much coffee. Michelle smiles, combs some hair back behind her ear. There's a swell of music, a crescendo of strings like you'd expect to hear in a movie at a time not entirely unlike this one. James's and Michelle's eyes are locked for an instant, and the music so perfectly coincides with James's increased heart rate that he believes this is all some sort of hallucination, a sixteen-year-old kid's overactive imagination, too heavily influenced by movies to let a moment stand on its own.

Turns out it's just a track on the overhead café speakers. And it cuts out just a moment after James and Michelle look into each other's eyes, not because of symbolism, but because the power has called it quits again, packing off and shrouding the airport in absolute darkness.

\\\\\\\\\

This time, the darkness does not flicker away in a moment. Nor does any remaining daylight from the outside make its way into the building.

After sitting up straight, as alert as everyone else around him (though he cannot see that he is not alone in his reaction), James freezes. He can't make anything out, but we can.

The clerk at the bookstore holds out the change for a recently purchased book, her fingers clutched tightly around the coins. A man who'd reached inside his jacket's breast pocket to proffer an engagement ring to his boyfriend never closes his hand around the box. Michelle, who'd been eyeing her new companion, watches for the movement of his silhouette, thinking, Don't go. A child calls out for their mommy, as if unsure she's still there. One person nearby starts hyperventilating; another curls up on the floor into a tight ball.

A moment later, the emergency floodlights lining the hallway of Atlanta's international airport come alive in a blinding flash of white, and hell breaks loose. Though, for now, it's not all hell. Just some of it.

Some people in the terminal, unsure of what else to do, simply start sprinting down the hallway, shrieking and waving their arms in the air the way a cartoon character might. Others shriek while standing or sitting (or, in a few cases, squatting) in place. Some, cajoled by their instincts into believing it is the best of all possible options, lie down on the floor and play dead. Still others, blessed by their phones' battery lives and a connection to a still-functioning wireless network, shrug off the turn of events and post mild-mannered complaints on social media. They text their friends or spouses that they'll be arriving late. Some try to google what's happening and find nothing.

A few, hosts to the looting gene that overtakes many a celebratory sports fan (and their defeated counterparts), decide that the best course of action in this unlikely dark is to run out on their restaurant bills and raid the duty-free store, maybe break a window or two. A group of Japanese business types in a private room of a first-class airport lounge continue their sales presentation bathed in the glow of their computer screens. Thirty or so people who happen to be using the bathroom at the time shake their heads and think, Of course.

James and Michelle look at each other, eyebrows raised. They have similar contradictory thoughts: that they should check on their families, that they should not split from each other's company. They remain seated as the airport collectively loses its shit.

Murmurs about terrorism start spreading, from the table next to them to the restaurant next door, gaining traction as they make their way across the B gates. James can't help but fall into that theory's grip, at least for a moment. A group of guys in military dress jog down the hall, trying to find a way to make themselves useful. Raised in the age he was, it's hard for James not to feel a creeping sense of panic. Fear, now, that makes his heart beat faster.

Beneath it, though, still joy. More delays are coming, and Michelle is still seated across from him. He feels like an asshole for thinking of joy, not knowing if anyone's hurt, not knowing if something seriously wrong that leaves no room for thoughts of happiness is going down.

Shit, what if this is something awful? What if he's one of those unlucky people who find themselves in the worst possible place at the worst possible time? This is what he expects of growing old: that the longer he goes on, the harder it will be to avoid tragedy. Everything he sees in the news will come crashing onto his lap. This, whatever it is, is at last the first of many horrors that will come his way. He can avoid them no longer.

Michelle, meanwhile, is wondering if her life is going to flash before her eyes. Like many others in the airport, she has the perhaps-paranoid notion that she is in danger. Unlike many others, though, she feels no panic at the thought. The future is not in her hands, and whatever will come will come.

If her life is indeed going to flash before her eyes, Michelle wonders if that means she's going to have to relive the past week with her grandparents. Them at the kitchen table in the morning, huddled over coffee, discussing their will with her dad as if it were a movie they'd all seen the night before. Mamie lifting the oxygen mask off her nose just to crack another joke about how to get rid of her body when she goes. Fuck, when your life flashes before your eyes, do the feelings pass through too? If that's the case, Michelle would rather opt out of that whole thing. She's had a good life and all, but some shit should only be lived through once, and the discomfort of the weeklong farewell definitely fits into that category.

James's and Michelle's thoughts fall apart when the regular lights all shoot back on, the emergency ones blinking out at the same time, as if passing the torch. The departures monitors light up. James watches for the flight cancellations to start rolling in, but they hold steady at DELAYED. Nervous energy permeates the airport. Leg jitters are at an all-time high, and there are more than a few aimless chuckles, bodies trying to ease the tension with uncalled-for laughter.

The café's speakers continue the song where they left off, crescendo of strings and harmonizing vocals (though James, not looking into Michelle's eyes at the moment, no longer associates the sound with any romantic notions).

The airport's speakers, which so far have only been used to repeat their standard PSAs to not let strangers pack or handle one's luggage, come on. Instead of a robotic feminine voice, there's the staticky hiss of a real person fumbling with a microphone. A man clears his throat, mumbles something unintelligible. Then: "Ladies and gentlemen, we apologize for the . . . um . . . you know. The recent power outages. Rest assured that the problem has been resolved and that there is no need to worry. Most flight schedules should not be dramatically affected. We are working with airline and airport personnel to ensure the smoothness of functionality that, um . . ." A few muffled voices in the background, the sound of a hand being clasped over the mic. "(I don't know, Gary, there's no script for this. I'm doing my best.) Please keep close attention to flight monitors and be aware of possible delays and flight changes. At this time there is no reason to think flights will be canceled. Please remain calm. Thank you."

The airport murmurs its collective response. James and Michelle exchange a look, and despite it all, they manage to smile.

THREE

\\\\\\\

IT IS STILL UNCLEAR IF THERE IS SOMETHING NEFARIOUS afoot in the Atlanta airport. The air-conditioning is whirring, strong as it ever was. The Wi-Fi signal is functional enough, though every fifteen minutes it forces users to click through and accept the terms and conditions again. In the too-bright white floodlights, the airport hallways look more like a film set, like the last act of an action movie, or the first act of a horror film. James would really rather not be in either. Where are the rom-coms, you know?

He's sitting stiffly in his chair, wondering what he should be doing. He wonders what he should be feeling, if his reactions should more closely mirror what others around him are doing. Is panic the move here? He doesn't feel panic, not yet anyway.

The screamers have exhausted themselves, so the airport is much calmer. There seem to be no explosions, no gunfire, nothing that points toward violence or imminent danger. A few people are still running around. Those who look official have not drawn any weapons, and despite the strangeness of the situation, this detail puts James at ease. James has not seen anything like this before, but he knows that if shit is going down, you probably don't have to look far to find a gun.

Next to him, Michelle has now kicked both her feet up onto the chair and is sipping her coffee. "Weird," she says. "My hopes for a slumber party might not be so crazy, eh?"

James manages a chuckle. He looks up and down the B gates hallway. A middle-aged woman wearing glasses has decided that in the present circumstances, it is okay to smoke a cigarette without bothering to look for a designated lounge. Her fellow passengers cast annoyed, disbelieving looks, which she chooses to ignore. At gate B17, the flight to Kansas City is now slated for a midnight departure, and it seems like every single person meant to be on board has lined up to have a word with the poor airline representative.

"What do you think is happening?" James asks. He doesn't feel as chill as Michelle looks, but he's trying to pretend these little signs of the airport unraveling aren't bothering him.

For Michelle, the truth is that, despite her exterior chill, the airport's status has sent her mind spiraling back to the past week. She's seeing her grandparents' faces in her mind's eye, no matter how interesting the scenes in front of her are. She's seeing herself avoiding her grandparents, not even offering to cook with them in the evening after the party, when it's become clear that they mean to stick to their plan. Michelle shrugs at James. "Nothing we can do about it anyway. I wouldn't worry."

James runs a hand over his hair, which he keeps closely shorn. His parents might be freaking out, or they still might not have noticed anything. He takes a look at his phone, and though its inactivity relaxes him, he wonders if he should return to them, if he should be calling for help, somehow. Make sure everything is okay, because it sure as shit seems like things are not. But then Michelle reaches over and touches him. It is just the slightest tip of her index and middle fingers, a simple tap on the bone that protrudes in a bump on his wrist. Possibly the least interesting way two people can touch each other. A call to attention, nothing more. But for a moment, it causes James's mind to empty of everything but Michelle, as if she has found a secret button on his skin. He can feel her coursing through his veins, and he wonders if his earlier rant about love was bullshit. Maybe all those other times he thought it might be love—making fun of Sandra when he was nine just to bring up her name; the hurt of not hearing back from a crush via text, the pain proof positive of love; Marcus's sister, Aubrey, all of freshman year, how he'd dream of her every night, then wake to see her at school, shocked that she hadn't shared in the dream, that she still didn't know who he was—he was wrong. This was it. A simple touch that pulls you into another being, that pulls them into you. Nothing else could be love.

He relaxes back into his seat, looking at her in awe. Then an airport cart rolls past them. A woman seated next to the driver is holding her crying baby close to her chest, trying to soothe the child though she herself looks flustered. The cart driver honks his little horn, then calls out to the people still in his way. The effect fades from James's system, and he starts to think that, yeah, this girl is cool, but maybe they shouldn't just be sitting around like nothing's going on. Michelle is looking across the hallway, where a man holding the hands of two toddlers has started yelling at the smoker. They watch the skirmish for a while, eyebrows raised, Michelle releasing little chuckles that sound like bells ringing, like the hum of summer bugs.

"So, what gate are you at?" James says, trying to bring his mind back to normal things.

"D-something," Michelle says. "I still have a couple hours, probably more now. I think I've walked the whole airport at this point."

"You wanna go check in with your parents or something?"

Michelle shrugs. "Sure, they'll like that." She pushes away from the table, legs swinging off the chair they've been resting on. Black sneakers with neon-green laces, no socks, a faded blue string tied high on her ankle. She stands up first, grabbing his cup off the table and walking their trash over to a nearby bin.

James calls out a thanks and slips one arm through his backpack strap. He stands there for a second, looking around at the airport, before he realizes Michelle is standing still and staring at the wall, the empty cups no longer in her hands.

"Come look," Michelle says.

James steps over to her, sees what she's seeing. The blinking green light is no longer blinking. It's steady now, as if soothed by the chaos in the airport. "Weird," James says, thinking: Fuck. What's that mean? Who knows, but fuck, right?

He doesn't want the light to hold his interest. He wants to focus on Michelle, wants to dive into the crush that's blooming with every one of her comments or slight touches, blooming despite his lack of game, blooming despite the airport. He wants this to be his whole world.

Instead he's thinking of people with hatred flowing through their veins and the ability to bring harm to others. He wouldn't want us to reveal this, because it does not show who he always is, just who he is occasionally, but he's thinking there hasn't been enough love or flesh in his life. If this day somehow gets crazier and this is the end of his life, it doesn't seem fair that he'll die knowing so little of either romance or sex. Even if there are far greater injustices in the world.

Michelle, however, is entirely captivated by the green light. Ever since she was three years old, she has been jumping off slides at playgrounds, heaving herself at puddles and patches of grass and the dark maroon leather couch in her mom's home office. She likes arriving full-force. This has resulted in broken limbs and hearts and the worst of all possible feelings: taste buds scalded by hot liquids. Yet she refuses to hesitate, hates the mere idea of it, hates the sound of the word in all four languages she speaks. And since it is not at all related to her grandparents, Michelle is happy to dive full-force into this light.

So while James is thinking about love and flesh and all of it getting wiped away from him, Michelle's arm is reaching for the light. This time she does not pull away. The green light flickers almost imperceptibly at her approach. Michelle catches on that she's just won this staring contest, and a smile spreads across her lips. She closes the last of the distance between her fingers and the small glass bulb, then notices that it's not entirely solid. There's some give, some room for pressure. It's not just a light, but a button. She does not hesitate.

\\\\\\\\

Things that happen in the ensuing moments:

The sun disappears entirely beneath the horizon, casting the airport in a barely noticed twilight. A brown thrasher perched on the security fence surrounding the elaborate runway system ruffles its feathers, sings its chirpy song. Traffic on the 285 slows, only briefly, only for the usual reasons.

The temperature inside the T gates drops thirty degrees below the airport's standard 68-degree Fahrenheit setting. At the other end of the airport, the F gates' temperature swells instantly to 98. Some of the hot air particles in the F gates, following some basic rule of science or decency, decide to scurry the hell away. These air particles rush up the long hallway, down the escalators, past moving sidewalks and temporary art installations, past a still-functioning tram sending people from one set of gates to the other—pointlessly for the time being—past tidily packed black carry-on bags rolling this way and that. The hot air eventually meets the suddenly frigid air from the T gates, which has been moving much more slowly up the same hallway. Somehow—we're a bit iffy on the science involved—the opposing fronts meet, clash, interact. Hartsfield-Jackson Atlanta International Airport gets its own climate.

At the same time, Roger Sterlinger, the socially anxious cyclist who tucks his pant leg into his sock, feels a wave of calm. He looks up from his book and finds his gait slowing. There are so many people around him, such a flurry of activity. For once, he does not think of biking, of the smell of fresh air and woods, the bumps of the trail, the way his mind focuses on the task at hand—controlling his bike and his body around the curves and the dangers in front of him—and is not burdened by floods of worry. Roger takes the nearest available seat, which happens to be a stool at the circular bar near the duty-free shops, and he orders a diet soda. He has no idea where this sudden ease comes from and does not expect it to last. But he is glad to have it before his flight, before the shitshow of a family reunion that he is destined for.

A nineteen-year-old TSA agent named Rosa Velarde clocks out of her shift and grabs her phone from her locker, checking to see what her friends are up to. Her phone is malfunctioning, though, and she is unable to switch away from a clock counting down from fourteen hours. She is swiping her finger repeatedly over the screen, muttering complaints to herself, when a snowflake lands on her screen.

Two men waiting to board the Kansas City flight (now set for a 2:15 a.m. departure) at B17 get a heart attack at the same time.

The control tower goes completely dark—not just the room at the top, but the entire building, and not just the lights, but the concrete and steel that make up the structure, darkening completely, as if the tower's been erased from the world.

Music stops working within the B gates; it won't emerge from headphones or speakers or even vocal cords.

Meanwhile, James and Michelle begin to sweat. This is the only effect, for the time being, that they notice, and they quite reasonably don't assign it to the light at all. "That didn't do much," Michelle says, pulling her finger away from the green light, which pops back up to its original position.

"What?" James answers, hands clutched to his backpack straps, trying to work out his nerves through his fingers. He didn't see her press down on the light at all.

Michelle keeps her eyes on the light for a second longer, then whispers a "nothing" and leads them away from the B gates, down the escalators that connect to the rest of the terminals. The airport is still running on floodlights, and Michelle's and James's shadows grow as they walk down the hallway.

James tries to think of something to say, remembering that

he was being pretty smooth and conversational earlier. That feels like so long ago, though. He wishes he could just get into that state of mind again, move his body a certain way and fall right into that ease he felt before. Instead he's just sweating up a storm, looking over at her every few steps.

They leave the B gates via an escalator that sends them toward the underground hallway that connects all the terminals. James casts a glance over his shoulder, wondering how far he should stray. But his cell phone is still functional, and all the flight monitors are flashing DELAYED, so he leans on the handrail and listens to the quiet whir of some unseen engine.

For some reason, the escalator ride takes James back to childhood, ten years old, some mall during Christmastime. The place crowded with scarf-wrapped shoppers, the same songs in every store, fake snow on the indoor tree while sleet slathered the cars outside. James's still-gloved hand warm in his mom's as they headed up the escalator to the video game store. It was also not long after the hard times, and though he hadn't really understood the financial reasons for them that day at the store, he lived in fear of returning to that frailty. Every video game he picked up, he looked at the price, trying to will himself to understand its true cost. Would they have to move again to a neighborhood where the nights weren't quiet? Would this purchase bring hushed conversations from his parents that he could hear through thin walls, his mom's choked voice saying, "We will figure this out."

James and Michelle step off the escalator at the same time, looking out at the hallway that stretches the entirety of the airport. A few people are sitting down near electrical outlets, phones and laptops plugged in, brows furrowed as they stare at their screens. A handful of others roll their suitcases, blank looks on their faces.

"Is it just me or does it feel humid here?" Michelle asks.

"A little, I guess. Weird."

They stand for a minute or so, looking up and down the hallway. Then the airport tram arrives with a melodious ding, and a handful of people push past them to get on the escalator. Michelle looks at James and nods in the direction of the tram, and they both squeeze inside before the doors shut.

The tram car is empty except for lone TSA agent Rosa Velarde, her dark, curly hair in a loose ponytail draped over her shoulder. She's got her phone in one hand and is looking down at it every few seconds, chewing her lip in concern.

"Excuse me," Michelle says.

James's heart quickens a little, even though this girl looks no older than Michelle and seems chill. He's never done anything wrong, and is lucky enough that nothing wrong has ever happened to him either, not really, but there's something about a uniform that sets him on edge. The world treats him like he's guilty, and guilt is what he feels.

The TSA agent looks up, startled, as if she hadn't noticed them at all. "Do you know what's going on?" Michelle asks.

For a second the agent just stares blankly at Michelle, gently tapping her phone against the side of her leg. "What do you mean?"

Michelle traces a circle in the air with her finger. "The lights? The delays?"

The agent nods, slipping her phone into her back pocket. "Oh, right. Don't really know. Not my area."

"They didn't tell you anything? Is it, like . . . a security threat or something?"

"I doubt there's a reason to worry," the agent says, crossing her arms and looking up at the display overhead just as they pull into the C gates. James thinks he sees a snowflake on her hair but dismisses the thought, and when he looks back for it, it's gone. The pleasant PA voice makes an announcement, and all three heads turn to the opening doors.

Loud voices fill the car well before James's eyes can take in what's happening outside the tram doors. There are about five or six guys in the foyer in front of the tram. They are all limbs and lips, angry spittle and angry words, muscles tensed, holding someone back, arms peeling away from those restraining them. A tall white guy in a puffy vest breaks free and takes a swing, but he gets pulled back at the last second, which only makes him angrier. Red-cheeked, he tries to push away the guy in the denim jacket who's holding him. "Let me fucking go, Jeff!"

A man whose back is to James stands between Puffy Vest and the other group. Both his arms are out and his voice carries over just enough to make out his tone, none of his words. He looks South Asian, dark-skinned and tall. The soft lilt of a British accent somehow floats through the mayhem, making itself heard, like leaves rustling in the wind despite the sound of a nearby waterfall. A peacekeeper, his T-shirt tight against his biceps, keeping the fighting men away from each other. His name is Taha Silva, and this is his first time in the United States. So far, it is not exactly what he pictured, but he is also not surprised.

Rosa stands in front of the scene, reaching for her radio, which she left behind in the locker room when she clocked out. There are so many angry people, and she has nothing but her uniform and a couple of training videos' worth of knowledge. She's almost a kid herself.

Another erratic swing from Puffy Vest, which this time his friend Jeff cannot restrain. It doesn't reach its target either, but it does land. The peacekeeper catches the blow directly on the nose, and that sound carries toward James, as does the sound of the back of Taha's head when it lands against the floor.

"Oh, goddamn it," Rosa says, and she jogs past Michelle and James toward the scene.

Michelle takes a step forward but stays inside the car. She looks over at James, eyebrows furrowed with concern. James looks back, jaw slack, stomach clenched. They're asking the same silent question of each other: What do we do?

They look back at the scene. Rosa rushes over to the peacekeeper, checks his breathing. The other men continue to shove each other, not even looking down at the knocked-out man at their feet. They yell, and then Jeff and Puffy Vest shake their heads and walk away as if nothing of interest has happened.

Right before the tram doors close, James sees the peacekeeper move his head up ever so slightly. There's a splatter of blood on the tile.

FOUR

\\\\\\\\\

THE PLEASANT PA VOICE ANNOUNCES THEIR ARRIVAL to the D gates, and though neither James nor Michelle has said anything, they both step off. The air is crisp, not in the usual way of artificially frosted airports, but something more authentic. It's like fall is in the air, or perhaps spring, depending on which way the airport (or science) decides to go with it. But for now: comfort.

"That was intense, no?" Michelle says softly.

James's mouth is dry, his hands a little shaky. He hides this by slipping them into his pockets. "Yeah." Every Hollywood-bred scenario of mayhem is unfolding in his head. More evidence: the world comes for all of us. It was that guy's turn. "I wonder what happened."

Another escalator, a ride up this time. "What always happens: people being angry." Her accent has been soft enough to miss for the last hour, but now a certain lilt has returned, a gentleness to the way her tongue sounds out her words that James finds impossibly enticing. He wants her to keep talking.

"Shit like that scares me," he says.

"People fighting? But it's so normal. Look at the world."

"Yeah, but that's exactly it, right? It's normal. That's wild to me. That every single day people are angry enough to hit each other." He doesn't want to ramble again, but he feels it bubbling up from inside. Plus, there's no one near them on the escalator, and when he pauses, he can still hear the wet smack of the back of that guy's head hitting the floor, like it's playing on repeat on the little speakers hidden everywhere. "And people are so chill about it. They say it's human nature, as if that somehow makes it cool. As if that erases the fact that some dude just got hit so hard he lost consciousness and maybe cracked his skull open." He shudders involuntarily as they reach another concourse, this one almost identical to the B gates, the storefronts only slightly different. "It sucks that I feel like I'm sheltered because I don't like seeing someone getting knocked out, that my sensibilities are called into question because I feel something for another human being. Why the hell is *that* the way the world works?" The question seems to echo down the hallway, turning a few heads.

James doesn't even want to think about it anymore, feels the steam running out of him. His voice has been quivering too, and he doesn't want Michelle to notice that. They pass by a chicken wing restaurant, and James peers in to take his mind off things. They've turned up the volume on a football game. Some businesspeople are sitting at the bar, ties yanked loose, shirts untucked, beers half drunk, making the most of their delay, laughing and joking. Weird how he's forgotten this is just a flight delay.

They start walking down the D concourse. A few people are lying down on the carpeted areas in their gates, heads tucked into sweatshirts, arms crossed over their chests, gently snoring. A few are still in line to talk to the airline reps, who look exhausted, as if they've been at it all day. But it's only been an hour and a half since the lights first flickered out. James glances at the departure monitors to his right. Everything is still delayed.

"I hope that guy's okay," Michelle says.

"Me too," James says quietly.

"You've never seen a fight?" Michelle asks.

"I mean, I've seen dudes fighting." James pushes his sleeves down to his wrists, suddenly chilly. "But that sound. The way that guy just swung and didn't give a shit that it had connected with someone. Maybe I'm overreacting or whatever, but he really could have killed that guy. The way his head cracked . . ."

"Yeah . . . ," Michelle says, her voice trailing off when the PA comes on.

"Hartsfield-Jackson Atlanta International Airport apologizes again for the unforeseen delays. We appreciate your patience and understanding as airport and airline staff attempt to get everything in working order and resume flights. . . ." A brief pause, though the microphone is clearly still on. Muffled voices again. "(Yeah, Gary, I already said that bit. Yeah. Yeah. Do *you* want to do this? Ahem.) Solutions are coming, is what we're trying to say here. We would not advise leaving the airport, as it could result in missing your flight without a refund. Meanwhile, we ask you to please remain calm, as it will make this whole experience a lot easier." Then a cough, and the mic goes dead.

James and Michelle don't comment on the announcement. D16 is on their right. A couple of guys are lifting a row of seats and moving them. James stops out of curiosity, and Michelle follows his cue. They watch silently as the two men move the seats toward the wall of windows. The men then walk over and pick up another row, flipping it upside down and stacking it on top of the one they have just arranged. In ten minutes or so, they've set up a barricade against the glass and another one blocking off a portion of the gate from the hallway. No one is stopping them, and, even stranger, none of the people at the gate are complaining that they no longer have a place to sit. Families and business travelers alike sprawl out on the floor. They read books or hunch over their electronic devices or sit staring blankly out at the world.

"Hey!" Michelle calls out. Almost everyone around them turns to look at her, but it is clear she wants the attention of the two guys moving seats around.

The older of the two, wearing a jungle-green button-down with the sleeves rolled up, a thin sheen of sweat on his forehead, puts his hands on his hips. "Yeah?"

"What are you doing?"

A tense silence follows. James feels the desire to get away, and he reaches out to urge Michelle to keep moving but doesn't want to make unwelcome contact with her. His hand pauses in the middle of the gesture. Instead he looks down at the floor, really starting to wonder what the hell is going on at the airport. This isn't just run-of-the-mill mass-delay frustration anymore. What else will they have to deal with?

"Preparing," the older guy says. Then he nods his head at his friend and they move over to another row of seats.

"For what?" Michelle asks.

The guy shakes his head, a slight smirk on his lips. "One, two, three," he grunts, and the men heave the row of seats onto a stack, blocking off the window completely. Twilight is just about over, the sky beyond the airport almost completely dark. Only a few smudges of color remain. James can see these slivers of pink and orange, and he feels a sense of foreboding as the colors wane. He pulls out his phone to check social media for what is happening; is there a storm or something, an attack somewhere else? What do these dudes know that he doesn't? The internet offers no clues, though. He has the thought—quickly quelled by a part of his brain that doesn't want to follow the thought any further—that it is a good thing his phone is fully charged, that he'll be able to call his parents, call the outside world, if things continue on this way. He doesn't yet notice that the battery life is not draining at all.

"Weird," Michelle says, and they get back to walking.

"I'm starting to think we might not catch our flights anytime soon."

"Slumber party." She laughs, but something about her enthusiasm feels forced. Something's changed in the air. James isn't sure if Michelle can sense it too, or if it's just his nerves coloring everything else. We'd love to be able to tell James that he's right. She does feel it. It's not just the temperature either, the slight breeze neither one wants to acknowledge. They can see it on the faces of everyone they pass by. People are holding their belongings a little tighter, the indents of their fingers on their bags, their knuckles turning white. Mothers and fathers corral children who have grown bored from all the waiting, while other children have cried themselves exhausted and fallen fast asleep on their parents' laps.

"So," Michelle says, "do you travel much?"

James looks up from his feet at Michelle, who is fiddling with her nose ring casually. There's something about this particular angle of her face that reminds him: shit, this girl is attractive. Even with all this going on, even with how great she is to talk to, it's hard to get that out of his mind, hard not to focus on this specific aspect of the day's craziness, him hanging with a cute stranger. "Not really," he responds. "Little road trips and stuff. A couple other times to Tampa. LA once." He bites his lip, wishing he had a more interesting answer. Most of the people he knows haven't done much traveling either, except for the new dude Marcus has been dating, whose family vacations are to places like Bali and probably don't involve picnics at highway rest stops in Michigan. "You've probably been all over, huh?"

"Yeah, I guess." If James were to look over at her now, he'd see that Michelle is blushing. But he is actively keeping himself from looking at her too much, and so the blush goes by unnoticed.

"Dude, your answer to 'Where are you from?' includes more countries than I've ever been to. It's okay to say yes."

Michelle laughs, and her cheeks return to their normal color, a discomfort easing within her. "Fair enough. I just hate the idea of becoming one of those people, you know?"

James shakes his head. "What people?"

"Someone for whom traveling is only a priority so they can talk about it. Someone who goes to new countries in order to increase the number of places they've been to, or only goes to a landmark just for the picture proving it."

"You don't really strike me as that kind of person."

"That's sweet of you," Michelle says, causing James's stomach to wring itself once or twice and send happy goose bumps down his arms. "But you don't really know me all that well. I know myself better, and I feel the potential of that person within me. I love keeping track of the number of countries I've been in, number of flights I take every year. I'm a lucky person and get to do it enough, but it's like I'm always hungry for more. And not even for the experience of it, but also for the stupid tally mark. To say I've been somewhere new, to check in to the country on social media. I hate that. There are people who live their whole lives in one place, not because they don't want to escape but because they can't. And I'm here just looking forward to the next place I can go to for the social media attention it'll get me. It makes me feel so shallow. Like I don't deserve to travel."

The air is getting colder in the D gates, the frigid drop in the T gates is bleeding over, or the warm air is scurrying away toward the other side of the airport (again, us and science). James's and Michelle's breath is starting to become visible. "You still don't seem like the shallow type to me. I know we've just met and all, but it sounds like you've given this a lot of thought. Which is, like, the exact opposite of being shallow."

Michelle cocks her head, studying James for a moment. "I guess. But bullshit motives that are well thought out are still bullshit motives, no?" Then she rubs her hands in front of her face and blows into them to warm up. "Is it just me or is it getting cold?"

"Yeah, I'm freezing," James says. In D10, a woman has unzipped her carry-on and is rifling through for extra jackets. Except she's on her way to Puerto Vallarta and so she ends up wrapping herself in sheer, thin beach shawls. "So, where's your favorite place to travel?"

"Well, the Eiffel Tower is always good for at least a hundred likes," Michelle jokes. "No, I guess it's my grandparents' house, a little outside of Bordeaux." Michelle goes on to describe the handful of summer visits to the little stone house in southern

France, the sprawling greenery that surrounds it. She skips over the fact that she was just there, not wanting to delve into the past week, instead wanting to describe the place as she means to remember it.

"The trips don't happen every year, but I remember my life according to them. The year of rain, the year I met and fell in love with Mathias, the year of the bombing in Bangkok, watching in horror from the coziest living room in the world, unable to contact my cousins.

"That living room . . ." She sighs, and James wishes he could see it as she does (ignoring that quick pang of jealousy at whoever Mathias is).

We can, so a tour while Michelle tries to paint a picture for James. Stone walls, a brick-lined fireplace. There's a wall that is entirely composed of dark brown bookshelves stocked with first editions of classic books and leather-bound journals her grandfather kept fifty years ago, the handwriting as elegant as calligraphy. A cast-iron chandelier hangs over the middle of the room, but it's not electric—it works off candles. It's never been used for fear that it'll cause more harm than light. In a corner sit two ancient, uncomfortable, high-backed chairs that Michelle's grandfather calls "The Chairs" and uses only when someone needs to receive "A Talk." A Persian rug beneath the ton-heavy coffee table. The wooden-framed portrait of a relative on one wall, a van Gogh print on the other. In that room, Michelle feels like the world outside her family does not exist.

Always arriving from the airport in a rental car, Michelle is constantly taken aback by the size of the driveway in comparison to the rest of the house, how long it stretches on. Especially when she's spent the last hour passing by behemoth Bordeaux houses that are more estates than homes. Her grandmother Mamie always smells of the garden—pollen and lavender and earth. Her grandfather Papi like the kitchen. Butter and flour and rosemary, heavy beads of perspiration on his temples. His nose is like a bulbous root vegetable littered with bright red veins.

"Like an online map depicting traffic," Michelle says with a smile.

"I like this," James says, barely aware he's saying it.

"Like what? Hearing me ramble about my family?"

"Sure. Poetry amidst chaos." He shrugs.

Michelle bites her lip, then continues.

Most nights her grandfather cooks. He didn't this past visit, but again, Michelle is choosing to ignore that this past week ever happened. On Wednesdays they all go as a family to the farmers market, and they don't leave each other's sides all day. They peruse every aisle of the market and pick the menu together, and when they return to the house they go straight to the kitchen, each one knowing their traditional task without having to ask. Her mother cuts, since she has the best knife skills in the family. She can slice an onion so fine the pieces come out see-through. Her dad washes vegetables, keeps the kitchen tidy.

Papi oversees it all, never ceasing to smile. Michelle peels. She loves the efficiency of that same peeler, year after year. How it never dulls, never rusts, never catches on a single bump of a carrot, never struggles to get over the hills of those heirloom potatoes. They let her stir sauce too. Michelle always remembers the stirring in those years between visits, the warmth of steam coming from the pot, the aroma released with each rotation.

When the hours of cooking are done, they all pull up seats on the patio and face the back garden. They watch the fireflies if they're around in the summer, or the rain coming down in sheets during those evening thunderstorms, or else the full moon crisscrossed by picturesque clouds. They never face each other, always hold their plates on their laps. The adults lean over to pull sips of red wine from tall-stemmed glasses that sit at their feet.

"I've never felt more a part of one corner of the world than in the house at Bordeaux," she tells James, "especially while feeling wholly apart from every other part of it. I know every path through the woods to get to the pond, know every inch of the meadow where I had my first kiss. I've memorized every crack in the enormous boulder that, together with the meadow and the pond, forms the last point in a triangle surrounding the house. It doesn't belong in a place like that." Her eyes are so far away that James starts to believe maybe she's really in Bordeaux. Maybe this girl can travel with her mind. He remembers throughout her speech how she said earlier that she might not ever see her grandparents again, and it paints everything she says with a shade of sadness he wishes he could ease.

"There's no geological reason for a boulder that big to be there," Michelle says. "Trust me, I did some research. The only explanation is that it came from outer space, but even that doesn't make sense because there's no crater. A meteor that big would have made an impact that lasts, you know?"

She looks at him as if she expects him to understand anything she's saying. "Yeah," he says, because how could he not?

"Although I guess even the world's largest catastrophes have been mellowed by time." Michelle stops, little puffs of cloud floating into the airport's atmosphere as she catches her breath from the walk and the talk and the unexpected cold. "Well, this is me. Those are my parents."

They sit right beneath the D3 gate sign. A slight white guy in beige linen pants, a dark button-up shirt with the top three buttons undone despite the cold. He has a book open on his lap. Michelle's mom is slight too. But she wears a long purple skirt and a cashmere sweater folded over her lap. She is knitting something with pastel-colored wool.

"Coucou!" Michelle says, approaching the two.

They look up from their respective distractions as if nothing has broken their concentration in hours. "Nous sommes retardés une heure de plus," her father says, almost immediately returning to the book. There's a slight glance in James's direction, but the page-long paragraph he's on calls out more fervently.

"Ces putain de compagnies aériennes américaines," he adds as an afterthought.

Michelle's mom stops her knitting. "คุณไปไหนมา?" James has never heard Thai before, at least he doesn't think so. Being from Chicago, it's hard to believe there's a language he hasn't heard. You just have to find the neighborhood where it's living.

"I was just walking around," Michelle responds. "This is James. He's delayed too."

Michelle's parents seem to take stock of James for the first time. He straightens his shoulders out, offers a smile, tries to remember the things his parents have taught him about making good first impressions. Which is a little weird, he thinks, because these people are strangers and will remain strangers when all this is over, in an hour when flights start to take off, or when the airlines start canceling flights and shipping people off to airport hotels.

"Hi, James," Michelle's mom says, returning a smile. "She's not getting you into trouble, is she?" Her accent is thicker than Michelle's, easier to pin down to one place in the world.

James smiles and is about to say one of those non-statements you make to parents, the kind where both of you laugh even though there's clearly nothing really funny about it. Something like "Not yet! Hahaha!" or "I wish she would!" or whatever, when he is interrupted by the loudest noise he has ever heard.

FIVE

\\\\\\\

IT WON'T BE KNOWN FOR A FEW DAYS WHERE THE explosion originated—a vending machine in the C gates—but every single person in the Atlanta airport feels it at the same time. It ripples the air and shakes the walls, sending several people to the ground. James and Michelle are thrown to the floor, landing almost on top of each other.

Roger Sterlinger, still happily perched at the central bar in the E gates before the explosion, is sent sprawling backward, thinking throughout the fall: Of course.

Rosa Velarde, who'd just succeeded in getting Taha the Peacemaker to rise to his feet, holding her TSA shirt to the back of his head while trying to get in touch with her supervisors, feels the shock wave of the blast and thinks: I just want to go home.

A large percentage of the panes of glass throughout the airport shatter, but only the internal ones, the storefronts and bathroom mirrors. The windows that face the outdoors—the airport tarmac, Atlanta in the distance—do not so much as crack, as if to assert to the people inside that whatever is happening is contained within the airport and is of no concern to the outside world.

Inside, the shouting does not subside for a long time. There has just been, after all, an explosion within an airport. People can't point at any smoke, or fire, or other telltale signs of a traditional explosion. There are no bodies. But the evidence of a huge wave of energy unleashed all at once is incontrovertible. Would-be passengers are on the floor, recovering slowly from the physical blow. At least a hundred of them have concussions. Dozens of coffee cups have been knocked over, bleeding their contents onto counters, paperback novels, the floor.

The glass is everywhere. People hide where they can, in bathroom stalls or under the rows of seats, hunkered down and holding their loved ones, crying, praying, muttering assurances they don't fully believe. They shut their eyes as tight as they possibly can and they wait for harm to come to them, or wait for the harm to pass. They send text messages and voice mails to their family members, to their significant others, to the ones that got away, to everyone they didn't get the chance to confess something to—guilt or love or regret. No one responds to them, but still they send their possible last thoughts out beyond the airport walls however they can.

People scramble to the exits. Whole hordes of them go in

search of how to get out, forgetting, for now, the option to leave by air. Their search only leads to more fear, though, when no one can seem to locate an exit.

There are many guesses as to what exactly is occurring. But not a single person really knows, and that makes the fear stronger.

The airport's weather continues to develop into its partitioned ecosystems, unfettered by the blast. In the T gates, the cold air builds upon itself and the inklings of a blizzard form. The passengers unconsciously huddle closer for warmth, and when their breathing returns to normal, they blame the snow on the airlines. In turn, the airline reps do their best to keep their customers happy, and they hand out seven-dollar meal vouchers by the handful. Some are used to sop up blood from gashes caused by the explosion. The three coffee shops in the colder terminals see their lines grow substantially. Aside from the blast itself, which slowed things down considerably, the baristas have yet to notice anything strange going on.

After a week and a half in Florida, James's family recognizes the feel of a thunderstorm building in the B gates. They can feel it in the air, on their skin. They look up at the ceiling, expecting to see clouds. They don't, but they're still sure rain is coming. They're not overreactors, James's parents. They took cover beneath the chairs in the moments after the explosion, and that's where they remain now. The only step they take for protection is to pull out their jackets from their carry-ons. James Sr.

resumes his crossword puzzle on his electronic tablet. After trying to call her son a few times, Jaquelyn Herrera finds her place in the magazine article she was in the middle of, though she's too worried about James to focus on her reading. She gets up to go look for him in the terminal. Ava messages her best friend, Josie, via three different apps on her phone, though every time she tries to mention something about the events at the airport, her words turn into a string of emojis even Josie can't decipher.

Over a dozen military personnel gathered in the Delta Sky Club by C37 arrange their chairs into a circle and confer. What is appropriate protocol for when an airport is under attack? they wonder. If that's what is happening, someone points out. No one knows what is happening, and without a cache of weapons at their disposal, they're not sure how to proceed. TSA must have some sort of arsenal in the airport, right? Twelve men and three women in uniform shrug in unison, awaiting orders from somewhere or another.

Approximately half of the airport uses the still-functioning Wi-Fi to try to figure out what's going on, but the internet seems to know nothing about the situation that is unfolding. Even those whose home pages peddle in conspiracy theories are none the wiser. There is not a single headline's worth of information or misinformation to glean, even if it seems like the internet is otherwise functioning regularly. Overhead, planes that were circling Atlanta waiting for clearance to land start to disperse as they get rerouted to nearby airports.

Meanwhile, on the ground at the D gates, faces only a couple of inches apart, James and Michelle look into each other's eyes. They know that pupils dilate in both fear and attraction, but neither can tell which is to blame here. "Sorry," James says softly, but he doesn't yet move away from her.

Michelle has one hand gripped on his upper arm, the other awkwardly wedged between their bodies. "It's okay," she says.

Neither of them stands up, because the shouts and mayhem of the D gates have not died down. No one is seriously injured, but no one knows that yet. Fear reigns supreme throughout the airport.

James studies his surroundings. People are crouched down, covering their heads with their hands. Like with the earlier blackouts, there are a handful of screamers, and this time around plenty of criers. There are so many who look prepared for more.

Michelle's parents appear at their daughter's side, bursting out quick sentences of concern that James can't understand. He crawls away, giving them space to care for each other. He stays close to the ground, though, trying to make sense of what is happening. What was that noise? Is everyone okay? Is he okay?

He's acutely aware that in a situation like this one, it's important to stay calm, to think rationally, keep yourself safe. But there's a steady backdrop of what the fuck, what the fuck, what the fuck reverberating through his thoughts. He's not ready to deal with whatever this is. Terrorism, nuclear war, whichever of the world's dangers has finally made its way to him. This is it.

The fire spared him, his parents made it through the hard times, he and Marcus were lucky that night with the cops. James has been lucky many nights in his life. Luckier than his friend Ozzy, whose dad got deported two years back. Luckier than Mau, whose mom got breast cancer. But this is it. It's his turn now.

He finds himself leaning back against a pillar, just breathing. Down the hall, at a kiosk selling premade sandwiches and salads, an employee wearing a red apron holds a wad of napkins to her bloody forearm. James catches the glint of broken glass all around her. She looks calm, ready to stay at her stand, as if selling shitty food matters right now.

A man with his shirt untucked half marches, half runs past James. "None of this makes any sense! Someone let us out of here," he screams. His eyes are wide, wild. He notices an airline employee and runs over to him, grabbing him by the lapels of his dark blue vest. "I don't care what you people say, I'm leaving." The airline employee looks terrified and tries to mumble something, but the man gives him a little shove and turns away. "I'm leaving!" he shouts out, not really aiming the statement at anyone in particular before storming off.

"James?"

He turns his attention forward again, where Michelle is looking at him, eyebrows angled in concern. "James, are you okay?"

"Oh, yeah, I'm good," James says, running a hand over his head. "You?"

Michelle chuckles, but barely. "I'm okay." Her parents are

right behind her. Her dad is dialing a number on his phone, but it doesn't look like he's reaching anyone. Michelle's mom is stone-faced; one hand is clutched to Michelle's shoulder. "My dad's trying to call people to figure out what's going on, but the calls aren't going through. We're gonna leave the airport."

"Oh," James says. He looks around again and notices that plenty of others are thinking the same thing. A horde is moving toward the escalators that lead to the tram, most of them walking hunched over as if bracing for another explosion. "That's too bad." A moment goes by before he realizes what he said. Michelle is biting her lip, still doing that angled-eyebrow worrying thing. "I just mean it was cool talking to you."

Michelle is quiet, a slight smile tugging at her lips. Then she turns back to her parents and says something in French. Her dad starts to argue, but then her mom cuts in with a simple line that must lay the law down, because he stops talking. Her mom looks at Michelle and nods.

James wonders if he's being weird, talking about enjoying his time with Michelle while whatever's happening is going down. Except Michelle's presence is the only thing keeping him from getting swallowed up by the craziness.

"We'll walk back with you to your parents. You should try to call them too."

Several babies are wailing, and the airport's usual steady backdrop murmur of hundreds of conversations and shuffling feet has been replaced by something that hums at a different frequency. Footsteps crunch over broken glass, and the voices that carry are fraught with a worry that goes beyond flight delays. Is it the sound of his world changing? James wonders.

"James?" Michelle reaches out her hand, and for a second he doesn't know what she's doing. He just sees her forearm (delicate wrist, barely noticeable hairs, a single freckle like the stray mark of a pen) and the sheer humanity of it. How it's a part of a living person. He reaches out tenderly and grabs hold of her hand, and the touch snaps him out of whatever funk he was mired in.

She helps pull him up to his feet, and he's quick to release her hand for fear that he'll do the exact opposite and never let go. "Sorry. I think that fall knocked something loose in my head," he laughs. "Thanks." He looks to her parents and smiles, offers a clumsy "merci."

They smile back, and after James tries to call his parents (his phone responds only with silence, not even a ring), the four of them start to follow the signs for the B gates, which is the same direction that leads toward baggage claim and the exit. The escalators down to the tram are packed, and Michelle's dad says that since they don't know where the explosion originated, maybe it's best to avoid crowds and/or potential sources of mechanical malfunction. James sends a flurry of messages to his family. *Are you guys okay?*

The corridor from the D gates to the C gates is lined with an art exhibit: *East Africans Living in Atlanta*. James wants to stop and read the plaques, but it feels like a weird time to do that. Michelle's parents are leading the march, walking at a hurried pace, trailing their carry-ons behind them. Michelle has a simple black backpack on now; she must have grabbed it while they were at the gate. A few pins adorn the straps. There's one of a strange white creature with wings and a goofy face, one of a cat drinking boba tea, and a simple black circular one that reads, *What the world needs now is nuance sweet nuance.* He feels his time with her running out now, and though there's been more than he could have imagined, he feels like it's a shame that there isn't more, a shame that this is when they had to meet.

"Crazy day," he says. On the right, there's a photography series by an Eritrean living in Atlanta, all portraits of cabdrivers he's met during his time here. The captions are paragraph-long quotes, and James wants to stop and read them all, half out of curiosity, half because it'll slow Michelle down too.

"Yeah, that's not an exaggeration," Michelle laughs.

"You don't think this has something to do with that green light, do you?"

He can't know this, but as soon as he's brought it up, Michelle feels her stomach drop, as if he's just accused her of something awful. He takes her silence as dismissal that it's a silly question. A light can't do all this.

"Quién sabe," Michelle says finally. "Who knows."

James understands a little Spanish, but now that he knows she speaks it, he wishes he took his grandparents' trying to teach him a little more seriously. The matter of the light is dropped.

Some flight attendants pass by them, talking casually. James thinks that's gotta be a good sign, all things considered. If they're not panicking, things are maybe not all that bad.

"Did you ever have a Sandra?" James asks suddenly, not sure where the question really came from.

"Sandra?"

"You know. The girl I loved when I was nine. You ever have something like that?"

Michelle fiddles with her nose ring a little, then sticks her hands in her pockets. "No, I don't think so."

Three portraits in a row of men with beards, the first a Sikh with a killer smile, the second a young Black guy with a gap between his teeth, the last an older white guy with sun-cracked skin and gray in his sideburns.

"I didn't get the whole obsession with love when I was a kid," Michelle adds. "I had my friends and I had my family. I didn't understand where a third thing could even fit in, much less fight for power over those other two. When my friends started getting crushes and talking about them, I felt like they were buying into some lie. Movie and story bullshit. I felt like the world had managed to convince them of this stupid, made-up thing and I was the last one who knew the truth."

"Shit. Bet they were super cool with that."

Michelle chortles. "Yeah, a thirteen-year-old girl not talking about love? My friends started giving me so many looks I had to make up crushes just to shut them up." She turns her voice nasal and high-pitched. "'Ooh, yes, Étienne, he's so charming.'" She switches into another cartoonish impersonation. "'You should have seen how Manu looked at me. He's in love with me! I know it!'"

They pass by a heavyset woman sitting on the floor, her head resting against the wall, a blank look on her face. She's got her boarding pass on her lap, her glasses serving as a bookmark on a hardcover lying open at her side. James isn't sure if a sight like that is just airport normal or if there's desperation on the woman's face, something deeper and scarier than boredom.

"What about Mathias?"

Michelle laughs, impressed he remembers. "Touché. That felt like love for a while." She's momentarily transported back to that summer, sneaking around, finding places to make out, finding new places to press their bodies together. She'd thought she'd hidden it so well, until her grandmother made a comment during one of their Wednesday cooking sessions, and everyone had laughed, unsurprised by the news. "The truth is, I don't think I've really felt love, and I don't know if I will. Not romantic love," Michelle says quickly, a finger up to quell any interjection James may have. "I'm eighteen and I think that's normal not to have. I don't care if it never happens."

"You really don't? What all these other people want? What people who write books and movies and everybody who watches that shit and swallows it up . . . you're not into it?"

"I'm not saying I'm above it. I just know I'd be content with something . . ." She pauses. "'Less' is the word that comes to mind. But that might not be true. Simpler. I'd be content with something simpler than love. Or a whole bunch of other things simpler. A perfect sexual relationship, sure. A perfect friendship, fuck yeah. One perfect conversation." She lingers for a moment on that last one, as if chewing it over. "I don't want to ask all of that from one person. If those things happen independently of each other in my life, I'm happy. I never needed a Sandra. Not when I was nine, not when I was thirteen, and not now."

They've naturally started to lag behind her parents, just far enough so that the conversation feels private, even with the swarms of people flooding into the corridor. Despite it all—the explosion, the broken glass shimmering in the hallway, the inherent temporariness of meeting Michelle at an airport during a layover—it's hard not to feel gutted by her words. "You think you'll always feel that way?"

Michelle sighs. "I don't know, James. The future is big and foggy. We're always making plans that the world has no intention of letting us keep."

She thinks now of the last conversation she had with her grandparents. How silent she was in her anger. She's been thinking about it since she left France, all those hours in the air, and only now is regret starting to sink in. Before, it was anger, indignity. She wonders why her feelings have changed. Is it the airport, or James, or just the way anger's fire eventually runs out of fuel?

They walk in silence, the traffic of pedestrians getting heavier as they pass the C-gate concourse and head into another hallway. Approaching the escalators that lead up to the B gates,

James checks his phone to see if his parents have reached out at all. The fact that even Ava hasn't texted him back makes him chew his lip and wring his hands.

And then there's a crowd at the foot of the escalators. At first glance it just seems like a normal sight, a large crowd getting bottlenecked into two sets of escalators. But after a minute or so, it's clear no one is moving.

"Ce l'enfer qui se passe ici," Michelle's dad grumbles.

"Calme-toi, Papa. Nous savons pas ce qui se passe," Michelle says.

People in the crowd are restless, and those approaching from behind James encroach on his space, their weight up against his backpack, their shoes stepping on his heels, as if it's his fault that no one's moving. Their murmurs start to build. "What now?" someone whines. The complaint is contagious, and soon enough everyone gathered at the foot of the escalators starts to voice their frustrations. James's heartbeat is back to pounding, infected by the panic of those around him.

Eventually the murmur takes on a single voice, one single concern repeated almost like a chorus in a play, dozens of voices delivering the message: "They're not letting anyone up."

SIX

\\\\\

WHEN JAMES WAS TWELVE, THERE WAS A FIRE AT A
neighbor's apartment. He woke up to his parents' frenzied yells
and the taste of smoke. The tenants scrambled out into the hallway and down the stairs. Mrs. Williams was crying, but aside
from that James doesn't remember any noise, no fire alarm, no
roaring flames.

They crossed the street and waited for the fire department.
His parents camped him and Ava out with some of the other
neighbor kids, and then they went off to help. He remembers
those few minutes while they were gone, when they both
went back into the building, even though smoke was pouring
out of a window on the third floor. It looked like something
from the movies, or a cartoon. Dark billows of it catching the
streetlights for a moment before blending into the dark, star-
less sky.

In the end it hadn't been a huge deal, a grease fire put out before the firefighters showed. But James remembers what it was like to watch his parents step away from him in the face of danger. They walked back into the building, and it felt like they were slipping away from him for good. He remembers not knowing what would happen, not knowing how much his life was about to change. Would they be homeless? Would someone die? Would he and his sister become orphans? Would the fire keep spreading and wipe away everything he was familiar with? At his side, clutching her blanket, rubbing sleep from her eyes, Ava took in the scene quietly. He was scared for her, and slightly ashamed that she seemed less worried than he was.

Now half the crowd disperses from the escalators and the other half grows increasingly restless, shouting questions at the humid air. James thinks of his parents sitting at B36, and he is reminded of the night of the fire. There is so little he knows about what is to come, but the mere fact that he can't see his parents right now puts the fear of the unknown at the forefront of his thoughts.

Michelle and her parents are speaking to each other in French, their voices hushed in comparison to the murmur of the assembled crowd. James texts his parents yet again: *I'm on my way to you guys. Everything okay?*

No response, even though the texts are marked as DELIVERED. He puts his phone away right as the PA comes on again. "Listen, folks, everything is fine. Seriously. We promise. Yeah, there's an obstruction at the airport's exit. But we have official word that flights will start taking off soon, so just everybody chill out." The murmuring crowd settles down a little to listen. "Make your way to your gates, check in with flight monitors. If you are in the B gates, we apologize for the wetness, but several stores do sell umbrellas, so please don't complain to airline personnel. They have no control over airport microclimates, and frankly they're tired of your shit."

To his surprise, James laughs at this. Despite the circumstances, despite being out of reach from his parents and sister, despite the incomprehensibility of this whole day and the fact that this might be the kind of day he's feared, laughter starts to bubble up within him and build. He makes eye contact with Michelle, who raises her eyebrows and chuckles a little, which only makes the laughter come stronger. There's some shuffling around on the PA, muffled voices as if they're not up close to the microphone. "(No, Gary! It's my mic. Mmph. No!)"

The laughter starts to tear through James, doubling him over. He doesn't understand it, but that does not lessen its takeover of his body, nor the goddamn pleasure of laughter itself, the serotonin-flooding feeling it spreads. The people immediately around him react in one of these two ways: they move on, or they join in. It's an astonishingly even split. Of the 240 people huddled at the foot of the escalators, exactly 118 of them do not laugh at all. They can't hear his laughter over their own conversations and concerns, or if they do, they ignore it, the way most of us do to public laughter. People laugh, it's a thing we do—as Michelle would say.

The other 122 find the same exact need to laugh. It's in the pit of their stomachs, the backs of their throats. Their facial muscles contort into unwitting smiles, then their expressions crack and laughter takes hold. It ripples outward from James and Michelle, who are by now wiping tears and struggling to catch their breath in between guffaws. Strangers share mirthful looks until the laughter causes them to close their eyes. They reach out their hands to support themselves, finding each other's forearms and shoulders. The laughter roars through the long hallway, turning heads as far as the E gates and even instilling a tiny glimmer of hope and joy in some who hear it.

We're pretty happy about this. We want some joy for all these people before things get markedly worse. Especially for James, and the fear that's been simmering within him since this whole thing started. Especially for Michelle, who doesn't fear what's to come as much as what she's already done.

Things don't get worse instantly. The laughter peters out, the way applause does. A few people stop abruptly, some slow to a chuckle. There's one audible giggle at the very end, that last clap that serves as punctuation. The assembled passengers start to disperse, some still wiping tears away from the corners of their eyes, their bellies sore from the intensity of the laughter. In a second they'll start to question what came over them, almost embarrassed, but for now they hang on to the joyful distraction as they walk. They don't really know where they're going; they just know they don't want to crowd at the foot of these escalators anymore. Some are thinking they'll find another way out, some are feeling the rumble of hunger and figure it's a good time to sit down and grab a meal.

And then it starts to take a hold. A stillness in the air. Uneasiness that goes beyond the obvious reasons for it (unexplained delays, the inexplicable explosion, incomprehensible happenings).

James straightens out, trying to catch his breath. It feels like he can't, though, like the air is failing to reach his lungs, like it keeps taking wrong turns. He turns his head and tries to smile at Michelle, but what his face does feels less like a smile, more like a quiver.

"I guess we should try one of the other exits?" Michelle asks.

"For sure," James answers, with absolutely zero conviction.

She turns around and has another polyglot exchange with her parents, and they soon turn away from the remaining crowd, which is choosing to wait out the blockage. Back down the hallway they go, as if they are just killing time by wandering the airport.

Their pace is noticeably quicker than before. James is leading the way, eager to see his family. He's started fiddling with his backpack's straps, swinging a dangling strap in wide circles in front of him. All around the airport, people are developing little nervous tics like this one. Most of the people will be fine by the time this is all over; they won't even remember the few hours where they chewed their knuckles or hiccupped continuously. Some will have the tics for years, pinching at their shirts to wipe their mouths, pushing up invisible glasses.

The escalators leading up to the C gates are busy, but foot traffic is flowing, and James and Michelle make it back up to the terminal quickly. James sets his backpack down at his feet and pulls his sweatshirt over his head. Sweat trickles down his temples. "Is it just me?" he asks, looking at Michelle.

"No," she responds, pinching the front of her shirt and airing herself out. "The AC must be down."

"I don't think it'd be this hot even if it were summer," James says. His eyes right away go to the overhead signs, looking for another way to get to the B gates. He catches sight of another bank of flight monitors. Every single flight is holding steady at DELAYED. Madness. "I gotta use the bathroom," James tells Michelle. "If you guys need to, like, go or whatever, that's cool." He finds himself looking away from her, despite the fact that he wants to do exactly the opposite.

"I have to pee too," Michelle says with a shrug. She relays this to her parents, gives them her backpack, then heads off into the bathroom.

At the sink in the men's bathroom, James splashes some water on his face. He feels like he just woke up from a bad dream, those moments right after when the dream is still clinging to you and you're not sure how much of it really happened and how much is just your own brain trying to scare you. He takes a few deep breaths, then reaches over for a paper towel. When he's done drying his face, he sees that a guy next to him is brushing his teeth, listening to music through earbuds, even dancing a little.

That's the spirit, James thinks. Through the mirror, he watches the guy groove out for a while, not knowing the guy isn't actually listening to music, but simply imagining it. Shit's weird right now, James thinks, but there's no reason to worry. It'll be okay, he tries to convince himself. He gives an appreciative nod to the dancer when their eyes meet. Then he looks at himself. Flecks of water stick to his forehead and eyebrows. He'll wipe them away before going back out, but the coolness feels nice for now. Calming.

Every now and then James gets stuck looking in mirrors. The way everyone does. Late at night, when they just meant to pee and wash their hands, but there's a lingering fear of the world beyond the bathroom door, something left over from childhood, when darkness itself was a terror. Or in the midst of anxiety-riddled afternoons, or perhaps even drug-addled nights, lost in a haze of thoughts, trying to stay huddled safely within those that feel like comfort, like warm blankets during a blizzard. The blizzard, in this case, being a queasy self-awareness of who you really are, some deep momentous truths about yourself, all of them mostly insignificant in the face of that one big truth: you are mortal. God knows no one needs drugs to find themselves lost in that particular whirlwind.

The tooth-brushing dancer spits in the sink, stirring James from his thoughts, breaking the hold his own reflection has on him. He grabs another paper towel, makes sure he's completely dry, then emerges out into a pitch-black airport terminal.

SEVEN

\\\\\\\\\\

"WHAT THE FUCK NOW?" JAMES SAYS OUT LOUD.

James hasn't really cried in a long time. Maybe he came close a few times during those weeks when Aubrey refused to talk to him after they'd hooked up. He'd been hoping silently for a certain kind of love since he was twelve, or maybe since he was nine, with Sandra. He really thought it was about to come into his life, and it was that peak of joy that had made the descent into heartbreak all the more painful.

But he hadn't actually cried. He hadn't even cried that night with Marcus and the cops. They hadn't been doing anything, just driving around the city, killing time, waiting for someone from school to say they were hanging out somewhere. Then those blue lights flashing in the rearview mirror, Marcus's hands going straight to the dashboard. It was that, more than anything. How Marcus knew he had to become a statue or his life would be at risk. James was so jittery he could barely speak, but Marcus did all the talking. Yes, sir; no, sir. Cop made them get out of the car for failing to use their blinker—and only because he found nothing else, and they deferred to him like he was God, did they get back in.

Afterward, back at Marcus's, they lit a joint in the backyard and put on a dumb movie to take their mind off it, both of them shaky in their laughter, their desire to not talk about how it could have gone wrong. Sonny texted about a party, but they ignored the text. When the movie was over, it had come out anyway. "How'd you know what to do?" James asked Marcus.

"Come on, man. You know how it is. My parents have been training me since I was seven. You don't think about it every time you're out? How everything can go wrong in a second, especially around cops?"

James hadn't answered then, but Marcus's question bounced around his head all night, keeping him tossing and turning in his sleeping bag on the floor next to Marcus's bed. He thought about the fire, about the hard times, living in Humboldt Park when the shootings were bad. Thought about Ozzy's deported dad, Mau's dead mom. There was a kid at school whose brother had been shot, another one who'd died in the military, another whose uncle died in the desert trying to make it into the damn country. The longer life goes on, the more it feels like the odds increase for you to encounter tragedy. How quickly everything can go wrong. Marcus's words hadn't left his head, tears or not.

Now James hears his own voice crack, and it doesn't matter

if anyone is around to hear it or not. He feels himself about to break. He just wants this wild layover bullshit to be over. He'd even go back to Tampa and its incessant rain, all those nights of playing Scrabble by the glow of a muted television with his loud-ass uncles and their loud-ass banda music, if it meant this nightmare could be over.

The darkness might not be so terrifying if it weren't paired with the silence. Hysteric screaming, crying, explosions—James would prefer to hear any of it. An unknown danger, perhaps, but one that could be guessed at. He waits for his eyes to adjust, straining his ears for anything. Maybe he hears breathing, but he can't be sure it's not his own bated inhale-exhale. Footsteps? The PA system crackling on? The panicked shuffling of thousands of frightened passengers trying to locate their loved ones?

Nothing. It's like sound has been sucked from the airport.

(False, James. In the B gates, a blinking green light has started to emit a high-pitched whine. But yeah, aside from that, sound has been momentarily sucked from Hartsfield-Jackson Atlanta.)

Each shaky breath James takes feels like it's pushing him closer to tears. In, out, that wobbly feeling in his chest. In, out, climbing to his throat. In, out, pressure behind his eyes like a sinus infection. If he breathes one more time without hearing a sound, he's going to break down like a damn baby. In.

Then he feels a hand land on his. Slender, strong fingers. Touch; marvelous even here. He knows it's Michelle before she pulls him toward her and speaks. It gives him back a semblance of sanity, of calm. Out.

"Stay near the walls," she says. "There's something here."

He feels himself getting pushed back. Michelle's still holding on to his right hand. With his left, he reaches out and feels the wall, cool and smooth. Then there's a gust of wind like something blowing past him. He tenses his free fist, ready to strike if that's what this has come to. He is not a fighter, but he'll gladly take a danger that can be fought with fists.

A pause. James narrows his eyes, trying to make out what he just felt, what Michelle saw. Then the sound comes. It's sudden, like when you get in a car and turn it on and the last person who drove was blaring the radio. It's a forceful cacophony, making him press his hands to his ears for a moment until the shock wears away and he can start picking out the sounds individually.

Now, as expected, people running. Heavy boot steps belonging to a Black woman named Justine clod past. She's in the National Guard and is certain terrorism is afoot and has broken away from the soldiers previously seen at the Delta Sky Club in order to do what she can to help. James can't identify what they are, but he hears the loud prayers of a Swiss woman named Johanna, begging the God she stopped believing in when she was fourteen that she'll see her kids again someday. The looting, which up until now had been mild, mostly contained to the few moments right after the blackouts, mostly contained to a few chaotic parties, now unleashes itself full force for the remainder of the layover. Two white twentysomethings named Brad and Chad, buzzed off their earlier choice to pair shots of Jameson with twenty-ounce beers, decide it is time for a little chaotic fun. Taking advantage of the darkness, they do what they've seen sports fans do for years. After some conspiratorial whispering, they each grab their stools and hurl them through the nearest pane of glass. It's one of the few that survived the blast earlier, but now it shatters with a loud crash that causes everyone in the vicinity to shriek, cry, get one step closer to reaching the end of their rope. The fire alarm system in the airport rings out. "We have detected an emergency," an automated voice drones in between the blaring tones. "Please remain calm while we investigate."

James is focused on one particular sound above the others. Something guttural, wet. Like Marcus's fat-ass bulldog, Freckles, anytime he tries to go upstairs. But a lot more menacing, like Freckles has finally had it with all these fuckin' walks and is looking to get back at someone. Like Freckles is in a horror movie and fell into a pit of something radioactive and it's dinnertime.

"The hell is that?"

"I don't know," Michelle says, still calm. "Putain," she adds under her breath. "Maman? Papa?"

James unconsciously squeezes her hand, only then realizing that he's holding it once again. The guttural sound seems to be getting farther away. James reaches out blindly at the hallway, as if that will tell him anything.

"I'd ask what's happening," he says, "but that seems to be a pretty pointless question right about now."

"Add another pickle to the shit sandwich," Michelle says.

He can feel her looking around anxiously. He doesn't blame her, wishes he could help somehow. But then he's distracted by the thought that the phrase she just said feels distinctly American. Like, no matter how good her English is, that specific thought feels so close to something his friends might say, to something he might say if he were being particularly funny. And she's saying it in her third or fourth language. "You're amazing," he says, the words slipping from his tongue before he knows what he's saying.

"Putain," she says again in response, or maybe just to herself.

The darkness does not dissipate. The noises do not either. James realizes that every scary movie he's ever seen, every scary situation in a TV show or in a book or in any story whatsoever failed to do its job, to really terrify. He's jumped at certain moments in the theater, felt anticipation. Loud noises, suspenseful music bringing their predictable yet unavoidably jumpy conclusion. But it never captured this. The true suspense of not knowing what is to come. The true fear of a world turned upside down. Even the fear he's felt in growing older pales in comparison to this.

James squeezes Michelle's hand again, and he mumbles a "sorry" for not asking if it's okay with her. But Michelle seems more focused on the thing that rushed past them in the hallway.

Seconds or minutes or decades go by (actually, two minutes

and forty-seven seconds, but we'll forgive James for not keeping exact track). James's eyes do not adjust to the lack of light. "Maman! Papa," Michelle half screams, half whispers. She swivels her head, trying to make out their silhouettes among the darkness.

In, out. James doesn't know what to do. He wants his parents near him, wants his sister near him, wants Michelle to hold on to his arm this entire time and be smarter than him, tell him what to do, where to go, how they will get through this.

Meanwhile, Brad and Chad, thrilled by the thought of living without consequences, run out of their bar without paying their tabs, in search of more glass to break. They want to steal things, want to break things, want to set something aflame without having to breathe in the ashes. They stumble around in the dark, giggling to themselves, calling out for each other, tripping on the feet of scared mothers huddling their children close to their bodies, trying as best they can to create a shelter. Tears and sobs flow freely, adrenaline is spiked throughout the airport. Brad and Chad cannot wrap their minds around the fact that anything could possibly go wrong.

After who knows how long, James and Michelle are half-crouched against the wall. Whatever it was in the hall has passed, or dissipated, returned to the ether from which it came. Impossible to know the details when the thing itself—if it even is a thing—is shrouded in obscurity.

Michelle's grip has eased, but their hands are still clasped within each other's. They're even leaning their bodies slightly toward the other, without acknowledging it at all. There are more important things to think about, and mentioning it at all would break some sort of spell. Even James knows this, unfamiliar with love though he may be.

"I have to find them," Michelle says.

James nods, knowing what she means. "If they went anywhere, they'd go to baggage claim, right? Toward a light at least?" He turns his head left and right, sees nothing of the sort.

No response from Michelle. Everywhere, muffled little cries. The atmosphere feels the way it does when you're a kid just learning about death. He vaguely remembers the night when he went through that. Waking up from a bad dream in hysterics. He was five or six, maybe, the realization first hitting him that one day he would be gone. He wants to protect people from this feeling, but he doesn't know how to break through it himself.

It's weird how little he knows about Michelle but how he knows that it'll feel so comforting to be near another person right now. Just a little closer, nothing real changes, just distance.

"What do you want to do?" he asks when she still hasn't answered.

A deep breath from his side. Her thumb ever so slightly runs over the length of his knuckles. "Find them," she says. "I think whatever it was is gone." Her hand unclamps from his, tiny little heartbreak. He feels her stand up straight, and it compels him to do the same. "They knew in which direction we were going; that's where they'll head."

James doesn't ask Michelle what she thinks the thing in the

hallway was. The wind that blew past them, its sound and smell chilling them both to the bone. He doesn't ask about what happened while they were in the bathroom, or how she knows it's gone. He will follow her no matter what she would say to these questions, so what point is there in sounding them out?

They feel their way down the hall, their phone flashlights on, though the darkness seems to suck up the light.

Touch is mostly how he's getting around, but James is so keenly aware of everything else. Namely, he's aware of the lack of what he should be seeing. Monitors, people, tile, fluorescence. No matter the hour, there are normalcies that a light going out should not erase. The sound of the airport is quickly relegated to the background, almost surprisingly so. Instead, the sounds he is aware of are Michelle's footsteps. The rhythm of her breath. Her softly muttered thoughts, which are spoken too quietly for James to fully grasp whether they are in a language he speaks or not. Was that Spanish or French or Thai or English? A statement meant for James or for Michelle herself? He's not sure of anything.

For some reason, he thinks of a Thursday when he was fourteen or so. No school the next day, he can't remember why. Usually his memories are inextricably linked to seasons. Heat, and the constant desire to escape from it. Schemes to get to the lakeshore. Air-conditioning. Shit, the joy of a dark, air-conditioned movie theater on a summer day. Fall in the Midwest. Chicago cold. Spring, such a fitting term for the feeling of shedding yourself of winter's constricting, heavy coat. To be sprung out into the world, that's how it felt.

But no, he can't place anything around this Thursday. The memory takes place indoors, but James can't remember dripping boots at the front door, can't feel the relief of central air within the daydream. It's just a TV screen, three of them laid out on the carpet, two more on the couch. James was on the carpet, that much he knows. A video game, a handful of controllers, bellies full of pizza and junk. The point of the night right before the 'rents went to sleep and he and his friends had to start keeping it down. Sound unleashed, as if they knew time was running short. Marcus, Karim, Mau probably during those days. The feeling that he never wanted this to stop. Not in those words exactly. Just that he would do this forever if he could. His friends, shouting without consequence, a game, their hunger sated. He'd felt a certain boyhood dwindling away back then. Or at least this version of himself thinks so now.

He's at a fucking airport, James has to remind himself. He's in Atlanta, a city he doesn't really know anything about, except for their sports teams and a rapper or two who he knows are from here. More shit has gone down tonight than in any other single night of his life. Inarguably.

"You all right back there?" Michelle asks.

"Fuckin' swell, man," James says with a chuckle, wondering if he took a hit to the head at some point. He's never said "swell" before in his life.

Michelle laughs. "Talk to me. My brain's driving me nuts here."

"Yeah, I think I know how you feel." Up ahead, the darkness starts to break. James can see the glow of cell phone screens lighting up faces. A few are being used as flashlights by frantic people calling out names over and over again. Soon dozens of cell phone flashlights are shining in the D terminal. There are storefronts coming up ahead, so James and Michelle move toward the middle of the hallway.

"James. Talk to me."

"Right. Sorry." But he can't find anything to say. He flashes his light on each gate he passes. Some people shield their eyes from the glare, some just stare blankly. This is not a sight James ever thought he'd see. It's a scene from a disaster movie, it's news coming in from a war-torn country. Although maybe he's exaggerating. There's no carnage, at least that he knows of. He turns his flashlight away from the gates, up and down the hall, looking for the thing that blew past them, looking for anything that could at least explain the sound he heard, the feeling it left him with. "You think this might be one of those 'life will never be the same again' moments?"

"You mean for us or for the whole world?" Now that there's a semblance of light, they're walking side by side again. Michelle is looking around, every now and then calling out her parents' names.

"Both, I guess." He sighs. "I wonder how many of those days

people have. On average, I mean. Throughout their lives. I think about that a lot, actually."

Michelle slides her phone into her pocket as much as it will go, the flashlight still shining forward. Then she pulls a hair tie from her wrist and does her hair into a half ponytail. "It's probably not hard to figure out. The day you die, I think, counts, so that's one. I don't buy that a wedding changes your life, but the day you meet people that you date long-term probably does change things. And everyone gets, what, one or two of those? People who really change life for you, I mean. Not someone you make out with for a couple of months and get sick of."

"Right," James says, as if he knows exactly what that's like.

"Then we can probably assume at least one life-changing event during childhood. Some sort of trauma that puts your life on a different path, maybe. I didn't quite have that, at least not that I can remember. But I did move around a lot, so I probably have a higher count than most people, since where you live changes your life." Michelle pulls her phone out again to point it upward at a nearby sign. Her hands are shaking, James notices. If his parents had suddenly disappeared during the blackout, he'd be a lot more freaked out than she is now. Though, now that he thinks about it, he hasn't seen his parents in a long time, and he is already more freaked out than she is.

She puts her phone away again and then leads them in the direction of the E gates. "So that's four or five life changers so far, including death. I don't think there's a ton more, on average.

Maybe one tragedy when you're an adult, or one great thing that happens."

"You think that's it, though? What about job changes? Breakups, fights, presidential elections? I feel like every year has been completely different for me. Just school alone, man. Every new year feels like a whole new life for me. Even week to week, I wake up being friends with different people, liking different girls. Whole new worries on a Thursday than I had on Wednesday. Shit, sometimes I have a crazy dream about a girl in class or about what I want to be, and in the morning I feel like life is not the same as it was when I went to bed."

It's getting hotter as they walk, more humid. (By our accounts it should be getting colder, but perhaps we should stop trying to understand the nuances of airport microclimates.) James feels like he's right back in Florida. Sweat makes his jeans stick to his legs in the worst way. He keeps looking over his shoulder, waiting for crazy things to come running at them, but all he sees is darkness and screen-lit faces.

"Those are just blips, I think," Michelle says, then calls out again for her parents. Her voice is steady, but it is growing quieter each time she calls out. "A new crush doesn't change your life, it just adjusts the details."

They're almost at the end of the hallway. James can see the curve leading toward the E gates, toward his parents, toward the exit. Somewhere up ahead, maybe four or five gates on the right, more glass crashes. James and Michelle pause to try to make out whether the breaking glass will unleash some fresh new hell.

Nothing. They keep walking.

"How many of those moments do you think are for the worse? More than for the better?" James asks.

Michelle kicks at something on the floor, a cloth face mask patterned with sea creatures in turquoise and orange. They walk on.

"So," James says, not wanting silence to take over and not wanting to hear anything else either, "how many times would you say your life has changed in a huge way?"

Before Michelle can answer, a swell of voices erupts. James turns to look at Michelle. There's just enough light emanating from who knows where that he can see her profile. He has the thought that he didn't flee when she wanted to take a walk. And now he'll remember her as more than someone he could have talked to but didn't. That little choice has changed his life, momentously or not.

Then the voices get louder, and James sees fear cross Michelle's pretty brown eyes. He only has a second to appreciate the fact that his vision's adjusting to the dark before he has to face what's coming. We'll let him have it. We'll let Michelle have it too, the slight joy, among all this, that she can see her companion's face for the first time in a handful of scary minutes. We won't show the scary thing quite yet.

Not yet.

Not yet.

Fine, to the sight:

From the bend leading to the E gates comes what can only be described as a horde. James knows right away that it is not what passed them in the hall earlier, because it is too mundane. Well, not mundane, but at least not indefinable, not just a feeling. Not to mention that if this was what passed them in the hall, they would have been trampled.

It's a horde of at least fifty people, and they appear to be drenched, droplets of water surrounding them like a mist, flung from their bodies. James can see these minuscule details because the water droplets are suspended in the air, moving in slow motion. There's a red-bearded man at the helm of the mob. We've caught him mid-yell, his jaw dropped wide open. James can imagine the guttural scream he'd be emitting if his sound was traveling the way it ought to.

Businessmen in their suit jackets and button-up shirts and no ties. One guy has wrapped a pink-and-blue-striped tie around his head like he's some sort of corporate warrior. There are three flight attendants from different airlines jostling for position, each looking like they're trying to pull ahead of the others, as if they're in some sort of no-holds-barred race. Other people seem to have just been swept up in the horde, forced to join by momentum alone. At least two people are holding crying children, hands cradling their tender napes close to the chest, pained expressions on their faces. Most people roll bags behind them, unwilling to abandon their belongings in this escape or siege or whatever it is.

James takes advantage of the slow motion to try to parse out whether these people are running from something or to something. A quick scan shows nothing that looks like a gun. No one is bleeding. One guy has an armful of potato chip bags, clearly swiped from one of those book/convenience stores called ATL Today News. A Latino dude is holding something that looks suspiciously like a torch, though it's hard to tell what it's fashioned from. In the glow of this burning light, James can see dozens more people behind, all soaked, their faces stretched into screams of anger. A fitting sight in this day of unleashed fears: the angry mob. He's never actually pictured an angry mob before; it's been a vague, shapeless thing in his mind that he equates with internet trolls, cable news viewers, whole parts of the country (and the world). Strange to think that the mob is made up of individuals, each face twisted into its own particular expression of anger.

The slow-motion effect fades away, and the shouts and footsteps get closer at a clip that gets James's heart beating. They're storming toward James and Michelle, and it's hard to imagine that they would stop for any reason.

There are only a few other people in the hallway between James and the horde. One guy is stopped in the middle of the hall, looking at his phone. The throng of people reaches him in a matter of seconds and swallows him up.

James tries to see what happens to him in the crowd, but he's simply gone, no trace of him, as if he's sunk below murky waters, as if he's really been swallowed.

The horde picks up speed, their footsteps quickening in time with each other, as if they've all rehearsed, as if they've moved as one before.

"Michelle," James says, reaching out a hand to make sure she's still with him. "Run."

EIGHT

\\\\\\\\

JAMES AND MICHELLE SPRINT BACK THE WAY THEY came, undoing all their progress. Their phones light the way, illuminating the universe of broken glass on the terminal floor, the people trying to sleep through it all, those hunkering down awaiting explosions, wiping away their blood, their tears, the filth that has somehow accumulated on their faces throughout the past few hours. The frantic pace of our heroes' movement makes it hard to avoid everything in their path, and James finds himself having to jump over backpacks and extended legs, avoid pillars and kiosks. The sound of destruction behind them continues.

James barely allows himself a backward glance, especially because he keeps seeing a bunch of confused people in his wake, and he knows that none of them will react in time to avoid the mob. He doesn't know if the mob means to harm people, if that guy who was swallowed up was hurt or just became one of them, but obviously James is not going to stop and ask.

Michelle, meanwhile, is calling out warnings in English. "Watch out! Excuse me! Run!" She speeds ahead, pulling in front of James and leading the way. It's a weird thing to think about right now, she knows, but she considers how she's particularly well suited for a chase like this. Those early years in Jakarta, maneuvering in the street markets. Pasar Mayestik and Taman Fatahillah, those trips with her mom for fabric and produce in the crowded corridors. Walking around in Bangkok with her cousins, racing each other past slow-moving tourists, always aware of the tuk-tuks and scooters speeding close to the crowded, narrow sidewalk. When she was younger, she used to believe she had a modest version of a superpower. A hint of seeing into the future—if only a second—a vision for what was in front of her, a sense of when someone might step out into her path or slow down.

As she sprints, she tries to take in the entirety of her surroundings. Hiding spots, restricted-access entrances, anything. But the only escapes from this hallway are restaurants and stores, and in each doorway, there are people huddled, emerging from their own hiding spaces as they investigate this newest ruckus.

She's glad that James is running with her. She imagines other people in the airport who came here alone, having to figure all this shit out on their own. She's glad that her parents are still with each other, regardless of where they went and why and how. She thinks of the way the green light pressed down beneath her finger, succumbing to her touch. For some reason, her stomach turns at the memory, but there's too much else going on for her to focus on that.

Onward they sprint. By the time they start to slow, they've made it all the way to the B gates, where all the lights are functioning normally, but it's raining. When their lungs and sides start to hurt and their ears tell them that they've put enough distance between them and the mob for the time being, they walk. They don't mention the rain, only give each other a look and shake their heads. James spots a water fountain nearby and takes long, yearning gulps. Michelle breathes heavily behind him, arms up, hands behind her head. The rain feels nice against her skin, washing away the sweat she's worked up on their run.

"Well, this is probably not a great sign," she says.

"People are straight up losing their shit," James answers, wiping at his mouth.

Overhead, more flight monitors. United 224 to Newark: DELAYED. Air China 7450 to Newark: DELAYED. Delta 1138 to Chicago: DELAYED. James wants to laugh at this, but something in him can't quite get the chuckle out. "Just say they're canceled, man."

At that moment, against the odds presented by the rain and the lack of lighting throughout the airport, everyone's favorite PSA guy cuts in. "We're definitely not canceling flights, everyone! This is still expected to be a temporary delay. So please stop saying otherwise like it doesn't hurt our feelings. It does.

We're trying our best. Also, we've been urged to remind you that airport police are on hand, and any criminal activity will not be tolerated, no matter how long you've been here. Just, you know, chill out. Please don't destroy the TGI Friday's. We love TGI Friday's. We'll get you home. Eventually."

\\\\\\\\\

Elsewhere, Rosa Velarde sits next to Taha. He is holding a bag full of ice wrapped up in Rosa's bloodied TSA shirt to the back of his head while Rosa stares at her phone. At this exact moment, it shows 10:39:24. Her battery life is at 100 percent, and she has not been able to switch away from the countdown or to turn the phone off and on again.

The man responsible for Taha's bloody nose and head scurried away and will likely face no consequences for his action. Rosa momentarily tried to find other agents to help, but when the lights cut out, Taha said, "Let's sit. I am okay, the bleeding has stopped, no use fretting." They waited out the darkness, Rosa wondering with each passing minute how long this could possibly go on for.

She knows all about airport safety protocol, the backup generators, the measures in place in case disaster occurs. Nothing is going the way it's supposed to. The lights flicker back on, just as inexplicably as they left. Taha shakes his head slightly, tsk-tsks a few times. "People must be so frightened," he says in his mellifluous voice.

They are sitting with their backs against the wall. In front of them are the escalators that lead up from the tram to the D gates. James and Michelle ran by not too long ago but failed to notice the two sitting there. Lots of people have gone up and down the escalators in that time, some of them lit by the glow of their cell phone flashlights, others shuffling past quietly in the dark. Rosa wishes she knew what to do to help. Her uniform is supposed to grant her some sort of authority right now, some sort of knowledge of what to do.

"Is your phone working?" Rosa asks.

Taha reaches into his pocket and hands it over. "It doesn't have a SIM card yet. I was going to get one first thing when I got to Savannah." He chuckles, then clicks his tongue again as he shakes his head. "My new landlord is probably waiting for me, wondering what's going on. I'm starting a new job on Monday."

"Congrats," Rosa says, delving into the world available within the phone. Her first thought is to call the office, but without a SIM card, that won't work. She logs off of Taha's social media and into hers, then messages all of her coworkers. *What's protocol right now? I'd clocked out already, don't have my radio.* She goes to news sites, reads her feed, sees nothing enlightening in the least bit.

"I suddenly feel very bad for people who grew up without technology," she says to herself.

But Taha hears it and chuckles. "Oh, believe me, those days had their merits."

Rosa only momentarily looks away from the phone. "I don't

have time for people who are nostalgic for ignorance. Say what you will about information overload, at least we're not sticking our heads in the sand."

Taha laughs now, and Rosa can't help but find the mirthful sound pleasing. The world can go to shit, but there'll still be people who can find joy in it. Taha composes himself, winces a little as he presses the ice pack tighter to his head. "Very well."

Now he rises to his feet. He's an imposing figure, muscle-bound and tall. That dickhead was lucky to get him down with one punch, Rosa thinks. The Birkenstocks don't help that image, exactly, but then again, Taha doesn't seem like a guy who wants to establish any sort of aggressive reputation. "So, where do we go?"

Rosa looks at him with a furrowed brow. "How would I know?"

"You know the airport better than I do, I would think."

"Yeah, so?" Rosa checks back to her social media, but none of her coworkers have responded. She goes to several news sites, most of them highlighting some political scandal and a typhoon in the Philippines. "We shouldn't go anywhere until we know what's happening."

"What can we do sitting here?"

"Stay safe?"

"Nonsense," Taha says, stepping over to her with a hand outstretched. Rosa figures he wants his phone back, so she hands it to him. But he waves it away and motions for her to grab hold.

"If others are not safe, we have a duty to our fellow man to try to help. Or would you rather bury your head in the sand?"

The guy smiles so confidently, Rosa is sure he's been in a toothpaste commercial or something. His teeth aren't pearly white or straight, but he somehow still works it like a model. She shakes her head at him, but deep down she knows what he says makes sense. When she took this job, it was for the money, but in the months since she's been here, she's most enjoyed those days when it feels like what she does helps. Not her country, necessarily, but the people around her. Long shot, she knows; the chance is greater that she provides annoyance and frustration more than anything. Sometimes she feels like she's helping by simply not being an asshole.

Rosa rises to her feet without taking Taha's help.

"I could tell you care," he says, beaming another smile. "Now, where to?"

Just then, a sound reaches them, the roar of hundreds of voices echoing down the hall.

\\\\\\\\

The rain in the B gates grows so torrential that James and Michelle cannot see where they are going and are splashing through rushing water. A veritable river flows through the hallway, despite the fact that there is no incline or decline in the airport and it makes no physical sense for water to rush.

They sneak away to a smoking lounge, which, for some reason, is a haven from the downpour. They stand inside, looking at the rain for a while, waiting for a break in order to continue. When it becomes clear they'll have to wait, they sit, facing the tarmac, which is shrouded in darkness save for the red and blue lights lining the runway and the orange glow of the planes that have been parked out there since this whole thing began. It's a clear Atlanta night out there.

James's mind is focused on his parents, fantasizing about finding them, about leading them toward the exit at the T gates. If he can do that, then life can still go back to normal. No harm has come to him, yet. He's chilly again, so he slips his hoodie back on. He can somehow sense that he's not done with this dance between cold and hot.

Michelle is quiet, dripping water onto the floor. They slump in uncomfortable chairs that smell of stale cigarettes. Except for the occasional crackle or hiss from the overhead speakers, the steady white noise of rain, it's quiet. James is hyperaware of his own breathing, and he tries to control it so that it sounds . . . normal. Why he thinks he should be breathing normally in this situation is beyond us.

Michelle wrings her hair out, the water splashing onto the maroon carpet. Which is a terrible choice for a smoking lounge but reminds her of the maroon bathroom floor mat at her grandparents' house. She spent the whole week in Bordeaux trying not to think about the permanence of the goodbye, so it's no surprise she's been avoiding the thought since she left too.

It had felt like a joke from the moment her parents had told her about the idea: a living funeral. Each of their diseases was progressing—Mamie's lungs, Papi's bones—and soon they'd be too sick to drink as much wine as they'd like on a final goodbye. And didn't Michelle know her grandparents better than that? No, no, it wouldn't do for them. They did not just succumb to life's indignations. They folded those indignations into a plan that worked for them.

They would throw a big party, see all their friends and family one final time, hear the nice speeches everyone would give in their honor, then retreat into hospice care, hopefully passing within hours of each other, since it would make a good story and prevent the heartache of one being without the other. They did not want their loved ones to see them shrivel further than they had, to see them sleep all day in pain. Those last stages of decline could be done over the phone, if they had to be done at all.

From when they called to tell Michelle's dad about the idea up until the goodbye at the airport security line, it never occurred to Michelle that they could be serious. It felt tongue-in-cheek, an excuse to throw a party and then forget all follow-through. But as the end of Michelle's stay approached, it became clearer that they meant it. Barring some miracle, years left instead of weeks, Michelle would never see them again, except on a screen.

How ironic it will be if Michelle goes before they do.

And why? It suddenly hits Michelle: the green light.

"This is my fault," Michelle says, breaking the silence.

"Yeah, I don't think that's even a little bit true."

"I'm serious. The green light. I shouldn't have pressed it."

"Michelle, listen to yourself. Are you saying a random green light caused people to riot like it's the end of the goddamn world?"

"Okay, yeah, it sounds crazy. But give me another explanation."

In the glass, he can see faint reflections of himself and Michelle. She looks just as drained as he feels, slumping so low in the chair that her head is resting on the back of the seat, her gaze set on the ceiling. He knows how close his family is, knows that at any moment the crazed mob could reach these gates too, if they can get through the rain. Right now it feels like he'll never manage to get up again.

The thought sends him sliding down the seat, matching Michelle's position.

"I've had too good a life, that's my guess," James says. "I've had some close calls with those big life-changing moments we talked about. But nothing terrible. How long can a person go on like that? Avoiding tragedy. Maybe all of this is the universe balancing shit out, or whatever."

She turns to look at him. He looks back at her. Usually James hates eye contact that lasts more than a second or two. It's like the hardest endurance contest he can think of. It makes him feel like his soul is fully exposed and that the person watching him will be able to run off with it. This is different, though. Like Michelle might not run off.

"Hm," Michelle says, right as she smiles at him. Her eyes look a little sleepy, and he gets that feeling he did the first time she touched him. Like maybe *this* is what love feels like. Comfort in another's gaze. He pictures them just a little closer together, maybe Michelle's head on his chest. The image lasts only briefly, until Michelle's smile fades and she turns back toward the ceiling. "If we die tonight, what will you wish you'd gotten to do in your life?"

"I didn't say we were dying. Ain't no way we're dying here, Michelle." He's a little surprised at the force with which he says this. He, too, has thought that death might be lurking in the terminal, so his adamance that it's not takes him aback. "Stop even thinking like that," he adds. Whether it's said for her benefit or his is unclear.

"But if we do—"

"Seriously, you're tripping. I know tonight's been crazy, but we're at an airport. The slightest bit of violence gets sniffed out as soon as it begins. I bet those people are all under arrest already. TSA and cops would be on it in a second."

Michelle sits up for a second, just to make a show of looking behind them toward the glass door. "You hear anyone coming, James? Do you see a swarm of officials parading down the hall?"

James bites his bottom lip, then angles his neck so he can look out the window. There are no sirens in the night sky, not even the usual yellow spinning lights of baggage carts or stair cars that patrol the runway.

"If this was a normal day," Michelle continues, "I'd agree

with you, it would end quickly. But something happened when I touched that light, and things are not the way they usually are. No one's coming to rescue us. We can't leave, and we sure as hell aren't getting on an airplane tonight." She takes a breath, calming herself down. Then she sighs and slumps back into her earlier position. "So, if we die, what will you regret that you never got to do?"

James waves his hand at her and clicks his tongue, but enough of him believes she's right that he can't bring himself to say anything.

Knocking her knee against his, Michelle scoffs. "Okay, I'm exaggerating. We probably aren't going to die. But I think the question stands anyway. If we *did* die tonight, if this was the last night of your life—what do you wish you would have done?"

"Like, what's a thing I've always wanted to do?"

"Not necessarily," Michelle says. She starts moving her legs nervously, knocking her own knees together and then spreading them out far enough that parts of her thigh start to touch his. "It could be that, but it could be something you only now thought of. Like . . ." She thinks for a moment, making a motioning circle with her wrist as she searches for an example. ". . . petting an elephant. That's one thing I wish I'd done, even though I've never had that urge before, never even really thought of it before now."

Part of James's brain is thinking: Are you shitting me with this game right now, man? Exchange numbers with this girl, go meet up with Mom and Pops and Ava, and then let's get the hell out of here. At the same time, though, the other part of James's brain is thinking: Skydiving. Finally trying raw oysters, even if they look like dead aliens. Telling people I love them. Not in that cheesy tell-them-more-often way that is mentioned in every story about a loved one dying. But tell them at all. I've never said the words aloud, not the way they're meant to be said. Not jokingly when you're thanking them for giving you an extra slice of pizza, or when you're talking about a musician or something. But the way people say it when they say it all on its own.

"Nothing?" Michelle says.

The first part of James's brain goes: Yo, enough.

And the other, latter part, which maybe you've already guessed is starting to win the battle, goes: Have a drink on the beach. Not, like, sneaking beers in fast-food soda containers and sipping through the straw while on the lookout for cops at Lake Michigan, not that kind of drink. But how cliché visions of a Mexican beach always go. That picturesque, colorful, fruit-rimmed drink, "lying in the shade on top of white sand while gentle turquoise water laps in the near distance" kind of drink. I wish I'd felt that joy at least once in my life. Felt the joy of the first sip, the slight cool breeze, the smell of coconut sunscreen.

"I wish I'd made beef brisket," James says finally.

"Beef brisket," Michelle repeats. It's not exactly a question, but a question mark is for sure lurking in the vicinity.

"I don't really cook or anything, which makes it weird. But

I've always had this"—he motions vaguely, his hands at either side of his head—"vision or something. I don't know what I'd call it. But I've had this image in my head for a while now of a big hunk of beef brisket. I make a dry rub for it, garlic powder, chili powder, some brown sugar. I dunno, I'd look it up. So I put this rub on the beef and then I put it in a smoker like the kind my uncle has at his house. It cooks for hours and comes out nice and burnt and delicious—"

"Wait, if you don't cook, why do you have this detailed fantasy of cooking brisket?"

"I have no idea." James shrugs. "It's just a weird urge. I can't explain it."

They look at each other again, and the go-see-your-parents part of James's brain gets a little quieter still.

"I wish I'd seen Prague," Michelle says. "It's been on the top of my list for so long."

"Made a movie. Just a short one or something."

"Played crokinole."

"What the hell is that?"

"It's a Canadian board game. It's, like, a tabletop thing with wooden pegs and little chips that you flick." She's trying to provide visual aid with her hands, but when she looks over at James to see if he knows what she's talking about, it's clear he has no clue. "I swear it's real. I learned about it when I stayed with some friends at their family's cottage last summer. It looks fun, but it's regional and you can't really find it in Quebec at all."

"What's it called again?"

"Crokinole," Michelle says.

James sounds it out once or twice, almost instantly forgetting the pronunciation as soon as he's done saying it. "Well, I wish I would have played croney-cole in my life too."

Michelle laughs, and it sounds like the crinkle of a candy wrapper as it's being opened. Not just any candy bar, but your favorite one. That's what her laugh sounds like.

Quickly quieting part of James's brain: Will you get off your ass and go find your family, man?

James: "Stayed up twenty-four hours. I don't think I ever did that all the way through without nodding off for a nap."

Michelle: "Sing David Bowie's 'Rock 'n' Roll Suicide' in front of a crowd. There was an open mic night every month at my school in Argentina, and even though there would never be more than fifteen people there, I always wanted to sing my heart out to that song. Probably a good thing I never did. I can't sing at all."

James's brain: Had sex. Had a steady girlfriend. Done the Blazin' Challenge at Buffalo Wild Wings. Gotten better at talking to strangers.

Behind them, the rain still hammers down like a typhoon. James focuses on a 747 out on the tarmac. It's parked right between the reflections of James and Michelle, and the glare on the window makes it so he can clearly see most of the plane. It's close too, enough that he can make out certain traits of the people in the windows. A woman wearing a red neck pillow has her head tilted backward, mouth open. James can imagine the snoring. There's a little kid wearing glasses, staring out the window, clutching some sort of stuffed animal. The people on the plane have been told nothing of what's happening at the airport, mostly because the pilots have not been able to communicate with the blacked-out tower. All those passengers inside have no idea how good they have it, in their annoyance. They are allowed to sleep, to watch movies while they snack on pretzels, to hang on to normalcy, albeit an inconvenient one. They share an armrest with their loved ones; what more could someone want?

James: "Volunteered for something. Like a charity or whatever. I don't have my own money or anything, but I've got time. And I wish I'd used more of it trying to help people, you know? It's not like I'm the luckiest dude on the planet, but I've had it pretty good. If my life just gets snuffed out tonight, if my time is over, I think my biggest wish is that I'd made someone's life measurably better. Someone who needed it, you know?"

The kid on the plane puts his forehead against the window, and little clouds of fog appear when he breathes. He holds his stuffed animal tighter in a hug, then exhales until the whole glass is fogged up. Something catches in James's chest, and all of a sudden he feels like his voice is about to crack. Pressure builds behind his eyes, and he turns his head away from Michelle so that she won't catch any of it. If he'd only known how short life might be, he would have been better. He would've spent his time helping someone instead of playing video games and riding his stupid bike with Marcus. He could have tried out one of those Big Brother programs instead of listening to music in his room with his headphones on, practicing dance moves in the mirror in case he got the chance to look cool someday. And, yeah, riding around with Marcus is one of his favorite things to do, and maybe the memory would look great in a movie or something, soft-filtered light and happy piano music overplaying the joy of it. Without the golden-hued nostalgia, though, what do those moments even matter? They get wiped away as soon as a life does, and didn't improve anyone's joy but his own.

Or maybe he would have spent more time riding around with Marcus. Maybe he would have spent more time playing video games late at night with his headset on, talking to his friends as they shot up aliens or dueled each other as NBA players. A screen and technology, yeah, yeah, a waste of a life they say; but when else can you have your friends' voices inside your head, feel their laughter deep within your bones, even across whatever distances lie between you?

Michelle happens to be looking at the same fogged-up window that James is, and she sees the little kid using his index finger to draw a dinosaur on the glass. She adjusts her nose ring, smiles at the kid's boredom. What a luxury, to be bored and not worried. She looks over at James, whose leg is jittery, his hands clutched into nervous fists. She rests her leg against his, hoping it'll calm him the way it calms her. She's somewhat sorry she brought up the subject of dying regrets, even though she's happy to know this guy whose company she stumbled into is a good person. If this is the end, there are worse people she could have spent her time with.

The reason Michelle brought this up is because she is trying to redeem herself. Her grandfather tried to have this same conversation with her two nights ago, right before they left. But she wouldn't hear of it, wouldn't admit that it was the last time they'd see each other, even if it had been the whole reason for the trip. Michelle wouldn't play a stupid life-affirming game for his benefit. The whole flight over the Atlantic, she felt sick to her stomach for it. Regret had never been more physical, wave after wave of shame and remorse. Some indie flick played on the tiny screen in front of her, and though she didn't once look away from it, she didn't understand a thing about what happened in the movie. It had about a dozen characters, none of whom she could name, nor could she say what their connection to each other might be.

"There's still time," Michelle says, even though she's not sure what she means.

NINE

\\\\\\\\

WHEN THE MOOD OF THE CONFESSIONAL GAME breaks, so does the rain. James gets up with renewed urgency to reunite with his parents. They're only a three-minute walk down the hall, and the shame that he was this close and decided to stop for a break is at least ameliorated by the relief that the rain has somehow drained away, leaving the hallway with only the occasional puddle instead of the river that was forming before.

It's still sprinkling. James wants to be protective of his backpack and its contents, and Michelle is walking with her shoulders instinctively hunched, but both of them are already drenched, and their break did nothing to dry them.

Gate B36, Delta flight 1138 to Chicago. DELAYED. Departure time: 1:45 a.m. James pulls out his phone, miraculously unbothered by the dampness of everything, and double-checks the fact that this is his flight.

James's parents and Ava should be right here where they were before. But they're not. No one's here at all. The gate is a sopping mess of carpet and puddles in the seats. There are a few abandoned bags, but his family's stuff isn't there, and the airline employees are gone too.

"They probably went to find shelter," Michelle says.

"Yeah," James says, though he doesn't know what shelter there is to find outside of the empty smoking lounge they were just in.

James thinks back to when he said bye to his parents. Thinks back to a week of being pissed at them for bringing them all out to the Florida rain. Thinks back a few years ago to the summer of barbecues, when his dad bought that new grill and couldn't get enough of it. Every single Sunday he invited who-ever he could think of. He had to keep rotating through people so they wouldn't get sick of it and would actually show up. His and Mom's closest college friends, any family member within a hundred miles, their work buddies, the family's work buddies, people from the block, James's friends, even though they were only thirteen. James Herrera Sr. made up a whole book club that summer just for the chance to host it and serve some food.

It was the end of the bad times, the grill a celebration of the move to a better neighborhood, one with a backyard they only shared with the renters downstairs. James remembers his dad staying out there as long as possible, scrubbing the grill clean. He showed James how to slice an onion in half and then use it to get the black chunks of charred past meals off the metal rods.

James thinks back to Ava hanging out with him out there as long as she could, even during those sweltering, sweaty Chicago days, when the breeze from the lake had been swallowed up by the concrete and glass. He thinks back to Mom sitting in the shade with a beer and a book, feet up, shoes off, pedicured toenails glinting in the sun. He remembers wanting to go back inside, the draw of video games and AC, but not being able to tear himself away. One day he even lied to Marcus. He called from inside his room, keeping his voice low while he said, "Sorry, man, my parents aren't letting me go." Then he sprinted back outside and added cheese slices to the burgers, fingers curled away instinctively from the flames that licked constantly at the meat, flaring every now and then when drops of fat fell and stoked their hunger. His parents' old-school music played from a crappy little speaker, not loud enough to disturb the neighbors, but loud enough that it could color this memory. He's sure he had fears back then, but it's impossible to remember any of them. It felt like his parents could protect him from everything. The hard times had ended, and the fire had passed, but all the other things hadn't built up yet, hadn't convinced James that the world was just waiting to unleash something on him.

James wipes the rain away from his brow. "Where should we go?" Now that he notices, the hallways of the B gates are nearly empty. And it makes sense that people didn't stay put, sought out shelter. The rain's starting to pick up again.

Michelle still doesn't look shaken. "Let me see my phone," she says.

They walk over to a phone-charging station that looks a little like a big desk for four. James hunches down under it so he can remove his sweatshirt and backpack. Inside the bag are James's headphones, a comic book he hopes isn't completely ruined, a half-eaten bag of chips. He hands Michelle her phone.

He tries calling his parents and Ava a few more times, but the signal is weak and the call never leaves his phone. The internet is just fine, though, and he even has a few notifications pop up. His battery is fully charged, miraculously, and the Wi-Fi works great after he clicks through the terms and conditions again. He uses the internet to send his parents a text, and another one to Ava. *Where the hell did you guys go? Im at the gate*

Nothing comes back.

He goes to the internet and tries every search term he can think of to try to glean some information, but there is nothing at all. No news articles from the past few hours, no trending social media topics, no announcements from government agencies.

Michelle puts her phone down on the floor, then leans away from it and wrings her hair out again as much as she can. From beneath the desk, she looks out at the abandoned concourse. Neon lights from the storefronts—operating normally again after the blackouts—now look hazy in the drizzling rain, like clouds of color stretching out down the concourse. A couple of people run past, jackets drawn over their heads.

James tries to suggest they get out of the rain, but they just did that, and now his parents are gone. So instead he says they should keep moving.

"Yeah," Michelle agrees. "The best thing to do is find the exit. I'm sure that's where our parents went."

They put their phones away in the backpack and then jog down the hallway. This time there is no exit leading to the other gates, and they have to go the normal way, down the escalators that lead to the tram, the long stretch of temporary art exhibits and moving sidewalks. The permanent installment they've chosen for the hallways between the B and A gates is apparently a fake jungle. There is a weak imitation of a canopy of trees overhead, plastic cutouts meant to look like a tapestry of leafy shelter. Green lights are aimed at this canopy for effect, and a soundtrack of birdcalls and insect noises follows James and Michelle's walk to the A gates. A patch of ceiling is made to look like blue sky.

"What's crazy is that this isn't even part of whatever's going on," Michelle says. "I walked by here earlier, and this was exactly what it was like when the rest of the world was still normal. Someone decided this was a good idea for the airport."

"I can't hate on it," James says. "It's refreshing."

They stroll right past the escalators that lead up to the A gates and toward the signs that read CONCOURSE T, DOMESTIC BAGGAGE CLAIM, GROUND TRANSPORTATION. Neither of them comments on their teeth chattering like cartoon characters being pulled from icy waters. They take the escalators to the T gates, eyes fixed up, probably having very similar thoughts: What the hell is waiting for us there?

The answer: snow.

It is not still falling, but everything they can see in the T gates is covered in a pristine blanket of white fluff.

"Yeah, why the hell not," James says. Funny enough, he's not sure he's ever seen snow look so beautiful before. In Chicago it always feels tainted. Even during the blizzards, it feels like as soon as it's landed on the ground, a plow has already smooshed it into dirtied ice.

The pristine stretch of snow is directly in front of them, leading all the way to baggage claim and the exit. James can see the glass door that's standing between them and the outside world. He can even see one of the baggage carousels spinning, a lone black suitcase that made it out before its owner could.

There are people visible in the gates along the hallway, sitting and waiting for this all to pass, or talking in little groups, huddled together for warmth. But no one is out in the fresh white snow; there aren't even any footprints on it. Maybe because they know it's useless, maybe because everyone has lost their damn minds. No sign of either of their families, but maybe they're already outside. Maybe the snow came down after a few people made it out. Who the fuck knows how anything works anymore? Why is anyone acting like any of this shit is in any way acceptable? Everyone should be curled into a ball until all the dangers pass. Everyone should be storming the hell out of this place.

To be fair, plenty of them are trying.

James and Michelle slosh slowly toward the exit. The snow

squishes beneath their feet. James is wearing cloth sneakers that were already soaked through from the rain, but now a fresh wave of freezing dampness comes in and chills his feet. He starts thinking that that's on him; he's flying to Chicago in January—he should be wearing some better footgear. Then he remembers he's inside an airport in Atlanta and no one can blame him for not busting out his goddamn snow boots.

He keeps his eyes on the exit, almost too afraid to turn his head left or right and see what kind of absurd shit is going on. It's weird, he thinks, that there's no one even at the door. That there aren't crowds, that there aren't policemen, that there aren't freaking National Guardsmen storming the place. Not even a dude parked over there making sure people aren't entering the airport without a boarding pass or whatever.

"There's, like, a zero percent chance that this door is open, right?" James says when they're a few feet away.

"At this point the only thing I think has a zero percent chance of happening is that we get on a flight tonight."

Michelle reaches the door first. She doesn't see any handle or knob, no push bar, nothing to indicate it's even a door at all. It's a barrier more than anything. She runs her fingers along the edge of what she thought was the frame, but she doesn't find any obvious way in or out. She looks back at James and shakes her head.

"Seriously, though?" James says. He doesn't even bother checking it for himself. Just looks away from that lonely suitcase spinning on the carousel, that sign that so clearly says EXIT, like an unfulfilled promise. His whole body is shivering now, his wet clothes becoming unbearably heavy in the cold.

To his left there's the security checkpoint, closed off with a metal gate that slides in from overhead. On his right there's gate T8, where a scruffy, gray-bearded white man in a heavy winter overcoat is barking orders at approximately twenty people, who are using broken-off seat rests as shovels to gather snow into huge mounds. James watches for a while as Michelle keeps running her fingers along what should be the door frame, trying to find a way through, muttering French curse words.

"I wish I knew curse words in a bunch of other languages," James says. Michelle doesn't hear him.

"Faster," the man in the overcoat yells, a slightly Slavic accent carrying over. "I can keep us safe, but I need your help, and I need it now."

It looks like he should have a whip. The people helping him accrue snow for who knows what purpose are red-faced, sweaty despite the cold. He's got a few people who happen to have gloves or mittens on them working the mounds, including some children, who look like they're welcoming the chance to play in the snow.

Beyond T8 there are people poking their heads out from each gate, wondering at what the man in the overcoat is doing. James is imagining their curiosity, but he isn't aware that only thirty minutes ago, there was a massive altercation between the man in the overcoat and several other people in the T concourse who had tried everything to break the glass door keeping them in. Shoes, keys, suitcases, a chair from the nearby Bojangles. A hulking beast of a human being, Clint Vandersnieze (not kidding), who had been waiting to board a flight to Austin, Texas, at gate T3 had even thrown himself directly at the door and was now nursing a concussion because of it. The tensions had grown along with the passengers' desperation, and a shouting match had ensued. Each gate had broken off into its own separate factions, with natural leaders emerging at each one. Many of them were right now choosing what form of government they would be ruled by if this was what the rest of their days would look like.

The man at T8, though, Ulf Pshyk, a Ukrainian national who's participated in the Iditarod twice, decided quickly that what they needed was shelter, first and foremost. He is set on building an igloo large enough to house everyone in his gate, in case the temperature drops even further, in case the other gates decide to take what doesn't belong to them. They will be safe inside an igloo.

Representatives from surrounding gates don't yet know his plan. All they see is this big dude in a coat barking accented orders at people, and they don't like it. They're sure he's planning something sneaky. Russians are sneaky people, many of these T representatives are thinking, even though most of them have never met a single Russian person in their entire lives and

Ulf is not, in fact, Russian. Beverly Bingham, a five-foot-three PTA president from Lawrence, Kansas, scowls at the scene she is witnessing. Ever since the blackouts, Beverly has been growing more and more distrustful, which will eventually bring more harm to the T gates than even the airport meant to unleash.

"That foreigner's up to no good, I'll tell you," she says to the worried group huddled at T5. "We should be ready."

"For what?" Auzelle Stalford asks timidly. She's a twenty-seven-year-old Black PhD candidate from Brooklyn, the only non-white person at her gate. She's got her legs tucked beneath her on the uncomfortable airport seat, which she has been on for what is starting to feel like her entire life. She's been doing everything timidly at this gate, especially right now, with Beverly Bingham riling people up. Auzelle is also really regretting her decision to fly to Kansas tonight instead of tomorrow morning like she had planned. She might be regretting choosing Kansas as the place to get her PhD at all.

"Everything," Beverly says.

Meanwhile, Michelle sighs deeply. Her breath leaves as a weighty cloud, not dissipating like warm exhalations in cold air always do, but lingering like fog, like cigarette smoke. James readies himself for her to kick at the glass in frustration, for her to shed a single dramatic tear, for her to curse at the French or Thai or Argentinean heavens. Instead she turns away from the white breath, which curls around her shoulders like an icy hand,

and she offers James a blue-lipped smile. "Let's find a change of clothes, yeah?"

James nods and follows her down the snowy corridor. She's got her arms crossed tightly in front of her chest, huddling in as close as she can into herself, though it's probably not doing much for her right now. "How are you always so cool, man?" he asks.

"Is that a temperature joke?"

James wants to burst into laughter but for some reason can only manage a chuckle. "That's what I mean, though. We're in possibly the most fucked-up situation anyone's ever been in, we can't find our damn families, nothing makes sense, and the most I've heard you say is a 'putain' or two."

They turn into an ATL Today News, drawn in by a rack of souvenir T-shirts and sweatshirts. "I just don't think there's much point in raging against things you think suck. It doesn't fix anything. It's shouting at the void." Michelle heads straight for the clothes, already pulling her wet shirt over her head as she talks.

Surprisingly, the clerk is still at her station, flipping through a magazine. She glances up at the two drenched teens walking in with what James feels is way too mild of an expression, considering one of them is already half-naked.

"I don't mind shouting at the void," James says.

He makes eye contact with the clerk and gives a shrug. "Mm-hmm," she goes, waiting for them to try some shit. James doesn't exactly know what consequences she could possibly enforce right now, but it's hard for him to think of anything except the fact that he's freezing, Michelle is now in her bra, and . . . yeah, that's about it. Those are the things he can focus on right now.

Michelle grabs one shirt off the rack and is about to slip it over her head when she takes stock of the store. It's just them and the clerk. "Don't look," she tells James, and then offers a half smile at the clerk. She reaches back to unclip her bra right as James forces himself to stare at a wall of overpriced candy. In a moment or two he feels a tap on his shoulder. Michelle's wearing a cheesy white sweatshirt with the Atlanta skyline on it. She's got a purple T-shirt in her hand, which she's using to further dry her hair.

"Plus," Michelle adds, "this is not the most fucked-up situation anyone's ever been in. There are worse things in the world than being stranded at the airport." She nods her head at him, motioning toward the clothes.

James tries to move past the image of Michelle undressing. True, it might carry him through whatever upcoming dark moments are to come, but it might also make him stand there like a moron while the world crashes down around him.

He pulls his sweatshirt off, and the button-up shirt he's wearing beneath it. For a second it feels like sweet relief, like he's never been warmer or lighter. Then the cold air hits him and he reaches for a tank top, a T-shirt, and the thickest, largest sweatshirt on the rack. It says something about the Atlanta aquarium, has colorful embroidered fish on it. "See? That's what I mean. This is for sure the craziest thing you've ever experienced. I don't even wanna hear you try to match this with some other bullshit. Yet you're all like—" He slips into a fake accent, a gross exaggeration of the beautiful way words come out of her mouth. He doesn't even know how to approximate that accent of hers, can't recognize the varied nuances of the globe on her tongue. "Zees ees no so bad," he says, at best a French person's impersonation of an Italian person speaking English. "When zere ees war in the world, how can we complain?"

Michelle stares blankly at him for a second, still wringing out her hair. For a second he's sure he has undone this whole friendship they were working on. Then her eyes get wide and her eyebrows furrow in confusion, followed by another stupidly cute smile. "Wow, you can never do another accent again in front of me."

"Yeah, that was bad," James says, running a hand over his head. He feels little drops of water stuck to his hair starting to freeze over. "But, seriously, you're way too chill about this. I know there are greater injustices in the world and all. People dying everywhere. I know we ain't dying. But c'mon, we're allowed to complain a little, right? We can look around at all this . . ." He starts by gesturing at the snow and catches sight of Ulf still barking orders at his cronies, the igloo starting to take shape. James realizes he can't just point out one single thing and waves his arms frantically. ". . . all this bullshit. And we can say, 'Damn. This is fucked up.'"

Michelle shrugs, then runs a hand through her hair to feel how dry it is, if at all. "Yeah, well. I just have a thing about superlatives. Fucked up, yes. 'Most' fucked up? Eh. Why does everything we say have to be 'most' or 'best' or 'worst' or 'funniest' or whatever? Why can't we just comment on a thing without trying to describe it as the most intense version of that thing? 'Best girlfriend ever! Funniest movie ever!' It's ridiculous. We can have experiences that are valuable even if they don't make humanity's highlight reel."

"That was the best speech I've ever heard."

"Shut up," Michelle says, cracking a smile. She looks down at her pants, which are still slowly dripping little craters into the snow inside the store.

James mimics the move, wondering if they're gonna go pantsless or if they're gonna let their legs freeze. "If we leave this terminal, we'll probably be okay?" he says, not quite sure of himself. "Maybe the other end of the airport looks like Arizona right now, and we'll dry up in no time."

Another breathy sigh from Michelle, the ensuing cloud wrapping around James like it's trying to keep him safe, like it's pulling the two of them closer together. She puts her hands on her hips and chews her bottom lip for a second, then starts to walk toward the front of the store.

"You gonna pay for those?" the clerk calls out. Michelle

doesn't seem too concerned. She hangs out in the hallway for a little bit, looking up and down, probably noticing Ulf and his shenanigans for the first time. The clerk stands up a little straighter, forgetting her magazine for a moment. She makes eye contact with James. "She deaf?"

With her back still to the store, Michelle raises a hand and waves it in annoyance. "Con calma, boluda," she says, just loud enough to hear, and James has to shrug at the clerk.

It's funny that James hasn't even thought about money until now. He thinks an adult probably would have at this point. The lack of cash or a credit card is not always on his mind, just sometimes, just the last couple of years, since he's started wanting to buy more video games than his parents are willing to, or wishing he had the cash to go out for Korean barbecue with his friends. When he thinks about growing older, going to college, there's a vague worry about money too, though it's usually overshadowed by deeper and more nefarious worries. But right now it is probably a not-good thing to not have cash. He already needs clothes. How long will it be until he needs to pay for food? How long until the societal rules holding the airport together decide to make like the rest of it all and start to fall apart?

Wait. Did he really just ask that? Indoor snow and shit, and he's talking about societal rules? C'mon, man.

We won't blame him too much, since he is trying to avoid eye contact with the clerk so that she doesn't realize he doesn't have any money. Thankfully, Michelle comes back inside a few seconds later. "I'm not sure if it's a good idea to move from here," she says, ignoring the clerk. "Your parents were closest to this exit. This is probably where they'll go. And my parents were in the middle, so they could go either way. Might as well assume they're coming here eventually. Otherwise we might be chasing each other across the airport all night, risking whatever it is that's happening out there."

First, James's mind goes to the shadows lurking in the hallway after the latest blackout. To the horde, and the explosion. Then he realizes that his family's gone, that what stands between him and them is rain and riots and unnamed terrors in the hallways. And that's just the stuff he knows about. There could be other dangers lurking. Aliens, terrorists, whatever it is that has caused this. Even if he is only counting the normal things that can go wrong in the world, it suddenly all feels so frail. It feels hopeless, like whatever might happen to his parents and Ava already has.

He blinks away from Michelle so she won't see him turn sad and small so quickly. "Sure, yeah," he says.

"You guys gonna pay for this or what?"

Michelle starts to talk to the clerk in some language or another. James stares out the window. Moonlight illuminates the treetops surrounding the airport. Clouds amble gently across the night sky. No snow falls. He sees the planes parked out there, and he's not sure if he feels bad for their passengers or jealous that they're likely safer. Maybe some people are going stir crazy in there, maybe they have less food. But it seems to be going just fine right now, and all they have to do is open a door and they'll meet fresh air. James pictures a few hundred people popping the emergency exit doors off a plane, the inflatable slides unfurling like big yellow tongues. He pictures them scrambling across the tarmac, hopping over the fence, scurrying away to freedom. In a few hours that is exactly what some of them will do. They will return home or check into their hotel rooms and Airbnbs, and they will try to make sense of what happened. They will sleep soundly throughout the night, and when they wake up in the morning, the vague memories they'll have of what they glimpsed through the airport windows will feel like the hazy images from a dream.

A reflection in the window breaks James's reverie. The TSA agent from the tram is at the entrance to the ATL Today News. She's with the guy who got knocked out, the peacekeeper, who is looking at the snow with the gleeful wonder of a kid seeing it for the first time. James feels another little surge of fear at the presence of a uniform. As far as he knows, the blame has not yet been assigned to anyone, and he does not trust the world, even this wild-ass version of it, to let him off the hook easily. But then he sees Rosa's face, how young she is, how scared and confused she is. Her blue TSA shirt is tucked into her back pocket, blood streaks still drying on it. He pictures her life, coming to work at this goddamn airport every day, maybe driving an old car that breaks down all the time, maybe having to ride the bus here, dealing with the same creepy old dudes hollering at her.

He's not quite right. Rosa gets dropped off every day by her stepdad, Steve, who, sure, is a bit awkward and unhip, trying to use too many slang words that don't sound right coming out of his mouth. But he drives Rosa out of the kindness of his heart. Unlike Rosa's mom, Steve believes that it's okay Rosa isn't trying to go to college. So he drives half an hour out of his way to make things easier for everyone, so that Rosa won't resent her mom, so that she won't grow up believing only one path is correct.

Rosa puts her hands on her hips as she looks at the closed-off exit. "That's weird," she says out loud, desperately wishing she had her radio with her. She tries her cell phone again, but the cryptic countdown continues and refuses to let her do anything else. Her mind hasn't even had time to wrap itself around the snow on the floor, and now this.

"That's not supposed to happen, is it?" Michelle asks. She leaves the store again, to the disbelief of the clerk, who shouts out something that on another day probably wouldn't be cool to shout out at a customer. Even if Michelle isn't technically a customer yet. She joins Rosa out by the store.

"No," Rosa says. "There are doors that only shut between one and four in the morning, when no flights are coming in or out. During an emergency, they should be open. It looks like they're not down, so it's something else. There should be other agents here."

"Isn't there an office or something inside the terminal, some place where people in charge hang out?" Michelle asks.

"We checked," Taha says, still smiling at the snow. He leans over and picks up a handful of it with his bare hand, packing it into an amateur snowball that tells James he for sure has never been around snow before. "No one was there."

"Where is everyone, then?" Michelle asks, directing the question specifically at Rosa, or maybe at her uniform. "Could they be at the . . . you know . . . source of this?"

"As far as I can tell, there is no source," Rosa says. She groans and pulls out her work shirt from her pocket, throwing it on despite Taha's blood. She rubs her hands together for warmth.

"Do you know what's happening at all?" James asks, lobbing the question gently, not wanting the girl to feel like it's on her.

Rosa shakes her head, eyes glued on the closed gate. "Anyone try that door that isn't supposed to exist?"

"It's less of a door and more an immovable obstacle," Michelle answers. "No handle, no hinges."

A shout interrupts them, echoing down the hall (although it echoes a little less than it normally would, the snow muffling how far it reverberates). Ulf again, commanding his troops. Rosa raises an eyebrow at James and Michelle, and they both convey similar "we don't fucking know" gestures.

Taha is working on another snowball. He's been picturing this moment for a while now. He grew up reading *Calvin and Hobbes,* marveling at Calvin's joy in the snow, the creations he would make, the way it colored what felt like a third of the strips. A childhood in Sri Lanka did not provide the same kind of seasons, and though he spent two years getting his postgrad in London, he has made it to the age of twenty-seven without ever seeing snow up close. He's imagined the texture so many times; he obviously knew to expect the cold. But now, actually touching it, sticking his fingers into the accumulated flakes, he understands that the anticipation of an experience is never the same thing as the experience itself. It could be so easy to find disappointment here too, after a lifetime of building up the expectation. Cold comfort, he thinks, knowing the phrase does not apply to this situation but thinking it all the same.

James watches Taha curiously, then looks back at the clerk in the ATL Today News. She raises her eyebrows and motions with her hands in a "what the hell are you two doing don't make me come after your ass" kind of way.

"So, what now?" Michelle asks.

No one knows what to say.

TEN

\\\\\

JAMES AND MICHELLE HAVE TAKEN SHELTER INSIDE THE ATL Today News, joined by Taha and Rosa.

Michelle now has her legs through the sleeves of a sweat-shirt. James is too afraid that the mob will arrive again and he will be forced to run, so he has draped several T-shirts over his bare legs instead, rubbing his thighs to get the blood flowing while his pants dry on a rack with earphones, chargers, and other less useful gadgets.

The clerk argues with Michelle for a while about the cost of the clothes, then decides it isn't worth her time and leaves the store unattended to go join one of the factions farther down the hall. The people at T11 have decided that lethargy is their ideal form of government and are just kind of lounging around idly, watching the TV, not wanting to be bothered by anyone. They still feel this is nothing but a layover and that normalcy will ensue soon. Until that happens, they will ignore all the signs that say otherwise.

Taha juggles snowballs for a little while, then tries to start a playful fight with the others, but no one else can match his mirthful mood. He tosses them anyway, down the hall, at the advertisements that line the walls. He builds tiny snowmen and kicks them into white explosions, laughing heartily each time. He falls onto his back and makes snow angels, crosses off as many snowy clichés as he can. If only this hallway had a slope for sledding.

James and Michelle are sitting on the checkout counter, trying to avoid kicking the assorted candy bars at their feet as they wriggle with anxiety and restlessness. Phone in hand, James keeps waiting for word to come through. His parents can go hours without remembering that there is a constant means of communication, but Ava hasn't gone more than fifteen minutes without sending a text message since she got her phone, all hours of the night included.

"Nothing," Michelle says. She's got her phone in hand too, scrolling through social media and news websites. She searches for information about green lights found at airports, but the search terms are too vague, and a million irrelevant results come in. "It's like the whole world is turning a blind eye."

"Maybe they just don't know."

"I found one post about someone whose flight got rerouted, but that's it." She taps her fingers on the screen, furrowing her brow. "And if I try to post about anything going on, it doesn't go through."

"Maybe the internet just isn't working."

"No, look, I can send other things." *Do you guys remember that duck-billed platypi are a thing that exists in the world?* she types, leaning over to show James. The screen takes a brief moment to load, and then a notification tells her that her thought has been successfully shared with the world. "It's only when I try to talk about the airport or use the word 'Atlanta' that it fails." She types out another example, and the app crashes, sending her phone back to its home screen.

Behind them, Rosa munches on a Twix bar, chewing slowly. Her phone is on her leg, showing 9:34:18. She's imagining what her friends are up to. Nothing out of the ordinary, probably. Doesn't ease the soft sadness of missing out. She was looking forward to spending time with them all day. Now here she is, hours past the end of her shift, shivering in the snow.

From the hallway, Ulf barks orders, Beverly Bingham bickers with the people in her faction. A couple of times the PA crackles on and provides no further information, provides no course of action, provides nothing but an assurance that normal flight activities will resume shortly.

James is staring off into the distance, his mind churning. There's a base layer of helplessness within his thoughts, sure, but something about that is almost comforting, helps him feel slightly more at ease than he has been since the first brief blackout. Nothing here is in his control. That's terrifying, but less terrifying than making the wrong choices, than knowing there was something he should have done but just couldn't. The airport is shrouded in madness, and nothing James does can change that.

"Is part of you kind of psyched that this is happening?" James asks Michelle.

"What part of me would be excited about this?"

"I dunno. The kid part. The still-believes-in-fairy-tales part." James leans back a little, moving a display of pens so he can set his elbows down on the counter. "Growing up has plenty of shitty aspects, no doubt, but one that I've been most disappointed in is that the world is just . . . the world, you know? That there is a set of rules life adheres to. I don't wanna say that I was looking for magic from the world. But you can't grow up with all those kids' books and movies and not hope that some of it is true. Every year it feels like more of that hope disappears. I don't say anything out loud because it becomes less okay as you get older, but I feel myself wanting to keep it alive. Peter Pan–style, you know, just clap so that Tinker Bell can survive. I want it to be real. I want things that can only exist in books to exist in real life. Time travel, monsters, superpowers, talking animals."

Michelle matches his lean, their elbows touching. "I'm not sure this is what I had in mind when I was growing up on Disney movies." In the hallway, snow has started falling again. Taha stands with his arms open, laughing, tongue out. A thin woman wearing a shawl ambles by, weeping softly. Ulf's barking persists; the sound of his minions working rumbles down the hall.

James laughs. "Yeah, I'd prefer talking animals too."

"I know what you mean, though. This definitely calls into question a lot of what I thought I knew about the world. And it's not like there was a ton I was sure about. Now? Pffft," she says, adding a hand gesture like she's throwing her knowledge into the hallway.

"Do you think everyone's like that? Quietly hoping that there really is magic in the world and it's just hidden?"

"No," Michelle says with a shake of the head. She sits up straight, reaches down to the candy bar display and grabs some Skittles, which she quickly tears open. "I think people would be too scared of that world. There's already so much in this life that doesn't make sense, so many things that are unpredictably cruel: natural disasters, terminal illness, human behavior. But at least those things are tempered by the rules of science. Can you imagine a world where a green light does this?" She gestures out at the airport, and before James can say she didn't do this, she goes on. "Can you imagine a world where nothing was kept in check? Can you imagine how terrifying that would be? Even if it was magic, and magic was mostly good, all stories about magic include its dark side. I think that would make people even more afraid than they are now."

"All right, maybe that's true," James says. "I'll admit that I have a hard enough time dealing with mundane scary shit. Having life be unchecked horrors all the time would be more than I could handle." He bites his lip, trying not to fall for the thought that this is what life will be like from now on. "But most people aren't that insightful, thinking about the deeper, long-term implications. I think that everyone still has a little of that hope inside. Maybe they're still hanging on to the idea that falling into a pit of toxic waste will give them superpowers. Or they believe that unicorns really exist and just don't want to be found. *Something,* you know? Some little part of them that keeps clapping, despite all reason."

Michelle chews thoughtfully on some Skittles, then offers the bag to James. "To be honest, no. I think that part gets silenced in most people. By other people or by their own experiences, by themselves. People get hardened by the world, their imaginations become less convincing." She sighs, pours the colorful candy into James's cupped hand. "People don't believe in magic because they don't see it. It's hard to keep believing in something that you see no evidence of."

James, for a moment, thinks of God. He thinks of Sunday church visits, those times he went with Marcus to his church, those gospel songs that he loved as a kid but eventually came to cringe at. Not the music itself, nor the feel of those mornings, which always felt like joy encompassed, but rather the words, when he came to understand them. He remembers the day when he realized that "He's Got the Whole World in His Hands" was about God. It seems obvious now, but when he was a kid he thought the song was about his dad, or maybe about himself. He thought it was a message that you could do anything you wanted in this life, that you could go anywhere you pleased. That the world was not a huge and scary place but that it was within reach. James thinks about how he believed in God though he never saw evidence of Him, other than what the preacher at church would say, other than how his grandma always used to bring Him up. Yet it felt like a betrayal to know the song was about God, whom he'd never really felt as connected to as he had to the "whole world." It reduced the song to propaganda, supposed evidence of a being that he never gave much thought to.

"I wish people were more like you as they got older," Michelle goes on. "I wish they walked around secretly believing in the fantastical. But I think they're more boring than that, sadly." Another offer of Skittles, which James accepts. "When I lived in Buenos Aires, it was in a pretty fancy neighborhood called Puerto Madero. There are a ton of high-rises, many of them with balconies overlooking the water. At a certain time of year, the sun would rise exactly when I was outside waiting for the bus. You know how many people I would see on their balconies watching that glorious sight?"

"Shit," James says with a laugh, "I'm guessing not many. I'm not a morning person at all. It would have to be a pretty sweet sunrise to get me out there too."

Michelle rolls her eyes. "It wasn't just at sunrise, it was at all times of the day. Dozens of buildings, hundreds of balconies, thousands of people choosing to look elsewhere. I've noticed that all over the world. Balconies are extremely underused."

"Meaning what?" James tries to pop a handful of Skittles in his mouth, but a purple one misses, bouncing off his lip and down on his lap, rolling its way to the snow, a stark drop of color embedded in James's footprint. "That people are blind to the magic of the real world?" He hops off the counter and bends over to pick up the Skittle.

"Just because it sounds cheesy doesn't mean it's not true. There might actually be dragons in the real world, but people can't be bothered to look for them."

At that moment James thinks of whatever it was that passed them in the hall, and Michelle thinks of her grandparents, and they immediately want to change the subject. They do that thing people sometimes do where they both start to speak at the same time, causing both of them to derail and let the other one go first. But James can't remember what he was going to say, and Michelle feels like what she was going to say is stupid, and so they both fall back into silence.

Taha comes in from the hallway, snow dusting his dark hair, beaming despite his shivering. Rosa is on the floor of the store, too bothered by the fact that she's still at the airport to give much thought to the cold, or her dampening pants. She's hidden her phone away in her pocket, and at this point she just wants to sleep. She wants to wake up in a simpler, more sensible world.

Meanwhile, Roger Sterlinger, socially anxious cyclist on his way to a family reunion, still riding a wave of calm that has made this the most pleasant travel experience of his life—emotionally speaking—has just crossed the barrier into the T gates. He is one of the few people in the airport, along with Taha, blessed with the ability to feel wonder at all these things that are happening. He is rarely able to appreciate the unexpected, and it makes everything happening feel like a gift.

Beverly Bingham notices Roger first. She's standing in front of T5, oddly protective of the people sitting at the gate. She'll eventually want someone else to be the watchdog, have everyone inside take turns while she brainstorms more important things. But she wants to lead by example first, and she doesn't quite trust the people at her gate yet, though she knows she needs the strength of their numbers. What for? That she doesn't know. When she sees Roger, a seeming outsider, not claimed by any of the gates or by the people at the ATL Today News, a rush of adrenaline floods her system. She stands up a little straighter, her scowl deepens, her fists clench. Beverly looks over her shoulder at the gate, eyes landing on Blair Stately and Corey Walford, the two largest men at her disposal. They sense her gaze on them and instinctively stand, though they are not entirely sure what she wants. Some people just have that ability to make others stand, and Beverly has honed that skill into perfection over decades of parenthood and PTA presidency. The two men wait for her instructions, which arrive in the form of a surprisingly intimidating index finger. Beverly stretches it out for a moment, then curls it back toward herself slowly, repeating the gesture only twice, which is enough to make its message clear.

ELEVEN

ROGER SEES THE TWO MEN APPROACHING HIM FIRST, and their build and purposeful walk should send his anxiety back into full gear. He waits for the familiar shortness of breath, waits for the immediate desire to turn himself small, waits for the clot of tears behind his eyes to try to fight through to the surface. None of it comes. Roger manages to smile.

Then he sees the small, stomping woman between the two men. His first thought is of a Pomeranian in a purse, some teeny furry thing baring its teeth. It says a lot about the strangeness of his state of mind that this makes him chuckle to himself, instead of flee in terror. He wonders briefly if someone has drugged him, if he got a concussion when he fell off the stool after the explosion. But he doesn't have long to pursue the train of thought.

"Can I help you?" the woman asks, her voice slightly hoarse, not in the way of smokers, but in the way of strained vocal cords.

She sounds like someone who's been trying to have a lengthy conversation at a loud bar for the last twenty years.

"Um," Roger says, because conversations with strangers are hard, anxiety or not. "I'm not sure what you mean."

Beverly narrows her eyes. "Can . . . I . . . help . . . you?" she repeats, as if she's talking to someone she thinks doesn't speak English. Airports these days, the country these days, it's probably not far from the truth, Beverly thinks, as if languages are to blame for all ills.

This no-gooder in front of her actually has the gall to crack a smile. "That's very kind of you, but no, I think I'm okay. Just walking around, exploring."

Beverly narrows her eyes further, exactly as far as her eyes can narrow before she's squinting, losing her intended effect. She's practiced this look many times; of course, not in front of a mirror, just by subconsciously paying attention to the effectiveness of her eye narrowing. She's taught herself how to pick up on subtle cues from the person she's interacting with, to recognize their fear, their nervousness. These are things she loves to see in other people, and it irks her that the man who's come parading into the T gates is demonstrating none of the usual markers. A handful of voices can be heard from elsewhere down the hall. Beverly doesn't have to turn her head to know that other factions are taking note of this exchange. She cannot falter.

"You should find somewhere else for that," she says, crossing her arms in front of her chest.

The man should furrow his brow right now. He should stammer or maybe even take a little step back, that'd be great. Instead he raises his eyebrows and quirks another damn smile at her. "Excuse me?" he says.

Beverly doesn't hesitate. She lifts her arm, extends her index finger to its straightest position (when it's in this position—and again, don't ask us about the science of it all, because we're iffy on that—she has the twenty-seventh-strongest index finger in the world), and jams it directly into this interloper's chest. "Find somewhere else," she says, keeping her voice low but giving it just that little edge. That same edge that gets her what she wants. Three weeks before her wedding, Beverly said the words "You will never lie to me again" with this same edge, and to this day, her husband, Larry, has not dared to.

"This terminal is closed to newcomers," she says, her finger still on the man's chest. Then she turns around, giving her two temporary enforcers a look that conveys they are now to stand in the most intimidating way possible. Though neither of these men, despite their stature, has ever been in a physical altercation, they both puff their chests and flex their muscles and do as they're told. Both Blair and Corey are worried about what will happen if the man decides to further the altercation. Blair is a Buddhist, morally against violence. He's not even sure why he's listening to the forceful woman's instructions, other than the mere fact that she is forceful. Corey, on the other hand, simply doesn't care enough to hit anyone, and he doubts he would now, even at this woman's behest.

Thankfully for them, Roger, whose right pant leg is still tucked into his sock, raises his eyebrows again in amusement and calls out a cheerful, if not entirely unsarcastic, "Thank you for your hospitality!" Then he smiles at the enforcers and tips an invisible hat. "Gentlemen," he says before turning around.

Blair and Corey watch him disappear back down the hallway toward the escalators, waiting what they believe is enough time so that Beverly will not yell at them. Roger, however, buoyed by his anxiety-free state, which he knows deep down could change at any moment, decides this is all some ridiculous joke and that he is in on it. He hides around the corner, practically giggling to himself, head poking out from the wall, watching the two hulking men retreat. The chest-poking woman follows them into T5. A few others litter the hallway, some looking in his direction. No one seems to spot Roger, and the thrill of sneaking around bubbles up within him.

He remembers being twelve, sneaking away from home for the first time to meet up with his friends when he wasn't allowed. No way was he going to jump out his second-floor window, and he was not afforded the luxury of a well-placed branch to climb down, so he had to time out his escape through the hallway, past his parents' bedroom, where his mom had already retreated to for the night, the door cracked open like always to let the cat in and out. Then down the stairs, past the kitchen, where his older sister—who would surely tattle—was doing homework. He hung back, listening intently until there was the squeak of a stool on tile, the sound of the fridge door opening.

He tiptoed past that too, then was left only to scurry past the living room, where his dad was surely propped on the couch watching television. He could see the glow of the TV in his dad's eyes, could hear the occasional wet-lipped sound of a pull from the beer can. For at least three minutes he stood there, trying to decide if he should walk quietly past, attracting as little attention as possible, or if he should try to move swiftly, be a blur of motion that his dad would think was the cat.

Leaving the house that night was exhilarating, and though his return later on was less stealthy, and he'd been grounded for a month upon his discovery, Roger remembers how alive he felt when the door shut quietly behind him, how breathless he was running toward the meeting spot by the park with his friends. Hard to recall anything else from that night, and hard to even associate with that kid he used to be, someone for whom a social gathering was a reason to escape from home, instead of the other way around. But Roger realizes now that he's been longing for this feeling for years. He eyes the hallway for a little while, waiting for his chance. When it comes, he runs down the hallway like he hasn't since he was a child.

\\\\\\\\\

At T8, Ulf's igloo is nearly complete. It was born out of a desire for shelter, and Ulf is sure that it'll serve its purpose well. But right now that is not at the forefront of his mind. He is feeling pride. Not for himself, but for the people who came together and built it. He feels it for their sheer humanity, for what it says about the species in the midst of the day's events.

In the face of fear, Ulf thinks, some people succumb, and some people unite. When all this is over, stories will emerge. Some will not speak well of mankind, and he is sure that the people here at T8 will face that inhumane humanity directly. But the story of T8 will be one of strangers coming together, of people knowing that unity breeds survival, that compassion is the correct response, especially in the most trying of circumstances.

He grabs a massive pile of snow and reaches up to pack it into the forming dome. Fortified snow, Ulf thinks. *That's* what we are.

\\\\\\\\

Across the airport, similar scenes play out. In the F gates, where most of the international flights are, people naturally separate into their nationalities. In the C gates, the Delta Sky Club sees people start to group off according to their frequent-flier status.

The looters, led by Brad and Chad, are running out of steam now that much of the glass in the airport has broken. They can't seem to find their way to the T gates, so they roar back and forth across the hallways until boredom sets in.

Concourse A, which, when all of this began, looked like any other terminal except for the weird fake jungle leading toward it, is now a full, honest-to-goodness jungle. A *Hunger Games*–esque/*Battle Royale* fiasco has broken out, and since we have weak constitutions and would like to avoid heavy hearts as much as we can, we shall pass over the events that take place there for the remainder of this narration.

\\\\\\\\

Back in the snowy T gates, James and Michelle have opened a pack of playing cards and are sitting cross-legged on the check-out counter, which they've cleared of all displays to make room. Still, their knees occasionally touch. James wonders about the joys of knees touching in worse situations than this. Like, if there was a line graph depicting knee touching, would the joy decrease the more fucked-up the situation, or would it increase? In a war, say. If bombs are going off and you get to sit with a girl you're into, do you give a single shit about the slightest of contacts? Or do you care about it more than you care about anything else? Do you hang on to that joy because all others have been wiped away?

"What do you wanna play?" James says.

Michelle fiddles with her phone. "I want to play some music, but this stupid thing isn't working." She taps furiously on the screen, then gives up and turns her phone facedown on top of her leg. "You know how to play spit? Some people call it speed, I think."

James scoffs. "Do I know how to play? Please. My hands are so quick that Marvel Comics tried to sue me for imitating the Flash."

Michelle laughs, a few quick bursts, loud and unfettered. It sounds like a knock at the door that you've been waiting for all day, it sounds like a person you love, arriving. "Is that right?"

"You know it," James responds, shuffling and dealing the cards. "I mean, I just won a game right now; you didn't even notice. That's how quick I am."

Quiet part of James's brain: We're moving on to games now? This is what's up? The 'rents are flat-out missing and we're playing mother-effing spit? Also, isn't the Flash a DC thing?

Michelle takes the cards and starts arranging them in front of her. "This is how you set it up, no?" James nods. "It's weird. I used to think my cousins invented this game. We used to play together in Thailand. The first time someone else wanted to play, I freaked out. I was like, 'How do you know my cousin? Who taught you this?' It felt like my brain was exploding, like my whole conception of the world was crashing down." She laughs again, shaking her head. "I didn't even jump to the obvious conclusion that the game existed beyond the people I knew. I was sure that the game had started with my cousins and spread to the other side of the globe. My friends looked at me like I was insane, which was probably fair."

"I mean, it is bizarre how there are little things like that that are worldwide," James says, adjusting the piles in front of him, pairing the overturned eights together and straightening them out, getting ready to start. "I don't even know how a card game makes its way across the world, but it's kinda cool that it does. I imagine it even happened before the internet, which is extra nuts. It's not like there are televised tournaments or anything."

"Yeah, I love that. It makes me feel like no matter how different we all are, how much people fear and hate others that don't look like them, we still play the same games. The phrase 'culture shock' exists because things are so varied across the globe, but yet everywhere I've been, people know how to play spit. It's almost enough to instill a little hope, no? As fucked-up as humanity can be, we do have things that tie us together."

"No doubt," James says. "Although how badly I'm gonna beat you right now might make you feel less hopeful about the world. You're gonna walk away emotionally broken. Like, you thought all the nonsense we've been seeing out here is traumatizing? Just you wait."

Michelle is smirking, biting her bottom lip and nodding along, and part of James's brain is completely freaking out that he can pull any of this off, that he can talk like this, especially while touching knees, especially when terrifying things exist in the hallway and the whole world is crashing down. Then Michelle starts to take off the rings on her fingers, setting them aside.

"Oh snap," James says. "Is that your version of trash talk?"

Michelle shrugs. "There's a hand-slapping portion of the game, right? It'd be rude to physically hurt you on the way to giving you PTSD."

James laughs and at the same time wonders what she thinks of the laugh, if she might be comparing it to something else, what that something else might be. All this time with her and still he doesn't know. Madness, that. How do people ever come to terms with the fact that they don't know what other people think about them? Not all people, just certain ones. "Ready?" James says, looking at Michelle put the finishing touches on her pile.

She looks up at him and smiles, holding his gaze for just long enough to make him squirm. "Ready."

Their laughter snaps Rosa from her daze. She's been letting her mind go blank, or rather trying to force it to. She keeps going into thought loops: This is the end of the world; this isn't the end of the world at all, things are going to be fine; how can those two kids be so chill about what's happening? God I wish I could be chill about what's happening; nothing's happening, it's just a little weird, things will go back to normal soon; this is the end of the world; this isn't . . .

She exhales as deeply as she has all night, and it feels great momentarily, her mind wiped clean by the act. Then the thoughts come back, and she decides what she needs is motion. Standing up, she brushes the snow from her pants. "I'm going to take a walk," she announces. James and Michelle offer a little nod. Taha, who's picked up a paperback from the bestsellers wall, holds his place with a finger and looks up.

"Would you like company?"

Rosa shakes her head. "If I'm not back in ten minutes . . ." She trails off, looking for a way to finish the sentence. But the start of the sentence doomed her. It can only end in cliché, or in a tongue-in-cheek acknowledgment of the cliché. Characters in horror movies say that line, not TSA agents who've clocked out.

"I will look for you," he says with that trademark beatific smile, then returns to his book.

Rosa stands in front of the store for a while, trying to decide which way to go. She opts to turn away from the shouts coming from the Slavic dude at nearby T8. Hopefully, this direction will have fewer things to deal with. Her shoes make soft crunching noises on the snow. She thinks that the airport looks rather lovely this way. Maybe there's a chance someone is doing this on purpose, just to try it out, and she somehow missed the memo. Some kind of holiday spirit thing?

Although it's January now, and that doesn't entirely make sense. Still, though. Wouldn't be a terrible idea.

Just in case, Rosa checks the exit. Still no way out. She sighs again, sticks her hands in her pockets, walks past T9. It seems like they're holding a town hall type of meeting. An Asian woman stands at the podium where people usually show their boarding passes. The rows of chairs have been moved, arranged to face the podium. The airline personnel are among the audience, looking perfectly okay with what's happening. Rosa can't bring herself to blame them. There are a million airport rules being broken right now, explicit and tacit and probably a few that Rosa doesn't even know about. Who the fuck cares? She's been at this job for three months, the pay's okay, she's nineteen. Who would expect her to be the enforcer here?

The Asian woman at the helm of the town hall meeting at T9 holds up a hand. She's Wendy Liang, a state representative in Washington, and before that she was a schoolteacher and principal for over twenty years. She knows how to quiet rowdy people. It's not so simple as the mere act of raising a hand, mind you. There's an art to it. We're not quite sure where the art comes in, whether there is a subtle flick of the wrist, a more commanding way of holding the fingers, an ideal height at which to hold up your hand to command attention. We'll refrain from conjecturing. Suffice it to say, the passengers at T9 fall under her spell, and what a moment ago were several voices speaking over one another now quiet down to let Wendy speak.

"It should go without saying that everything discussed here tonight will be voted on," Wendy says, her voice clearly projecting all the way to Rosa, who listens with mild interest.

"Can we vote on that?" some dude calls out, making another guy nearby laugh.

Wendy fixes the class clown with a stare. "It's unclear what is happening here, of course, but it's clear that the current concourse we are in is dividing up by gates. What the other gates are doing, we can't be sure. I tried speaking to some, but people seem to have fallen into distrust and territoriality rather quickly. It's fascinating, since I would think that w—" She licks her lips and looks down as if she had notes on the podium. Then she tugs on one of her sleeves, which are rolled neatly halfway up her forearm. "It feels rather arbitrary that our community should be our gate and not our terminal, or, say, profession, age group, whatever. An interesting question for sociologists when this is all over. Regardless, I believe in community. And if this is the way it is, then this is the way it is. I believe in democracy, and I believe this should be our approach."

A few heads in the crowd nod. One man in the audience, Johannes Nowles, has long been an avid believer in communism, even joining a semi-militant group while in college. He nods too, since that experience in college taught him that his belief in avoiding confrontation is stronger than his belief in communism.

"Whatever decisions we make from here on out," Wendy continues, "should be decided by a majority. I count sixty-seven of us, so there should be no ties. . . ."

Rosa finds her mind starting to wander, so she continues on down the hall. T10's approach to this situation appears to be hibernation. Nearly a hundred bodies, from what Rosa can tell, are huddled together in the middle of the gate. Carry-on bags and suitcases have been emptied on top of the mound of sleeping bodies, presumably to provide warmth. Rosa wonders who were the kind souls who volunteered for that job. Hard to tell, since it looks like absolutely everyone is completely covered by one garment or another.

T11 looks like any other airport gate during a layover. Most eyes are on some screen or another. They seem to prefer not to think about what's going on at all. Rosa can't blame them.

T12 is another town hall meeting, but this one is considerably less civil. The guy at the helm looks familiar, not just in the typical way of angry middle-aged white men. James noticed him, Joseph Flint, earlier on, before all of this began, when James was sitting at the café with Michelle and this man was screaming into his phone. His rage has clearly increased, and it does not seem like a productive way to hold the meeting. Several people are standing and shouting, pointing their fingers at the man, while he does the exact same thing back. "We gotta get guns!" someone bellows.

"Yeah," twelve people respond.

"Where the hell do you suggest we get guns?" the angry leader responds.

"I bet it's terrorists!" someone else shouts, clearly not caring whether this particular item is fully addressed before moving on. Actually, this seems to be the way everyone is thinking. "I'm hungry!" one woman yells. "Where are we gonna get food?"

"Yeah, what if people try to take all the food? We gotta get it first."

"We need guns!"

Voices bouncing off each other, no one listening. Rosa thinks this is basically how most adults deal with government anyway. She continues to walk.

One gate has turned itself into a de facto fort of suitcases and seats, and outside of the fort, three men and a woman are fashioning weapons from whatever they can. At T17, the very end of the hallway, Rosa has to immediately turn around, since it's clear what the moaning and flashes of nudity signify. She blushes, comes close to laughing hysterically, but finds the laughter unable to break through. This must be the quickest that human civilization has come undone, Rosa thinks.

She hurries away from the apparent orgy at the end of the hallway, wondering what could possibly be waiting for her at the other end. The snow is still falling softly, accumulating ever so slightly. Of all the approaches to this madness, she thinks Taha probably has it most right. Playing in the snow, reading. She wishes she had that ability some people seem to have of finding beauty in anything. Artists, maybe. She bets Taha makes some sort of art.

The two kids aren't far off either. They looked for their parents, tried to leave. When that failed, they turned to flirting. Rosa wonders if they realize they're flirting. The boy probably has no clue. But from Rosa's experience, girls are just as likely to be clueless. Everyone's goddamn clueless about everyone else, clearly.

She walks past ATL Today News again, sees the two still playing cards. Spit, by the looks of it. The girl slaps her hand down on the counter in front of them and cackles gleefully, showing off the small pile she's come away with. The boy nods and laughs, good sport. The girl does a little dance, cute as hell. When Rosa first saw the pair on the train, she recognized her attraction for the girl instantly.

She goes through these moments all the time, especially when she's checking passports. When Rosa is attracted to someone, there's always a moment that seems to stretch out. First, a desire to make eye contact so that the person will know. Have her eyes confess the attraction and see what comes of it. Nine point nine times out of ten, of course, nothing does. But that's the second step: the hope. How it floods, how it lays its finger down on everything, if only for a moment. Rosa can't really say what the hope's aim is. Certainly not a happily-ever-after with the stranger. Even hope is more practical than that. It's just a hope that *something* will happen. Some change of pace from life's constant flow of mundane moments. The slightest of exchanges, that's this hope. Returned attraction in the other person's eyes. A brief conversation. Her hope remains modest, if all-encompassing.

The following step in the moment—amazing, isn't it, how all of this happens in less than a second?—is hope's escape. Because what comes next is almost always the lack of requited attraction. At this point she's usually handing back the person's passport to them, and they see her as nothing but a uniform. They've barely even noticed her looking at them. And that's when a mild despair starts to take over. As modest as hope, this despair has only come to spread its message that, yeah, nothing's gonna happen. Maybe someday, but not soon. Not here, not like this. No one is looking at her.

Rosa went through all of this when she first saw Michelle. Her heart quickened when Michelle asked if she knew what was happening at the airport. Then the fight broke out and Rosa ran to help, and when she turned back to look at the train, it had carried Michelle away. She'd shrugged off her attraction to the girl, until she'd found Michelle and James at the ATL Today News, where it had come bubbling back up as if it didn't know exactly where this was going.

Farther down the hallway she goes, toward the bustle of T8. She stands and watches the scene for a while, because at least it's unexpected. Everyone is standing in a circle around a massive igloo, arms around each other. Rosa did pretty well in science class at school, and though she'd confess she has very little igloo-building knowledge, none of the conditions of the airport seem to support the igloo's construction, especially given the amount of time since Rosa arrived at the T gates. Although, really, at this point, the more surprising part of the scene is the people standing peacefully around the igloo.

Ulf is speaking some other language, his head bowed and his eyes closed. Everyone is quiet, shockingly respectful. His cadence sounds like a prayer, and Rosa finds herself rooting for T8. She's not sure what that means in the context of the day's events, but if this is heading toward some sort of battle, these are the people she wants succeeding. Not quite enough to stick around with them, though. Onward, exploring the terminal, escaping boredom and despair.

Behind her, Roger scurries from the bathroom into the nook where there's a water fountain. It's an absurdly short distance, especially in terms of sneaking around. The bathroom is only three or so steps away and much harder to spot someone in. He giggles a little, then rushes diagonally across the hallway to hide behind a large vending machine selling electronics.

Another explosion rings out through the airport, knocking a few more things to the ground, handing out another dozen concussions or so. Few people panic this time.

TWELVE

\\\\\\\\\\\\

THE LATEST EXPLOSION, WHICH ORIGINATED AT THE massage chair locale in the C gates, again has caused only minimal damage to the airport and its occupants, despite everyone having felt its reverberations. Joseph Flint, the angry, red-cheeked man at T12, decides he is done with blaming this on mere notions: terrorism, the government, liberals. He needs to direct his anger at something real, and he needs to do it now.

Practically screeching with rage, Joseph barrels down the hallways toward the only person around who he believes might be responsible, and therefore probably is. He storms into the ATL Today News, making everyone inside jump. The teens sitting on the counter jolt upright, kicking over playing cards onto the snow. The other guy, the object of Joseph's scorn, stands up, bigger than Joseph expected.

"Is everyone all right?" Taha asks.

Joseph knew he'd have a fucking accent. He'd expected something other than British, but whatever. Fuck accents. He knew this guy was trouble as soon as he saw him walking into the terminal.

Joseph wants to push Taha over, but the dude is for sure bigger than he realized. All right, no need to go all out. Joseph unholsters his index finger and becomes the second person in as many chapters to shove a digit into someone's chest. "You know, don't you? You fucking know."

James watches Taha look down at the finger on his chest. He feels the tension rising in the silence as everyone waits for Taha to react. Although James would bet more money than he has that it's the white dude who's gonna escalate. You can see it in his eyes, how he's hoping for more.

All right, maybe "hoping" is not the right word; Taha is built, and Joseph doesn't look like he actually wants to come to blows. But Joseph would sure as hell welcome being proven right.

Instead, Taha meets Joseph's eyes and slowly brings his arms up, hands out. He fucking smiles. James wants to applaud, it's such a badass move. But the tension hasn't dissipated and James himself is feeling shaky, so he's not about to call attention to himself that way.

"Why don't you start from the beginning, so that I can understand?" Taha says.

Joseph moves one hand to his hip, ready to shove his finger farther into the guy's chest. But he can't quite bring himself to shove again, held back by what, James can't quite tell. He'd guess muscles, but Michelle, watching just as intently, guesses it's the smile.

Instead, Joseph raises that index finger up, gets it real close to Taha's face. "Don't get cute with me, pal. I know you know what's going on here. And you're going to fucking tell me. You're going to tell everyone!"

"Sir," Taha says, his voice so calm James wishes he could record it for nights when he can't fall asleep. The old white guy, on the other hand, looks like he might get a fucking heart attack. "I am just a fellow passenger—" Taha continues.

"What, you think 'cause you work out I'm scared of you?" Joseph interrupts, loud as ever. "I'm not scared. You think I'm gonna let you win? You think I'm gonna let you get away with any of it? You're in America, you fucking jihadist. We don't let terrorists win."

Both James and Michelle, only a few feet away, want to step in, but neither knows how. James wants to knock the hell out of this prick, and he wishes he were the kind of guy who did that. But Taha is keeping his cool, and he motions for James and Michelle to do the same. Which is just as well, since James is more scared than angry, and his anger usually unleashes itself only in the form of impassioned internal monologues and sweaty palms.

"I understand you're afraid right now," Taha says, hands still up, voice steady. "But I advise you to think and be calm."

"Oh, you advise *me*, do you?" The index finger becomes emboldened again and goes right into Taha's pectoral muscle. Joseph regrets the move when he feels the strength of the muscle, even when relaxed. But the move causes Taha's smile to fade, and without it around, Joseph's rage comes on full blast. He turns to look at the teens, then gives his back to Taha and shouts out the open door. "This guy's a fucking terrorist. He knows what's happening." Joseph turns back around and bumps Taha with his belly. "I'm onto you. All of this, I know it's you."

Taha's voice turns. It's like hearing a puppy growl for the first time. It catches James, Michelle, and Joseph by surprise. Taha's tone remains the same, but there's something just under the surface, something he clearly doesn't unleash often. "Sir, first of all, please do not encroach on my personal space. Secondly, if you would only take a moment to think about the—"

"I don't need to think for a fucking second, buddy."

Naturally, the commotion has started attracting the attention of the surrounding factions. Several of the leaders leave the confines of their gates and find themselves standing outside of the ATL Today News. Many others follow, and soon a crowd is gathering. A handful of people find themselves agreeing with Joseph, sure that the tall, dark-skinned man knows something. A handful more feel a moment of agreement and then an instant wave of shame that they sided with the clear racist, even if it was just at first. A good number stay quiet, thinking others should intercede. That others will. Still more feel the urge to come to

Taha's defense but don't know what to say, or the words are swallowed by reticence, by cowardice, by fear. Several people do speak out but fear what the raging white man might do to them in response.

This, perhaps more than anything else that has happened so far, embodies real-world things that James fears. The easy ways people can turn their anger on each other. The way irrationality leads to physicality.

"Tell us what is going on," Joseph shouts, starting to feed off the presence of the crowd. His index finger basks in the spotlight, eager to strike again. "Tell us!" He wields his finger like a sword and jabs it toward Taha's chest. James flinches, as if the impact of the finger will bring with it a new explosion. He looks at the playing cards scattered on the floor around him and feels a sharp pang of longing for the past; the briefest rewind will do.

Before Joseph's finger can make contact, though, Taha has grabbed it with one hand and Joseph's wrist with his other hand, then twisted so that Joseph's arm is behind his back and his finger is some slight pressure away from breaking. The audience gasps, but no one comes near. James exclaims a soft "Oh shit!"

"I warned you not to encroach on my personal space," Taha says, loud enough for others to hear. "Now, if you would remain calm, I have some questions for you."

Joseph grunts in pain. "Like what?" he mutters, spitting out the question, little flecks of drool stuck to his bottom lip.

"First and foremost, what do you think gives you the right

to come charging at the first brown person you see and accusing them of terrorism? You don't know me, you don't know my religion. What has gone so wrong in your life that makes you feel like you have the right to do this? What has failed you in its misinformation to make you believe the things you believe?" Taha sighs, loosens his grip a little. This guy's a fucking hero, James thinks.

"My real objection is," Taha continues, "look around. Does any of this actually feel like a terrorist attack? Where is the gunfire? Where are the masked men shouting instructions? If I were involved in something like that, don't you think I'd be doing something other than reading at a bookstore and playing in the snow?"

Voices of assent from the crowd. Those who hadn't found it in them to speak out before find the courage now, among others. "Leave him alone, racist prick," someone yells. "Ain't no goddamn way this is terrorism," someone else says, to a chorus of approval. James speaks too, just a "yeah" tossed out there, almost inaudible, but enough to make him feel like he's made it clear where he stands, as if there might be a question.

Now Taha leans in a little closer to whisper something in Joseph's ear. Everyone around leans in too, trying to catch what Taha says, entranced by his voice, his control of the situation. James, so close to him he can almost smell Taha's shampoo, can just barely make out what he says. "I understand you are afraid. I am afraid too. I don't know what's going on, and I am praying for my safety as well as the safety of those around me. Let us not turn this fear on each other." He reapplies a little pressure to Joseph's finger, leans in a little farther, uses the deeper tone from earlier. "Agreed?"

Joseph brings himself to nod.

Taha lets go and then moves to pick up his book to resume reading. But almost as soon as he is free, Joseph returns to his bellowing. "Even if you're not a terrorist, I'm gonna sue the hell out of you. Who do you think you are, assaulting me?" He turns to the crowd. "You all saw that. This man attacked me and threatened me with violence."

"Are you joking?" Michelle says. She turns to make eye contact with James, but he can't look away, and it seems like he's bracing for the inevitable escalation.

Joseph ignores Michelle and the exclamations from others. "I know what you're up to, buddy. Just 'cause you've got these people buying your bullshit doesn't mean I will too. I've got my eye on you, and I'm gonna make sure I find some officers or soldiers to take care of you."

Taha shakes his head and flips through the pages to find his spot.

The crowd lingers a little while longer, waiting to see if the conflict is truly over. Joseph continues spouting angry epithets, trying to rile others up to his level. A few concede, mostly others from T12 who seem to genuinely enjoy elevated blood pressure. When it's clear that Taha is becoming enrapt in his book and is not going to engage further, those looking for excitement start to disperse. A few of those who spoke out against Joseph hang around, in case they get another chance to do the right thing and interject.

Beverly Bingham is in attendance. Her mind is churning, her fingers fiddling with the cross on her neck. She sees the man reading calmly and is not fooled by him. She's still more worried about the Russian, but this shouting man is bringing up good points. He's doing it in a barbaric way, sure, but that doesn't change the validity of his message. If this isn't terrorism, what is it? And if this foreigner with the— She catches herself before she thinks the specific words that she knows are there but would rather not put into words. It's simply more likely for a Middle Easterner to be a terrorist, Beverly thinks, as if it's a fact.

Oh, if only people didn't take nonfacts as facts. The Atlanta airport would be a much better place.

While others start to lose interest in Joseph's rant, Beverly looks around at the T concourse. She's come to accept that this temporary situation might stretch out for longer than she hoped. This is a reality everyone here must accept. But they don't all have to accept lawlessness and terror. Beverly will be the protector of the people in the terminal, she will save the children here, save the mothers and Christians. While she is in the T concourse, law and order will reign supreme, gosh darn it. Civility will reign supreme.

She approaches Joseph, who's still wielding his index finger, just looking for someone to point it at menacingly. He doesn't notice Beverly until she's right by his side, and he instantly recognizes within her a kindred spirit. "Ma'am, you agree with me, right?"

Beverly nods, and she reaches up to lower his hand. "Not like this," she says, giving his hand a gentle tap.

Elsewhere in the terminal, Roger Sterlinger rolls his way across the hallway, hiding behind pillars, re-creating that night when he was twelve.

Rosa, returning from her lap around the terminal, sees the crowd in the distance and slows down, not wanting to deal with whatever the fuck that's all about.

At the moment, James's and Michelle's heart rates are nearly identical. They spiked during the altercation and have been gradually calming in the ensuing moments. James and Michelle are standing protectively near Taha, though it is clear he doesn't quite need the protection of two teens. Most of the playing cards are on the floor, the game ruined.

Michelle walks over to where the cards are and starts to gather them. James joins, their hands occasionally brushing in the snow when they reach for the same cards. "Do you think there's *anything* that could happen today that would surprise you?" Michelle asks.

James takes a deep, long breath. "I dunno, man. Dinosaurs?"

"God, can you imagine? Velociraptors roaming the halls?"

"I honestly don't know if it would make me feel any different than I do right now."

They set the playing cards on the counter and stand up. Michelle looks down at her bare legs. "Should have gone with the pants earlier." She reaches for some on the nearby rack, cheap fleece with *Atlanta* written along the leg, tosses them to James.

"Thanks."

"You're welcome, *man,*" she says, teasing.

After slipping the pants on, James checks his phone for the first time in a while. Still nothing from his parents. The airport Wi-Fi makes him accept the terms and conditions again. He checks his email, deletes the promotional messages that have filled up his inbox in the last few hours.

Across the hallway, the flight monitors continue to flash their DELAYED designations, refusing to say anything has been canceled. The crowd continues to disperse, returning to their gates and town hall meetings, deciding who they want to be for the remainder of this delay. After conversing with those around them, a handful of people switch factions, unaware up until that moment that they had an option. Auzelle Stalford desperately wants to switch over to Representative Liang's faction, but the rest of the people at her gate keep casting suspicious looks at her as if daring her to try it, and so she ends up dragging her feet through the snow back to T5.

It's unclear why Rosa, Taha, James, and Michelle aren't compelled to join a faction, or to form their own. Technically, maybe they are one. Maybe they are the outliers, those still hanging on to the hope for normalcy to return. Everyone else seems resigned to the fact that this weird thing is going to continue to happen, and they may as well act accordingly. Maybe this happens because we are focusing our narration around these four, or maybe we are focusing our narration around them because they are not succumbing to this social restructuring. Hard to tell.

"We haven't heard from the PA dudes in a while," James says.

"What do you think is happening on that side of things?" Michelle asks. "Are airport officials scrambling to figure out what the hell is going on? Do they have any clue? Is it on purpose?"

"I dunno. The announcements they made earlier seem to really prove your theory that adults are just pretending they know what they're doing." James fiddles with his phone, flipping it in his hand a few times until it accidentally drops into the snow.

He picks it up and they fall into silence, as if waiting for the PA to take its cue and offer some instructions. Nothing, though. The adults who gathered for a scene have dissipated, likewise awaiting instructions, likewise unsuited to the situation.

Within moments the terminal feels emptied out. Presumably, everyone has settled into whichever concourse/gate suits their specific needs at the moment. James doesn't know that people are actually disappearing from the airport. He has the notion that his parents and Ava, that Michelle's parents, they're all somewhere else in the airport. But if that were the case, they'd have access to their phones, and they would surely let him know they were okay. That's not what's happening, though. They are gone, and we're sorry to say we don't know where they—or the 347 other people missing from the airport—currently are.

THIRTEEN

WE ALL PICTURE OURSELVES AS THE HEROES OF OUR own stories, and no one reading is a stranger to fantasies of becoming a savior. Michelle is as guilty, but she also knows that there is no shame in these fantasies. She even believes them, every now and then. She knows that eventually an opportunity will present itself where she will be able to at least attempt to save the day, and if this isn't that moment, then what else could it be?

"I think I might be to blame for this whole thing," she says, standing up.

James chuckles, "Still not true."

Michelle thinks back to the moment she touched the light, desperate to remember if that was when everything started to fall apart. In her memory, the order of events is muddled, the whole day a concatenation of weirdness. She can picture herself standing in front of the light, reaching for it, realizing that it's a button and pressing it down. James was somewhere off to her side, lost in thought. What happened the moment right after? Did one of the explosions happen then, or did that come later? The blackouts? Try as she might, all she can see is that moment, her and James, a photograph of the past, not video footage. She's trying to make sense of the sequence of events. Might as well try to make sense of disease, Michelle. Might as well make sense of the way tragedy gets handed out to people, a little here, a little there, like petals thrown by a flower girl at a wedding, indiscriminately tossed about. Sometimes it lands in one place all at once.

"We should go back to it," she says. "Do something about it." She's still reaching into her memory, trying to grasp more than just the image. This happens to Michelle a lot. When she thinks back to friends she's left behind in Jakarta, in Buenos Aires, in Basel. That night two years ago when she had friends over to watch a movie, the still frame in her mind: Lisa sitting on the floor at Gabriel's feet, her arm casually thrown back to rest on his knees. The glow of the screen reflecting on their faces, the look in Gabriel's eyes, which to Michelle is a clear indication that he was falling in love with Lisa right then and there. But she can never access the memory the way she wants, move a little forward in time to see if she can still see the look in Gabriel's eyes, or if it's just something she's added into the memory.

The thought that memory is fallible terrifies Michelle,

the fact that the narratives we create from our experiences are fabricated by faulty minds, stitched together like fiction, no bearing on reality. Right now it feels like she's responsible for everything happening at the airport, that the moment she pushed the green button was when hell started breaking loose. Who knows, maybe this all started because she was an asshole to her grandparents, because she didn't treat a goodbye as a goodbye.

It's a ridiculous notion, and it might just be how her brain is weaving the events together to create a narrative, but that is little comfort against the possibility that it's true. That she did this, and now it has to be undone. She pushes back from the counter, standing up abruptly. "Let's go. Now."

"Where? Why?" James asks.

"It was a button, not a light. I pushed it."

"And you think that caused the rules that govern reality to freak out?"

Michelle shrugs, but she calls out a "be right back" to Rosa and Taha and leads James out of the ATL Today News and toward the escalators, her strides long and quick. "I'm not saying I'm confident in the theory, just saying it's a theory. Got any others?"

James sighs, struggling to keep up with her. "I mean, no, but can we pretend I have a theory that involves us hunkering down somewhere chill and waiting for adults to take care of this?" He thinks of the fire, the feeling, at least, that it was not up to him to figure out what to do next. "Like that smoking lounge we were at. Or playing cards. That was the best I've felt all night. Let's go get some snacks and hang out in that room and look out at the runway and shoot the shit."

They're back in the hallway with the tram. The crowds from earlier have dissipated, who knows where to. The overhead marquee by the tram doors reads: TRAIN ARRIVING SHORTLY. "We can call that a backup plan," Michelle says. She stands in front of the tram doors, peeking through the windows to look for the approaching car.

Eyeing the escalator behind them, James wonders if they're making a mistake. Shit was getting intense up there, but at least it was typical human intensity. Heading back into this hallway, back onto the tram, it feels the way trips to the bathroom in the middle of the night felt when he was a kid. Especially if he and Marcus had watched a horror movie recently. His childhood bathroom was across the hallway, the toilet facing the door, so his options were to either pee with the door open, not knowing what might be lurking behind him (which, fuck that) or close the door and then have to endure that terrible moment when it was time to go back to bed. A world of darkness beyond the fluorescent glow of the three bulbs over the mirror. Even if the journey to safety entailed that same hallway he had already crossed, there was always an added sense of danger on the way back. No matter how much he tried to reason with his imagination, it still conjured up monsters, literal demons or their human counterparts—dudes with guns.

The tram arrives. An Asian woman in her twenties or thirties is lying on top of the seats at one end. Her body is curled up away from other passengers, arms clutching her hiker's backpack, which is jungle green but scuffed and faded. James and Michelle walk to the opposite side of the tram, not saying much the whole ride to the B gates. Only one other person gets on the tram during that time, but he changes his mind for some reason and steps away before the doors close behind him.

Back to where our heroes met. The bookstore/café is crowded, every potential seat taken up. Several people wear somber expressions, and the majority of the others have dived into books or the isolating comfort of their headphones, the nourishing sanctuary of food. James is surprised to hear the chatter of several conversations, both from the tables here and from the restaurant next door, whose staff have taken on the day's events with resilient smiles. There's no music playing from the overhead speakers, and over in a corner, some high schoolers with empty instrument cases at their feet are trying as hard as they can to get a single note to ring out. Their instruments remain mute. The rain has cleared, but a mugginess lingers in its wake.

Michelle strides right up to the green light, as if she's about to tell it off. It's not an unfair assessment, since that's exactly what she wants to do. Two years ago, when her school in Argentina fired the widely loved principal, Michelle stormed into the head of school's office and delivered a tirade that is still discussed by the board members with equal parts admiration and resentment. Her grandparents on her mom's side once made a racist remark about Chinese people, and Michelle underwent a tireless month-long campaign to get them to see that they were dehumanizing others based on cultural differences. They had apologized by day three, taken it all back. But Michelle did not forget wrongdoings easily, and she did not stay quiet in the face of injustice.

Not that this situation is either of those things. But there is a chance that she is at fault here, that she unleashed this madness on the world, either by her callousness or her recklessness, and the green light is the face of this madness. Except she's not quite unhinged enough to yell at a wall, so she stands there for a moment with her hands on her hips, feeling like the caricature of an angry teenage girl. Should she press the green light again? Bash it into oblivion? Stare at it and will it to correct the course of the airport, of the world?

Then the PA speaker crackles on again. Most of the airport is fairly quiet anyway, but throughout the seven concourses, people hold their breath and strain to listen. Information, they beg from the voices overhead. Instructions. Give us something. Those with missing relatives and friends think this a little more desperately. Airport passengers collectively look to the flight monitors, hoping for a change.

False hope, though. The crackle is some mistake in the wiring, some fluke in the system. Or Gary and his nameless coworker have changed their minds about the announcement. The speakers go quiet, the monitors hold their message.

James sighs and sticks his hands in his pockets while Michelle seems not to notice the blip. Then a nearby voice loudly says, more annoyed than anything, "Not again."

The ground starts rumbling. James cannot find an ounce of disbelief left within him. He only looks around to take in what it is this time. It's hard to tell at first what's causing this fresh disturbance, because so much of the airport is unrecognizable. Puddles line the hallways; glass is broken over everything, causing the overhead lights to reflect in little pinpricks of light throughout the concourse, like a planetarium turned on its head. A food kiosk is on its side, most of its products still splayed on the floor, not enticing enough to ransack. Some people were apparently traveling with tents, or were resourceful enough to fashion them out of the materials at hand. A small colony of them has sprung up near the fast-food court, and they have even built a fire to sit around, the sight a jarring reminder of refugee camps. Out the window, there's a blacked-out chunk of the world where the airport tower used to be. One plane on the runway has deployed its emergency exit slides, its passengers long gone, clambering over the fence where the brown thrasher still sits.

Since there's no immediate sign of something that would

cause the ground to rumble, James finds himself guessing: earthquake. Or maybe a volcano forming in the middle of the airport. Part of him is almost rooting for this thing to get madder and madder, to crank it up to eleven. Let's get all the trauma out in one go, and if he somehow survives this, then maybe he'll be able to stop waiting for the world to attack. This is probably that same part of him that is disappointed when the horde from earlier turns a corner and comes barreling through the hallway again. How unoriginal.

They're still in slow motion, but they've doubled in number. A woman talking on her phone, or at least holding it up to her ear as if it's functioning normally, crosses the hall in front of the mob, not noticing them at all. She even drops her passport and boarding pass and leans down to pick them up, the mob roaring toward her at a snail's pace in the background.

The people at the bookstore start grumbling, and then they go into a set of movements that feels choreographed, like they've all practiced their roles plenty of times already. For some, these roles entail only the momentary complaining about the disturbance while they continue sipping their drinks and nibbling at their pastries. The bookstore employees and a handful of customers who are seated in the little fake patio in the hallway get up and move the tables indoors. Then, together, they reach above to the rolled-up metal gates that usually only come down during closing time. It sounds like a roller coaster climbing its way up to the top, a satisfying, rhythmic clacking.

A tall Black employee with a seventies-style 'fro walks along the edge of the store, fastening the gates to little metal loops on the floor, then securing them with padlocks. The friendly restaurant nearby is going through a similar lockdown procedure. James watches with a mix of curiosity and growing panic.

"Um, Michelle?" She's still running her fingers along the wall, careful not to touch the light, fighting the burgeoning urge to do just that. She doesn't notice the rumbling, thinking that it's just her nerves. "I think more weird shit is going down, and we should probably not be in its way."

"Hmm?"

The horde approaches. They take up nearly the entirety of the hall, climbing over each other and stomping whatever's in their way, albeit slowly. There are now several torches among them, and weapons fashioned out of a variety of items: carry-on luggage handles, travel-size liquid containers turned into diminutive Molotov cocktails, the stanchions from TSA lines being hoisted like javelins.

For some reason James thinks of zombies. His mind goes to that time he and his friends went to a zombie-themed escape room, the thrill of pretend danger, the way adrenaline started pumping even in the face of something he knew was not real. It was a crazy feeling, his body working against his brain, muddling his thought process. The whole time, trying to work out the clues peppered around the room, James had marveled at the incongruences of his own body. Sweaty hands, rapid heartbeat, all under the guise of survival, at odds with how his clouded thoughts rendered him useless. Anxiety creeping in, but also the mad desire to act intelligently, to figure out the problem at hand.

James sees that the café has not yet closed completely. At the rate they're advancing, the horde won't be on them for at least a couple of minutes, but by then the only recourse might be to flee. And James senses that Michelle will resist this above all else, that an idea has wormed itself into her mind, that the green light is what matters to her.

He reaches out, lays the tips of his fingers on her bare fore-arms, trying to act like, after all this, it's no longer a big deal. She turns to look at him, her eyes wild, unfocused. "We have to go," he says, and when a look of concern passes over her face, he points out the bookstore. "Just right there, just for now."

She still isn't convinced, so he gestures to the mob. Some-one within the horde throws a shoe, and it sails through the air in slow motion. James follows its trajectory as if it's a video moving frame by frame, the shoe's laces undone, untethered like wings.

"Okay?" James asks. "We can come back to the light when they pass."

"What if . . . ?"

Michelle's eyes go back to the wall. Then the shoe breaks through whatever barrier separates real time from the horde's lethargic alternate reality, and it comes sailing toward them, landing a few feet away with a muted thud. Michelle snaps out of her daze, nodding to James, quietly wishing he won't pull his hand away. He doesn't. Instead he's emboldened, and his fingers slip down her forearm and past her wrist, resting heavier and heavier until they close around her own.

The world is a school hallway now. They are between classes, catching stolen moments of joy amidst the innocent drudgery of the everyday. Michelle feels her heartbeat quicken, feels her palms start to sweat. She feels a smile creeping onto her lips, joy fizzing in her belly. It's as if they've been trading notes for a whole school year, friends building up to more. She can picture James being the kind of boy who would orchestrate run-ins in the hallway, time his day so that they could see each other. He'd wait outside her classes, one shoulder leaning against the wall, earphones in, feigning innocence. She knows it. She also knows how those last few minutes of class would feel, hoping he was out there again. Never any specific urge for escalation in those moments, just the complacent desire for repetition. Simple joys, those.

Michelle doesn't dare break the spell by acknowledging this unexpected surge of happiness, but she can't resist squeezing James's hand. She finds herself looking at the slope of his jawline, the side of his young face. Sixteen, she thinks, the number sounding strange to her. Sixteen was the move to Canada; sixteen was the transition from clubbing in Buenos Aires to the quiet rules of Quebec. It was the year she ached for tattoos and boys, both of which she now dismisses so easily that it doesn't feel like she is the same person. Chuy, her cousin, turns sixteen this year, the same red-cheeked, chubby menace of a child she used to babysit, used to lift in her arms as if he weighed nothing.

James's eyebrows are furrowed, his lips tight with concentration. She wishes they would just turn around and walk like this for a while, hand in hand. Play pretend. Something else lands behind them, a louder thump than the shoe, heavier. Michelle flinches, draws herself closer to James, still envisioning the walk to their next period, the thrill of their hands together, and how long that sensation might linger in the space between her fingers. Crushes; she misses that about sixteen.

They reach the café right before the tall Black employee is about to bring down the last gate. "Can we come in?" James asks.

The employee doesn't hesitate. "Yeah, bro, get your ass in here." He slams the gate down behind them, and James hears the click of it latching into place. He feels a sense of relief, then realizes he's still holding Michelle's hand and quickly lets go.

"Sorry," James says softly.

Michelle starts to stammer something, but she doesn't say it loudly enough for James to know what it was.

"You guys seen this shit yet?" the employee says, marching past them. "Goddamn world done lost its damn mind." He chuckles and shakes his head. "We're out of chairs but we got plenty of drinks and food, so if you guys see anyone in a white shirt, just holla and we'll serve you anywhere in the store." He's about to head away from them, through the crowd gathered at the bookstore, people littering most of the aisles, some sitting cross-legged on the floor, but then he pauses, fixes them with a worried look. "Try to stay back from the gates."

FOURTEEN

MICHELLE AND JAMES MUNCH ON FRIED CALAMARI and watch the horde pass by up close. They sit cross-legged with their backs against a display of books, several feet away from the gate. Every now and then some member of the horde will hook their fingers through the metal squares and rattle the whole thing. James can't help but jump back every time.

Mostly, the horde passes by uneventfully. The violence they attempt to inflict is ameliorated by their still-active slo-mo. One guy with a torch manages to catch a magazine rack on fire, but the flames fail to spread, licking out tentatively like tongues testing out a Popsicle. An employee with a fire extinguisher snuffs out the flames before any damage can be done. A few other horde members shove weapons through the little holes, knives and blunt objects, but everyone inside the café is at a safe enough distance to watch unharmed.

James stabs another panko-breaded ring and dips it into the generically pan-Asian dipping sauce. It's surprisingly good for airport food, and by the time the plate is done, James realizes it's been hours since he had a meal. Shit, he should be on the ground in Chicago by now, swinging by Portillo's on the way home. Eating fries out of the bag in the car, still so hot they could burn your tongue, dotted with spilled grease from the Italian beef sandwiches. Everyone eating in the kitchen as soon as they get home, Mom and Ava at the table, Pops on his feet, fries resting on top of the bag, a beer on the counter, sweating beads onto the linoleum. Inhaled sandwiches, quick recount of the highlights of the trip (Uncle Ray's made-up Spanglish Scrabble words, the lone day of sunshine in Florida, a goose chasing Grandma through the park), then everyone would go off to bed. The house dark and his alone to enjoy in the night. He loves the feeling of being the only one awake, of filling the hours up. Not with anything productive, just video games, movies, a book. Sometimes he leaves the house, takes a walk around the neighborhood, counting how many lights are on inside the buildings. The faint blue glow of a television left on, a hallway light here or there to make nighttime bathroom trips easier. He knows how wrong it could go, brown kid walking around in the middle of the night in a gentrifying neighborhood. The cops called in, again. He pushes that thought down, thinks of himself as the only person awake in the whole city. Still a few days until school starts up again, forcing him into everyone else's schedules.

"You want to order more?" Michelle says. "I'm still starving."

"Yeah, me too," James says. "Kinda low on cash, though."

"I'm sure the airport will resort to a bartering system soon," she says, reaching over to grab a menu off a nearby table. Her assertion is spot-on. Across the airport, people have already begun to trade. A coat for some food, space within a shelter in exchange for a printed boarding pass (Gerald Harrington of Dubuque, Iowa, has been collecting as many of them as he can, hoping he'll have a pass to the first flight that leaves this damn place, wherever it may take him). Food itself has become the most widely accepted form of currency, to the dismay of the employees at the currency exchange locales peppered throughout the airport. They look to their computers, begging for the system to know what the exchange rate is from euros to potato chips. In the T gates, more and more people come knocking at Ulf's igloo, hoping for space within his creation, offering pillows, offering headphones, offering their hands, the strength of their backs, their sweat, anything he needs. "Don't worry, though," Michelle adds. "I'll cover you if they're still using real money."

A waiter comes by, and they end up ordering a veritable feast. "Everything sounds so good," Michelle says. "Who knew this tiny place would have so much food." She frowns at the menu, wondering if it was this lengthy when they were here earlier.

"Yeah, let's do the gobi Manchurian too. And some guac."

"This is probably too much food," the waiter says, "but I get it."

The food arrives before the horde has finished passing by. A bit strange, sure, eating while staring at people through a cage. But it feels like dinner and a show, a blessed break from the madness.

Michelle's attention shifts away from the horde and the blinking green light, which she's been watching nervously, trying to will the zombies away from it. Now she focuses on the food, giving little moans of pleasure as she takes a bite of a biscuit, a nod at the short rib slider. James's attention volleys between the food and the horde. As good as the food tastes (was he really that hungry, or is it something else—how survival can coat the taste buds with appreciation?), he's engrossed by the faces going past, their distorted features of rage and destruction. He wonders who these people are and why they were unlucky enough to get caught up in this particular madness. Why isn't he out there, swinging some sort of strap over his head in a circular motion the way this guy passing by now is, smashing a laptop bag into the walls with a thunk that tells James there used to be a computer in there. He's in his sixties or seventies, his white mustache the only recognizable feature on his face, the rest hidden by aviator sunglasses and a cowboy hat. He looks like he might be a regular at a dive bar in Tennessee, some old converted inn that now holds bluegrass jam sessions. James has the strange urge to approach the gate and rummage through the guy's pockets, unveil the hidden details of his life, some clue as to why he's in the horde. A leather-bound flask, a cheap Velcro wallet with pictures of a wife, grandkids, himself as a young man on a motorcycle. Dried tobacco flakes mixed in with lint, so old they crumble between his fingers every time he reaches in.

This thought hits James and sends through him a mad desire to know the contents of every single pocket at the airport. He looks over at Michelle, who's right now taking the lid off the bamboo dim sum container and scooping out a soup dumpling with a spoon. "How much stuff do you have in your pockets?"

Michelle chews, pulls her phone out. She hits the button as she does so, checking for notifications. Nothing on the screen but the time and a picture of a setting sun somewhere James has likely never been. A queasy feeling in his stomach that his parents are still MIA, that the fears of adulthood he's held on to will never come to pass, that *this* is what he has to fear now. Cold floods his veins, what he imagines is the onset of a panic attack. He keeps it at bay by taking another bite, looking at Michelle.

"That's about it," she says, patting her legs. She slides her European Union passport out from her back pocket. Its corners are creased with use and maybe carelessness. It's bigger than any passport James has seen too, the pages thick with ink. "Why do you ask?"

James reaches out to the passport, little head nod to ask if it's cool to look through it. He starts to flip the pages, looking at the stamps and visas. "I just had this thought. It's kinda stupid, fake-deep."

Michelle doesn't press. James tries to identify the languages it contains, the airport codes. What a life she's led, he thinks. He wants the passport to tell him exactly what her life has been, wants the information to take shape. He wants to know all about Michelle, not just the details that have emerged throughout the layover. Which of the pins he saw on her backpack match the stamps in these pages? Which of these trips did she take with her grandparents? Silly to think the contents of her pockets would give much away, but there the thought is anyway.

He tries to give voice to this, share the thought with Michelle, but a few moments of silence stifle the desire. Then her eyes flit up to the light and back down to the Mediterranean appetizer platter in front of them, which James realizes he hasn't dipped into yet. He combines the eggplant dip thing with some tabbouleh on a pita chip, licks his fingers. He should learn how to cook, learn how to provide this joy for himself. When this is over, if it's ever over, he'll ask his dad to teach him how to grill.

The horde is nearing its end, sweaty stragglers whose hearts don't seem to be in it. One guy is just running his fingers along the wall, a constant, weak "Ahhhh" escaping from his open mouth, more of a groan than a yell. No one in the horde looks back; they just keep marching forward, intent on their destruction.

When the many plates James and Michelle have emptied have been cleared away, the same tall employee pulls up the gate again. The café returns to relative normalcy, though the horde can still be heard down the hallway. A family of four gets up and goes, and James wonders why anyone would leave. Then Michelle stands and says she'll be right back, running over to the green light to continue investigating. James thinks to ask what exactly she hopes to accomplish but swallows that down too. He feels something slipping away, but that's probably just the little part of his brain that constantly feels this way.

Back to his phone, trying to text Ava, call his parents. Nothing. Like those three silent weeks from Aubrey, but worse. His imagination conjuring up nightmares. Back then it was nightmares that she had used him somehow, that she had no interest in him. A blow to the ego and the heart, sure, especially when it turned out to be mostly true. She'd enjoyed the making out but wanted nothing more from him. Now, though, the potential blows are not to his feelings but to his entire world. Ava and his parents, lost in the midst of the horde, maybe, or whatever other hells the airport has conjured up. All that food turns to stone in his stomach.

As his manic thoughts quicken his heart rate, James stands up and brushes off the crumbs from his sweatshirt. He rubs his hand over his hair, tries to fall into a relaxing breathing rhythm, fails. He walks over to Michelle, who's now just staring at the light with her arms crossed in front of her chest.

The meal and its pleasures are so quickly forgotten. No one even comes chasing after them asking for payment. It's as if the café has disappeared into its own reality and cares little about what happens beyond its borders. Another horde, basically, just happier and inclusive.

"I have to fix this," Michelle says. Almost to herself.

"Michelle, you didn't do anything."

He thinks for a moment that she doesn't hear him. A loud whooping sound rings out behind them, and James turns to look. Just a couple, a Latino-looking dude giving a girl a piggy-back ride. Michelle speaks again, chewing her bottom lip. "Even if that's true, doesn't mean I shouldn't try."

There's a desire to argue with her, but he doesn't know how to, exactly. So instead he falls silent. James notices the lack of music, doesn't bring it up. He thinks of the snow of the T gates, that dude Taha. The TSA agent. He felt good being around them and wants to find a way to guide him and Michelle back there. Looks around at the airport for the millionth time. These tiles and hallways have seared themselves into his brain, and he imagines he'll be having nightmares about them for years. Far down the corridor, people are huddled in blankets, sleeping the time away. How they survived the horde, who knows. There's a huge vending machine about thirty feet to his left, bright red lights humming in the silence. A couple of storefronts have been boarded up for construction. How the hell do mundane things persist in these moments?

When he looks back, it's too late to stop her. Michelle made up her mind before he even turned his head, convinced herself that it was a simple on/off switch. Again, she presses the light.

Harder this time, willing it to undo all the hell it's unleashed. Poor Michelle does not know it has not yet unleashed everything it can. The light compresses with a slight click, pops back up again as soon as she pulls away her lovely thumb. This time, the airport does not hold back.

FIFTEEN

\\\\\\\\\\\

THE THING FROM THE HALLWAY IS BACK. THIS TIME IT'S less of a feeling, more like something real. It has a shape, though James can't quite say what the shape is. He thinks of it as a creature now, though he has the suspicion that he's miscategorizing it, somehow. That it's not strictly alive, not even strictly singular.

What he sees: Great swaths of darkness. Moving black holes, absorbing light and life. Multiple legs and tentacles, the stuff of childhood horror movies. Bathroom halls at midnight. The dread-inspiring thought that people are generally more bad than good, that humanity is truly intent on destroying itself, and James will be a witness to the moment that it does.

Like in a nightmare, James finds himself unable to run away. His legs don't function; the synapses in his brain are firing orders to run, but the message gets lost along the way. James sees a thing he cannot escape, a cruel embodied truth: tragedy befalls us all. And here it comes for him, his family gone, violence in the air, the world flipped on its head.

Michelle sees something very different. Her grandfather in a hospital robe, shuffling down the hall alongside one of those IV-on-wheels things. He's smiling at her but won't say a word. She lost her chance to tell him anything, she cannot regain the past.

Basically, it seems, the creature—or creatures, or monster, or whatever—is like that thing from Harry Potter that shifts according to each person's specific fear. Not that the monster's unoriginality makes anyone feel better. The B gates return to mayhem.

\\\\\\\\\

Elsewhere, Roger Sterlinger continues to sneak around behind Beverly Bingham's back. The joy just doesn't seem to fade, and he'd be content to soak every inch of his clothes in the airport snow to keep on doing this. He barely pays attention to what else has been happening in the T gates. It's the first time that he can remember *not* being hyperaware of his surroundings, and he isn't going to ruin that because the surroundings are maybe more interesting than usual. Fuck interesting. There've been enough worries holding his interest his whole life.

The factions in the T gates have settled further into their roles. Beverly polices her gate and the wider terminal. Ulf protects his with the resources at hand and his own inventiveness. Joseph Flints scowls, looks for an outlet for his aggression. He keeps his eye on Taha, who he believes has infiltrated the airport ranks (proven by that treacherous TSA agent by his side, probably not even an American). The citizens of T11 have figured out how to change the channel on the three TVs in their gate and have started playing a *Die Hard* marathon.

All the others wonder if they should be taking sides or if they might remain safe in neutrality. They wonder if neutrality is the moral choice here. Auzelle Stalford is wishing she could really be anywhere else but is too afraid to retreat. "We need to stand together," Beverly says. Auzelle wonders just how far that "we" extends.

Then Michelle presses the green light again, and a fog starts to rise from the snow in the T gates. Thick, like it's been encroaching for hours. Thick enough that the overhead lights can't fight their way through it.

Beverly, having apparently concocted a plan, barks out orders, and then everyone files into two lines, flanking down either side of the hallway toward the other gates. They're hunched down below the fog, as per Beverly's instructions, everyone's hands unconsciously mimicking the act of holding a gun.

Those for whom Beverly's message has sunk in deepest are the most convincing. They start shouting at the people inside T6, T7, that this is now their territory. "Nobody better try anything," one woman growls. Her perfectly coiffed hair and stern demeanor point at some time in the military. Beverly's faction starts to take over land. As if that means something.

People submit. What else is there to do? Fight for a seat at an airport terminal? Some just surrender; they put their hands behind their backs, roll onto their knees, duck their heads and avoid eye contact. Most others go back to whatever it was they were distracting themselves with. Some welcome the observers, happy to have one less thing to worry about. Even Wendy Liang at T9 relinquishes her faction. Great politician though she may be—smart and fair and interested in others' well-being—she can do nothing about force. Curse of the world.

The plan is to surround Ulf and the ATL Today News. They don't want to engage, Beverly explains to Joseph. Not yet, no reason to. Not when they have the manpower to intimidate without action, and not till they know what these damn troublemakers are up to. Until they know what to do, they'll use the fog to their advantage, set up barricades below the fog line.

Taha and Rosa see them out there, slinking around like children playing war. "I hope this is being recorded," Taha says. Always such calm in his voice. "What you could learn about human nature by studying this phenomenon." He lets loose a low whistle, chuckles.

"Like what?" Rosa asks.

"That we all have no idea what we are doing," Taha laughs. "That we are beholden to rules and customs we don't understand and don't particularly believe in. That if the rules of our world change, we are a lot more likely to fall into a new lifestyle than to lose our way."

Rosa wants to crack a joke at this but lets the words sink in. She eyes Taha, wondering how a person can land on optimism amidst everything that's been going on. He's right, she knows. About humans adapting. A year ago, spending every morning with her stepdad stuck in rush-hour traffic would have sounded like downright torture. Now she almost enjoys the routine, the way they've landed on taking turns with the music, the smell of coffee in the car. Not quite the same as adapting to a world where the laws of nature no longer apply, but still. Humans adapt.

She clicks her phone on. 8:15:32. Before the dread can build up, she reaches into a bag of spicy beef jerky, tears off a chunk with her teeth.

\\\\\\\\\

In the F gates, the fragmentation of the passengers into their respective nationalities has not brought forth a T-like desire to conquer territory or fight. Instead, a rather playful notion sets in. They want to re-create the world within the concourse. The best mathematical minds start to crunch the numbers so that this new world will be to scale. Everyone else makes sure their country within the terminal looks like the real version, at least as close as can be expected. The Swiss make Alps out of furniture and luggage. Russians fiddle with the vents until a blast of cold air sweeps over their minuscule Siberia. Somehow the Italians find fertile soil beneath the carpet, and they begin growing grapes for wine. Who knows where, Mexicans find buckets of brilliantly colored paint, and they decorate their corner of the world with bright swaths of joy.

In the E gates, Chad and Brad, former looters, have now tasked themselves with throwing the best party the Atlanta airport has ever seen. They know there probably haven't been that many parties in the airport, but just because a goal is easy does not mean it's not worth achieving. They've procured speakers from that weird tech-and-gadget shop that no one ever goes into unless they need an overpriced pair of replacement headphones. The center bar in the concourse, where Roger Sterlinger earlier realized his anxiety had flitted away, now becomes the DJ/MC booth for Chad and Brad. They rig up a mic system and, every now and then, encourage people to get lit, get wasted, tear this shit up. People submit. What else is there to do?

\\\\\\\\\

This running bullshit again. James did not sign up for this. His backpack bounces, sweat forms beneath his shirt. Michelle's hand clasped in his. Slight whimpers coming from both of them in between deep, gasping breaths. Slight whimpers from the whole concourse, which, moments ago, witnessed a slow-motion mob of people and barely batted an eye. This is it, James thinks. This is how life is now. A succession of fucked-up events he either has to run or hide from. Exactly what he feared growing old would bring.

He doesn't know where they're running. It's not like the creatures are only behind them. They're everywhere. They reach their tentacles from beneath rows of seats, from the vents overhead. Dozens of them are out on the runway, moving toward the poor planes parked there, ready to envelop the people trapped within. Dozens of others have chosen to run too, so James and Michelle's route through the B concourse looks like a pinball's path, sharp turns to avoid running into others (or worse).

Five, ten minutes of this. No one shows any signs of wearing down. They're just sweatier as they run, their cheeks shiny with tears they don't have time to wipe away. Michelle's hand is still in James's. So different from earlier, when she pictured them as a developing high school crush. She squeezes tighter as they run, as if that might help push away thoughts of her grandmother coughing up blood, of her grandfather closing his eyes for a minute at a time to breathe through the pain in his bones, thoughts of their absence from the world. You can't run away from a thought like that by just running. Michelle knows it's necessary to dive into something else.

That's when she sees an inconspicuous door just off to her right, in between the men's and women's bathrooms. She imagines a hallway beyond that door, a hallway that will lead away from this, and though she knows escape will not be that easy, she leads James toward it. They have to avoid another couple running hand in hand, a slightly older version of them, Latino guy, Asian girl. Maybe strangers at the start of this too.

Michelle reaches the door and yanks it open, leading them inside even though it's nothing more than a janitor's closet. Shelves line the walls, loaded with industrial-grade cleaning products. A single mop rests in a bucket, as if this is just a school closet, the hallways easily cleaned by one person and this simple tool. No grandparents here, though. No dark truths about life either. Just a closet, a door easily closed to the outside world. James hesitates for a moment in the doorway, but Michelle pulls him all the way in and isolates them.

Darkness at first. Benign, though. They wait to see if the peril from the other side will join them in here, but a moment passes in peace. Another. They catch their breath, facing each other. Hands still clasped. Their eyes slowly adjust. James's jaw-line emerges first. His eyes, the glimmer in them. Lips slightly parted. Michelle feels drawn to them in a way that's easy to identify. Before she can think herself out of it, before it's even clear they're completely safe, she moves toward him.

That surprise of a first kiss, flesh made real. Michelle holds her hand to the back of James's neck, presses herself tightly to him. Blissful distraction from everything else. Whatever the critics would like to say of kissing, give it that. In a darkened airport closet, two kids mostly strange to each other. Happiness spreading, a flicker kept alive in the madness of the world. More to it, maybe. James feels like, yeah, maybe. Michelle feels something too. Who knows if it's the same thing. Who cares, for now. Let it spread its joys.

SIXTEEN

\\\\\\\\\\\\

JAMES AND MICHELLE ARE CURLED AROUND EACH
other on the closet floor, still clothed and mostly chaste.
Michelle wakes up first, closely attuned to the joys of the physical. Her flushed cheeks and lips, James's fingers in her hair. His
heartbeat and lungs working beneath her, rhythms of the body.
The smell of rain on him, that musk of male deodorant. Warmth
of his skin. Skin feels better than it should. Good to know that
feeling is not diminished in the face of other things.

James is still asleep. We kind of wish that they could stay like
this until the morning, cramped and safe and happy. Then they
could awaken to normalcy with this thing behind them, rose-
tinted now by something good.

Alas.

But let's not rush ahead. They get this, for now. James sleeps
nearly an hour. Michelle is in and out of sleep, resisting the
urge to wake James up and make out a little more. She keeps an

ear out for what may be happening, what else she's unleashed. Whenever that thought strikes, she nestles farther into James. There is comfort in the silence, but terror too. How long has it been? How long can this keep going?

Finally she has enough of her thoughts and the quiet and she stirs James awake. Quick kiss to the jawline, a hand on his chest. Shifting against him with a fake yawn, a mumbled "How long have we been out?" She's not sure why she feels the need to pretend.

James, still half-asleep, can't process the question. He re-awakens to the fact of her touch; everything else takes a moment. He has never woken up with someone in his arms before. The silver linings just keep piling on. Something he doesn't always consider: the joys life hands out.

Does he hold her closer, scurry away and apologize, stay perfectly still? He wants all three, and so his body freaks out and just goes stiff. What's a sane thing to say in these situations? He can't even guess.

Michelle senses all of this happening. It's equal parts cute and frustrating. Sixteen, she thinks. "Heyyy," she says with a smile. She hooks a leg in between his, doesn't let the touching get awkward.

"Hey," James responds. Very little moves other than his lips.

Quiet, again. Then a giggle. Another one. Since the outburst a few hours ago, the airport's seen very little laughter. Here it allows another bout. The closet fills with their giggles, and within a few moments, they're kissing again. The things we get used to.

"When did it start for you?" Michelle asks.

"When did what start?"

"The wanting. For this. At what point?"

James laughs, absentmindedly starts to massage her upper-shoulder area. His fingers are strong, good at finding little knots and easing them away. "I mean, to be honest, right away."

"Oh, shut up with that."

"What? It's true." There, in his stomach, the joy of knowing he can just be honest right now. He doesn't have to play anything up, be coy, hide the truth. What'd be the point? "I'm not trying to be romantic or anything. I'm not talking love at first sight. Just saying you're cute, you know? You came up to me and started talking. Being funny right off the bat and playing with your nose ring and stuff. I was so freaked out I almost sprinted down that hallway."

"You would not have sprinted away from me."

"You were intimidating! All cute and shit. I'm not good at talking to cute girls," James laughs. "In a different version of all of this, it's years from now, and you're telling this story about your crazy night at the Atlanta airport, and it starts with the story of the weird kid who just ran away from you."

"I don't think you running away from me would have cracked into the story of tonight, no offense."

"Some taken." His hand moves its way up to the hair at the base of her neck. Goose bumps appear on her skin, and James draws some pleasure from feeling them pop up. "What about you? When did you start thinking about yanking me into a closet and making out with me?"

Michelle sighs, props herself up onto her elbow to look at James. Strange just how much her eyes have adjusted to the darkness. She can see the details of his face. She traces a finger over his lips, trying to phrase her answer in a way that won't hurt his feelings. "To be honest, I didn't think about it until I did it."

"Whaaaat? How dare you not find me instantly attractive? I'm leaving," James jokes. He's surprised there is a moment of hurt beneath the joke.

"Don't get me wrong, I'm glad it happened. But . . . you're young," Michelle says, slight shrug. She reaches for his hand to assure him, laces her fingers between his. "We're at an airport. It's not the sexiest place in the world."

"I beg to differ. This closet is gonna be in all my fantasies from now on."

"I did daydream about holding your hand, though," Michelle goes on. "When you led me to the bookstore, away from the mob. You grabbed my hand like this, and it was like it transported me to . . ." She gestures weakly in the dark, reaching for words. "I don't know what to call it. Not a fantasy, per se." A couple of finger snaps. "Merde, comment on dit? It made me want to hold hands with you again too, but it kind of made me realize how great hand-holding can be. I know it gets a pretty good rap, but I've always thought of it as being a little overrated, a little sentimentalized. But when you took my hand, it was like all of that fell away. They have this expression in English, no? I felt like a schoolgirl."

James wants to kiss her, but it feels like she's not done.

"It made me feel like I'd had a crush on you for a long time and was finally getting to hold hands with you. I'm not the most romantic person on the planet, and I'm pretty certain that everything gets better after your teen years, but I will recognize this: hand-holding probably peaks at this age."

Fuck, if only music hadn't stopped playing in this part of the airport. Some lovely piano melody right now, sparse and pretty and light. That's what holding hands with Michelle feels like. "But you didn't want to make out right away, that's what I'm hearing," James says.

Michelle lets go of his hand. "Exactly, glad you're listening."

Their eyes meet. James can't contain a smile. "I gotta be real with you, I'm not too good at this. I'm not experienced or whatever. So, I'm sorry if I say something stupid." So different to say this with her in his arms. Without the benefit of touch, it'd be such a complaint, it would feel like sinking into himself. A few hours ago, he would have run from comments like this.

"It's okay," Michelle says. "I don't know how much experience really matters here. The first time you do this with a person is always pretty weird and wonderful, I think."

"How many times have you done this with a new person?"

Michelle knows what boys are like, their weird obsession with numbers and statistics. She rolls her eyes, and even though it's at his expense, James finds it unbearably cute. "The boys I've been with," she says, "forget gradients of sexuality; we're talking intimacy here, lie-in-the-dark-and-talk-deep-shit intimacy— they've all asked some sort of question related to numbers. How many others? How many times did you do this? Boys want to quantify experience, rank it within a spectrum. Delineate the spectrum. I don't understand the urge at all. There's value in comparing one moment to another, but what's the point in counting how many there've been? What is there to gain?"

James doesn't know what to say, and so he gives a little chuckle, trying to hide the shame he feels swirling around in his stomach.

"Three," Michelle says.

James is quiet. He waits to see what the number means to him. Michelle holds her breath, trying to read his eyes in the dark. This feels like a movie moment, and she wishes there could be some movie lighting attached to it. Mostly darkness, yeah. But just some soft glow so that all their features were visible. That fake blue tinge meant to indicate nighttime. Or just a picturesque orange spotlight, something that cast flattering shadows all around them. The latter option would be really easy, since all they would have to do is reach up and flick the switch by the door. But neither of them has thought to try, comfortable in the dark.

"That's kind of weird," James says.

Michelle's heart sinks right away. Shit, please don't let him be what this comment suggests, judgmental in such a superficial way. Beyond the closet door, everyone's fears still lurk. Human-size tarantulas. Cancer incarnate. Public speaking, turbulent flights, the thought of being entirely alone. Who knows why these fears don't slip beneath the crack in the closet.

"Like, in every other facet of life, an experience stands on its own, regardless of who was there. You try sushi for the first time in your life once; you don't get to add an asterisk because the person you ate sushi with was a new person. Why is sex or making out or whatever any different? Why do we value a variety of partners in this one facet of life?"

Michelle breathes a little easier. Her arm is starting to get tired, so she lies back down next to James, her head leaning onto his shoulder. "I appreciate that thought, but it kind of points to your inexperience. No offense."

"None taken. How?"

"Because of the intimacy involved. The act no longer matters, not really. What matters is the person. You don't get comfortable in the act, or the mechanics of the act. You get comfortable with the person. When the person switches out, it doesn't matter that you know how to unhook my bra while still making out, or that you know what to say in the stillness of the moments after. It matters how comfortable we are with each other. If it's a new person, the experience always feels new."

Thumbs rub against each other. Somewhere beyond the door, someone screams. They both hear it, the first cracks in this private moment. "Human beings are so damn weird," James says. "That's the only way I can ever think about it. It's just so damn weird being alive."

Without any warning or reasonable segue, they're making out again. Hungrier than the other times, more in sync. They celebrate that thought: how weird it is to be alive. They run from it. Escape into the weird thing itself. Hard to tire of this.

SEVENTEEN

THE CLOSET DOOR OPENS, AND OUR HEROES EMERGE.

A glance to the left, a glance to the right. No specific, visible threats. Michelle leads, James follows tenuously behind. Once again it feels like he is on the set of a movie. This is a scene from sci-fi. Characters in jumpsuits avoiding faceless villains in uniform as they sneak around the enemy base. This is a scene from fiction. Nothing to prove that, though. Strange as any of it may seem, there's no reason to believe it's anything but reality. No convenient wake-up from a dream, no deus ex machina. He's gotta carry on in this reality.

"So, any specific order in which we're gonna try to do these things?" James asks. When they finally found the strength to pull away from each other, they knew they had to venture back out, set their minds on some mission to accomplish beyond the closet doors.

"I mean, ideally we fix all of this at once. Hit some other

magic button. A red light, maybe? Find the Death Star weakness to this place. That maybe doesn't involve us blowing up." She scoots along the hallway, back to the wall. They're both on the lookout for something, but they wouldn't be able to say what that something is. "Failing that, we find our parents first. They have to be around somewhere. Then we reunite with Rosa and Taha; it'll be helpful to not just be the two of us. We destroy the green button. We get out."

Back to the C gates. They take the tram, and instead of spitting them out in the lower hallway where the tram belongs, the doors lead to the concourse itself, the long row of C gates ahead of them. James and Michelle share a look and almost find it in themselves to laugh.

The first thing they see is that they are at the very end of the concourse. An airline employee wearing a fluorescent vest stands at a window facing the runway, bashing it with a plastic stanchion. It connects with a dull thwack, causing no damage. His face is blank, sweat trickling down his temple. A thin stream of blood leaks out from between his clenched knuckles, his skin cracked from the efforts to break free.

James and Michelle pass quietly behind him, afraid that he might turn his anger on whatever else catches his attention. There are a few more like him in the first handful of gates, bedraggled individuals, as if they've been stranded for weeks instead of hours. Beards and tattered clothing, the smell of filth and alcohol coming off them. A couple are huddled around a garbage fire, passing a brown paper bag back and forth. James wants to hurry along, worried at what else may be waiting for them in this concourse. But they have to search every corner of this place to find their parents. They understand that there's a possibility their parents have been whisked away to some other plane (no pun intended), but there's no comfort in that thought. Better to assume the best.

James thought it would keep getting worse, but the farther they go into the concourse, the better things seem to be going, as if the window basher and the dudes who look like they've seen better days are just in the bad part of town in an otherwise safe city. That, actually, is the exact point.

You may recall that in this terminal, the residents of the Delta Sky Club separated their factions by social standing, as designated by the dubious and confusing rules of Delta's Sky-Miles program. Naturally, an oligarchy blossomed.

Diamond members kicked everyone out of the lounge, and Platinum members set up in the surrounding gates, especially the center point, where the real estate is rich with restaurants and stores. The Silvers and Golds established a sort of suburb nearby. The vast majority of the terminal's passengers, who are not of any special status within the frequent-flier program, could not argue with the fact that they didn't have as many miles as some of those other passengers. They accepted the societal construct and set up their belongings accordingly. Most of them were used to being lower middle class anyway. They cast the weirdos away to the outskirts of the concourse.

James and Michelle dip into every gate. They duck down to look under seats, behind the check-in counters. They enter every restaurant, most of which are still functional. Any staff who have wandered off replaced by common people looking to fill their time. Jillian Reynolds, a marketing executive from Cincinnati flying back home, has always secretly believed she would make a fantastic line cook. She's the one running the kitchen at a burger joint when James and Michelle sneak in to look for their parents. Seeing them walk into her kitchen, it is the first moment Jillian realizes what she's doing, how much flipping burgers has pulled her away from the horrors of the terminal. If she ever gets out of this, she's quitting her job, surrounding herself with food.

James and Michelle aren't holding hands, which hurts James in a small way that doesn't really make sense to him. He tries not to think about it too much, keeps his eyes peeled for anyone who might be related to him. Ava should be easy to spot. She's been into neon green for a while, and she has all the accessories to show her love. Headphones, a backpack, sneakers. The kind of outfit that matches how loud she is as a human being. Wakes up early every damn day, which James knows since she calls her friends as soon as her hands are on her phone, her voice carrying all over the house. Weekends too, the psycho gets up like she's got a damn job to get to, James thinks. She sits on the couch with a bowl of cereal, her friends on speakerphone while they each watch the same musical on TV. Singing along and shit.

James knows his thirteen-year-old sister about as well as could be expected from a sixteen-year-old boy: not all that well. He knows some of her habits, could rattle off a handful of her personality traits, mostly misremembered from earlier versions of her. He knows what annoys him.

"What are you thinking about?" Michelle asks him. This part of the concourse is busy enough that it almost looks normal. A hippie-looking couple at C41 are holding up a picture book to a circle of toddlers and their parents, reading out loud in singsong voices.

"I wasn't a very good brother."

Michelle sighs. "Putain, don't use the past tense."

"Sorry. I'm not a good brother."

"Yeah, that still sounds awful. I'm sure you're fine. You still have time to be a better one."

They continue walking down the hallway. More and more suits appear, as do the sleek carry-ons common among frequent fliers. James notices the looks they're getting a little more than Michelle does, but he takes her lead and carries on. "Do you have any siblings?"

"Two brothers. They're almost ten years older than me, though, so we're not super close. I don't see them much."

"Hey!" someone calls out to them. "What are you doing here?"

James and Michelle look at each other and each raise an eyebrow, certain that the guy in the blue suit is not talking to them. They keep walking; the man stares at them as they go. "Are your brothers still in school?" James asks.

"One's getting his MBA in Paris. The other's kind of a bum. He travels around. I think he has a job online, or several of them or something. That's not really the kind of stuff we talk about when we do talk."

One of those airport carts drives past them. An airport employee is at the wheel, and a woman in a green blouse and charcoal blazer is in the back, looking down at her phone. She doesn't notice them, but the driver scowls.

"I know this is going to sound redundant, but does something feel a little weird here to you?" Michelle asks.

"Yeah. Can't put my finger on it, though."

They veer off from the hallway, toward the bathrooms. After what happened last time, James is a little worried about splitting off, so he's relieved when Michelle follows him into the men's bathroom. There's a forgotten red duffel bag beneath the row of sinks. The sight of it would be menacing under normal circumstances. But James and Michelle pass it without comment, both certain that there's no bomb waiting in there. Maybe something worse, but definitely not as mundane as an explosive.

There's only one other person inside the bathroom, a balding man in a polo shirt using the urinal, his sunglasses on a bright string around his neck. He furrows his brow at them when they come in, then returns to his business. James and Michelle start knocking on stall doors and then pushing them open, as if after all this time, their families have just been hiding out in the C-gate bathrooms. James almost laughs at the idea, both sets of parents and Ava cramped into one stall, exchanging pleasantries, then turning to their reading materials once conversation has run dry.

"Do you think," James asks, pushing open the stall door in front of him, "that if you add up all siblings that are out there, add up all the individual relationships between brothers and sisters worldwide, that there are more siblings who get along or more who don't?"

Michelle gently kicks open the door to his right. "I'd say it's probably pretty even."

"Really?"

"Yeah, you don't? I feel like there's a balance to the world. Plenty of people get along great with their siblings. If I'm just thinking about my friends, most of them can't stand their siblings. There are a few who are friends with each other. But most aren't."

They move down the row of stalls, both of them momentarily lingering, as if waiting for their eyes to adjust and reveal their families, or maybe just searching for bathroom graffiti. "Why do you think that is?" James asks. "Age differences? Or just seeing them every day of your life and getting sick of them?"

Michelle shrugs, and they head out of the bathroom toward the women's, which Michelle walks into first before waving James in. "I think that a lot of people just flat out don't get along. Not in a hateful way or anything. But we're all so different from each other. That's why friends matter, you know? They're the few people you've encountered in the world whose company you truly enjoy. Human beings are weird. We're mean and selfish, and our brains are a mess half the time. It's a miracle anyone ever gets along."

James laughs. His chest flutters. This happens at the same time that he laughs, and at the same time that he then responds to Michelle. He's aware of this chest fluttering, of the fact that he's applying what Michelle said to the fact that *she* likes him. That this rarity they're talking about is happening right this very moment, between them. "I mean, sure. But the way I see it is that family's the one group of people that you don't really get to make quick decisions about whether or not you like them. At the very least, until one of you is an adult and can choose who you spend your time with, you're stuck. And that means that you've got time to stick around and change your mind from a first impression. My dad and my uncle, his brother, they always talk about how they used to beat each other up when they were little. How my dad never let my uncle hang out with his friends, would do cruel shit to him. And now they spend so much time together it's like they can't even get sick of each other. Like they're immune to each other's faults."

More stalls opening. A woman carrying a hiker's backpack and wearing a bandanna on her forehead walks into the bathroom, freezes when she sees James. There's a tense moment, during which James is trying not to seem menacing as a dude but also wondering exactly why this woman is freezing so obviously, like he's some kind of monster. Michelle has to say they're just looking for someone, and the woman laughs it off and apologizes, then steps into the stall Michelle just checked.

They leave the bathroom, head farther into Platinum territory. To them it just looks like more suits, lots of middle-aged people. A well-off artist here or there who's not a fan of this social stratification but will not shrug off its benefits. Another employee-driven cart rolls past them, two fifty-something white guys in cowboy hats and leather boots sitting in the back. They make some passing comment that James can't quite hear, though he picks up on an unpleasant tone.

Farther into the realm of the rich and well-traveled. At a bar, a bunch of people are arguing over who gets to pay the tab with their corporate account. They decide that whoever can prove they get the most miles will get to. Weird that anyone is paying, thinks James. There's a bit of a DJ-scratch moment when James and Michelle walk into that bar. They look around in silence. The bartender dries off a single glass for way too long, eyeing them the whole time.

"I'm looking for the Herreras," James says to the men at the bar, whose chattering has stopped completely. "They're my parents. They're, um, Latinx. In their forties."

"Or the Bouchers," Michelle adds. "Cute Thai woman about my height, probably knitting. My dad looks kind of WASPy, so you probably would have acknowledged him?"

Blank looks. A few background grumbles, complaints about damn kids. Someone shouts at them to leave. James is more than happy to comply. A couple of them are smoking cigars, bright orange glows from the ends when they take pulls. The smoke is thick and white, rising slowly to the ceiling.

Michelle lingers defiantly. "Cool," she says after a beat. "Thanks for the help."

Back in the hallway, they walk near the windows. The sky is bright with stars. The moon hides behind perfectly fluffy clouds, which gently float across in an unseen breeze. James is just about to wonder whether he'll ever experience weather again when he catches himself, derails the train of thought.

They enter the innermost circle of the C gates, the Delta Sky Club, which the passengers around them have dubbed Diamond Village. No fires here, no tattered clothing. A beefy baggage handler who is clearly being compensated somehow follows James and Michelle the entire way across, like a mall security guard checking for sticky fingers. They go through the entire concourse, looking in every possible corner, opening every door. No family members to be found.

Eventually they pass through another outskirt full of outcasts, and, when they can't find the escalators down to the hallway below, they have to go all the way back to where the tram now apparently operates in this part of the airport. They wait quietly for it to reappear.

Back in the B gates, the green light starts blinking again. Quickly this time, like it's gearing up for something.

EIGHTEEN

\\\\\\\\\\\\\

ROSA'S COUNTDOWN HITS 6:00:00.

The time keeps ticking down, but the numbers make her think of 6:00 a.m. Every day now for three months, she's been thinking about 6:00 a.m. The night of Chucho's frat party. She didn't really want to go, but as soon as she got home, she could sense her mom looking to pick a fight. So she texted Lisa for a ride to get away.

The frat house, thumping music and spilled beer. Guys trying to act casual about walking around shirtless, thinking that the display alone would get them laid. A crescent moon that night, she remembers seeing it in the backyard. Smell of roses in the air, somehow, despite all the spilled beer, the drunkards sneaking to the edge of the fence and pissing in the corner. She was counting down until it was 12:30, antsy to go back home but wanting to wait until her mom was asleep. Then the smell of roses got stronger, and that's when Rosa met her. Micki was looking up at the moon too, a smile to her eyes. Lavender eye shadow on, pulling it off admirably.

At 6:00 the next morning, Rosa woke up on a carpet. Micki was next to her, back pressed to Rosa's stomach. Missed calls on her phone, a sense of panic to get back before consequences worsened. But there was Micki. Breathing softly, one dark tress strewn across her cheek, the very tip tickling at her lip. Rosa half sat up, wondering what she should do. How could she pass this up? That look in her eye had been met with reciprocity, desire. Now here she was. Not a happily-ever-after, but a stepping-stone. A tiny step that allowed her to hope for more.

Then she thought of how pissed her mom would get. Another sit-down lecture. Privileges lost, as if Rosa were still a kid.

5:59:59. Rosa tucks the phone away, staring at the fog alongside Taha. They're on the floor, their backs resting against the checkout stand where James and Michelle were playing cards earlier. She wants the men crouching outside the store to act, goddamn it. Do something. Shut down this anxious anticipation and just bring on the stupid thing they will do. But they remain crouched, shockingly adept at playing their militaristic roles, though they are a financial adviser from Dayton, a middle school principal from Tallahassee, a Brazilian nightclub owner. One man in the crowd used to get his toy guns taken away by his mom, who'd been in the Israeli military and learned to hate the sight of them. Even those brightly colored toy guns that shot out fluffy darts she confiscated on sight. He crouches in the fog, hands held in the shape of a gun. It feels like he's disappointing his mom. They await orders.

After the memory of Micki passes by her, Rosa is left with a lingering tug of desire. She hasn't seen Micki since the party—she was a friend of a friend, in town for just a weekend—and there've been no other chances for desire to properly unfurl. Just those glances with strangers at work, hope that doesn't quite build. Always a surprise what brings it around, though. A memory, Taha's way of speaking. The slight sense of excitement to the evening. As if they're all having a slumber party.

It's different from a normal night, at least. Even now she can hear snoring from down the hall, the quiet of the airport settling into itself. There's something automatically intimate about sleeping in the presence of others. Taha turns a page in the book he's been reading quietly for the past hour. He's hardly made any progress. A slow reader, or maybe his mind is more focused on the events at hand than he would like to let on. Expressive too. Smiles at the pages, squints at them. Rosa's never been that into reading, so she can't remember a book ever drawing these reactions from her. If she could laugh at a book the way she does at a TV show, if she had to hide tears welling in her eyes while she was reading, then maybe she'd do it more often. All she recalls of books are the ones from school, which she hated just because of the association. She never retained any of those stories.

"If you had to guess what was going to happen next," Rosa says, wanting to draw Taha back out, "what would you say?"

"I'd say Gen and Carmen are going to fall in love," he says. When Rosa raises her eyebrows at him, he holds up the book and smiles, then sets it down again, open on his leg. He sighs, a cloud of breath leaving his lungs and joining the fog. Rosa had almost forgotten about the cold. "If you're asking whether you should worry, I would say you should not."

"Not what I asked. What do you think is going to happen?"

Taha rubs his hands together, blows into them. She likes how he doesn't jump to answer right away, the pause before his words. "I am guessing that things will continue to go strangely. I hope for a peaceful, quiet night leading to an order-restoring morning. We can't know the future, though, and I'd expect that we might still have a head-scratching moment or two ahead of us." He smiles at her, one of those smiles that don't reach the eyes. She feels like she's staring and has to look away. "What do *you* think is going to happen?" he asks.

Rosa tries to imitate his thoughtfulness. Whatever comes of this day, at least she's got a new appreciation for pauses. "I dunno. I keep expecting the cavalry to come storming in. And I can't help but think that that's how it ends. Like the last scene in an action movie. All flashing lights and sirens, all of us wrapped up in blankets in the rain or something." She looks at her cell phone again. 5:55:12. She shows him the screen, tells him how it's been counting down all this time. "But I have no idea what it's counting down to."

He frowns at the screen, not bothering to attempt to restart the phone or anything, since Rosa mentions that it hasn't worked so far. "Who's to say? Maybe the cavalry, as you said." He hands the phone back.

"But if that hasn't happened yet, why would it happen in six hours? And what the hell are these fools gonna do before that even has the chance to happen? What if it's not our rescue but something worse?"

Taha turns his palms up to the sky; the skin there is a similar shade to Rosa herself. Quick vision of those palms on her thighs, on her hips. She wipes away something invisible from her pants, trying to keep herself from flushing.

"It is out of our hands," Taha says. A long while goes by before he adds, "Mostly."

Quiet reigns. The kind of quiet that happens in old or unfamiliar houses. Creaks and groans that are louder than they should be. Like the airport's got old floorboards or something, pipes that get funky in cold weather. Rosa feels like she should be able to hear something from the guys outside—chatter, someone moving to scratch their nose, the snow shifting beneath them. Nothing, though.

She uses her hands to lift up off the counter a little, her muscles coming alive with the effort. A pleasant awakening in that slight pain. When she sets herself back down, she's a little bit closer to Taha. Their thighs touch. Funny how much she hates that feeling among strangers on the bus back home, but how context makes the sensation wonderful. Is there anyone who isn't into that first instance of thigh touching with someone they find attractive?

"Tell me something about yourself," Rosa says. "We've been hanging out all this time, and I feel like I don't know anything about you."

"What would you like to know?"

"I don't know. Just talk. Tell me something." She leans her head back and closes her eyes, waits for his voice to take her away from this. He takes his time, downside to the thoughtfulness. She tries to picture being anywhere else but can't even escape in her mind. She's stuck in this ATL Today News, in this concourse, in this airport.

"I hope this does not make me sound self-centered," Taha finally begins. The sound of his voice relaxes Rosa immediately. "It's a thought I've had for years and years now, something that comes up at random, it seems. On dates, while spending time with my family, at an interview, once for a job I didn't get." Taha looks over at Rosa, whose beautiful dark curls are now free from her ponytail. Her eyes are closed, and it feels like she might fall asleep at any moment. He likes the thought of that, for some reason, the intimacy of his voice bringing her to rest. It frees him from the pressure of being entertaining. "This is the thought: I don't know if my life could be framed into a story." Taha keeps his eyes on the doorway leading into their store. "Something about that bothers me."

"Why?" Rosa says.

"I'm not sure. Maybe it's because I've always been a reader. Maybe I have this romantic notion that a life matters more if it can be turned into a story. Something with a beginning, middle, and end. Some sort of unifying theme. God knows I wouldn't want my story to include a moral, but I would like my life to amount to something."

"And you think a story counts?"

A little chuckle from Taha. "Why wouldn't it? Among all the things a life can surmount to, a story is not so bad." He claps his hands together to bring some warmth to them. Throughout this night, he's felt the unfulfilled urge to laugh. It's there somewhere, unwilling to come out. "I first thought about this when I was looking at this man's face. I was at a pub in London with some friends from school. Two separate conversations formed around me, which I couldn't quite find my way into. We were outside, beneath a slight overhang that protected us from the rain. My friends were smoking, and I had just stepped out with them because I don't like sitting at a bar alone. Then I noticed someone else on the patio. A young man, looking out at the Thames, not minding the rain. He was sitting with his profile to me, and in just those few seconds of looking at him, I had this idea that he had a whole story to his life, something unknown to me. I thought about the possibility that I could have a conversation with this man, that he could tell me the details of his life, and maybe something deeper than that, something the beers within him would deem fit to confess. But still, what notion would I get of his life? What notion would he get of mine?" Another look at Rosa. She hasn't moved. He's been boring enough already. But it feels good to talk. It makes it all feel a little more normal.

"I don't know why that thought stuck with me so long. It's just another thought. But for some reason, it really has stuck around. The notion of a life as a story. The need to think about my life in a way that could be retold."

Rosa speaks again, so much softer this time, like she's stepped halfway into sleep. "Tell me your story." It's barely audible. Not even the men in the hallway outside can hear it, though they've been eavesdropping for entertainment.

In the pause before Taha answers, Rosa falls asleep.

NINETEEN

\\\\\\\\\\\\\\\\

A PLEASANT SURPRISE AWAITS JAMES AND MICHELLE on the way to the D gates. The hallway has sprung a plethora of flowers. Tulips, dahlias, lilies, carnations, chrysanthemums, sweet peas, and a dozen other varieties fill up every inch of space, except for the moving walkways on either side of the hall. Vines climb up the walls, creating new frames for the art displayed. James and Michelle are among the first to discover the spectacle.

Two tween girls chase each other through the stalks and stems, trying halfheartedly to avoid stepping on some of the unexpected beauty. A woman, maybe their mother or guardian, kneels at the edge of the garden and cries. They're quiet tears, unaccompanied by any sharp intakes of breath or moans of sorrow. James gets the sense that they're tears of happiness, or relief, maybe.

James and Michelle stand at the edge of the garden, speechless. He extends his hand, brushes Michelle's knuckles, not wanting to press the issue too much. But she immediately grabs hold. A person in an orange tank top steps around them, squats down directly in front of them, and turns their phone sideways to snap a pic. Not happy with the first few attempts, this person, named Tilli, backs up a little and bumps into James, who was too distracted by the sensation of Michelle's hand to notice them approaching.

James and Michelle step around them and wade into the garden, unwittingly providing Tilli with the exact shot they were looking for. Tilli goes to the photo-sharing social media app of their preference, tweaks a few of the settings to their taste. This has been their saving grace during the layover. Some connection to the outside world. Every hour on the hour, they post a picture from the airport, caption it *Another hour at ATL,* share it with the world. Or at least their little portion of it. For reasons even we do not understand (science?), these are the only pictures from within the airport that make it outside the building.

It's clear from the persistent crickets on the internet that no one outside the airport knows what's happening, and Tilli likes the idea that their friends and family and semi-acquaintances from college will only know this version of the story, only their version. Wandering the hallways like so many others, they've found joy in this amateur photography, which is more about the sharing of pictures than the pictures themselves.

"Well, this is pleasant," Michelle says, taking a step forward into the plants. She runs her free hand over the petals at her side. Her fingers come away chalky, and though she sometimes suffers from allergies, she can't help but bring the pollen up to her nose and sniff. "Spring," she says with a smile.

"Yeah, I noticed it's hot again," James says, just as Michelle slips out of her cheesy souvenir sweatshirt to reveal a tank top beneath. James follows her lead and laughs at the fact that he's wearing the same tank top she is.

Michelle smiles and nods, then cranes her neck to kiss him. When she pulls away, he sees the background of flowers, grass in between the stalks now, though it wasn't there a moment ago, he's sure of it. Bees and butterflies too, whipping around. As if they've been at this airport long enough that it's created its own ecosystem. This really is spring, he thinks. Michelle keeps her eye contact with him, and everything threatens to go into slow motion. How will he ever get over this image of her face, framed by the sight of colorful flowers that shouldn't exist?

She turns away from him, takes his hand again. They do their best to tiptoe around the flowers, though more and more people are showing up and don't have the same instincts to preserve. A few people rip out the flowers by the handful, stuffing as many as they can into their carry-on luggage. One guy rolls up the bottom of his shirt and fills up the pocket with as many bulbs and stems as he can manage.

"What the hell are they doing?" James asks.

"Tulip Mania," Michelle says. "In the 1600s, there was a

weird craze in the Netherlands where the price of tulips went out of control. Single bulbs were sold for ten times the price of . . . er, something. I don't remember; my grandmother told me about it a while ago. It was basically currency."

They watch the guy with the rolled-up shirt scurry away, petals flying out in his wake. "I guess that's the stage we're at now, then. Fools thinking flowers are money," James says.

"At least there's a historical precedent, you know?" Michelle says. "People have survived this particular absurdity, so we know we can too."

They continue on at a leisurely pace, swiveling their heads more than necessary, as if to prove to the world that they're really looking for their parents. James plucks a purple daisy from among the swaths of options. It feels like there are more flowers growing with each step they take.

"You know that 'she loves me, she loves me not' game?" James asks, twirling the daisy so that it spins like a propeller. He sees Michelle hesitate to answer and realizes how what he said could be taken. "Let's play a different version of it. Harness the flower's future-telling abilities for something else."

"Like what?"

"Like . . ." James thinks awhile. The tween girls run past them again, squealing. Flowers in their hair, in their hands, green stains on their knees already. He hasn't even thought about how kids must be taking this fiasco. "Like . . . we will get out of this by morning." He plucks a petal from the flower.

Michelle smiles, then reaches over and takes the next petal. "We won't."

"We will get out of this by morning," he says again, getting into the game.

"Or we won't."

One by one they strip the petals from the flower, little trail of purple behind them. They don't see this happen, but as soon as each of those petals hits the ground, another full daisy starts growing from the dirt. Tilli watches and tries to take a video to capture it, but their phone freezes and resets, and by the time it's running again, James and Michelle are farther ahead and out of petals.

"We will," James says. He chuckles and tucks the petal-less flower into his pocket. "That's actually reassuring. Weird, right?"

"Who knows what crazy is anymore. Maybe flowers are really aligned with fate. Maybe they exist outside of our understanding of time." Michelle picks another daisy from nearby, this one turquoise. Right before they exit the hallway garden, they pause at the edge and look back, both thinking that they don't want to go on, both knowing that they should.

"I will see my grandparents again," she says, ripping a petal a little more forcefully than she means to.

James sighs, puts his hand on Michelle's cheek, and holds her to his chest. This, before he realizes what he's doing. Strange gestures becoming familiar, actions taken in seconds when he would have tortured himself over them just a few hours ago. "You never told me about them. You want to?"

Michelle thinks about it for a second. But talking about it will not change the fact that she did not properly say goodbye.

"Play the game," Michelle says softly. "It's just a game."

James kisses the top of Michelle's head. A smell he wants around him all the time. He obliges her, plucks a petal gently, speaks the words quickly so that the universe might dismiss them. "Or you won't."

TWENTY

\\\\\\\\\\\\\\

JAMES AND MICHELLE SEARCH THROUGH THE D GATES, finding nothing but heat. There is condensation on the windows facing the runway, obscuring the planes still out there. Clothing lines the hallway, shed and abandoned by some passenger or the other. At least here the disorder is subdued, people lulled to sleep by the time of night and the ninety-degree temperature. The few who are awake fan themselves languidly, sweat drenching their shirts. No sign, even, that the horde has torn through here. It makes it harder to look for their parents, since they have to crouch down and get a look at the faces of those curled up into themselves.

They move quickly through the terminal, thankful that they're finding nothing imminently life-threatening. Then it's down the escalators, back to the long hallway to the E gates. A shared look when they hear the thump-thump of the music reverberating down the hall. The lack of music for the past few hours—absent from any of the coffee shops or restaurants they've passed, not even emanating from someone's phone with the earphones unplugged—has been one of the eeriest parts of the night, and they can't help but think that this is a good sign. A return to normalcy, maybe.

There's a slight vibration to the walls. It reminds James of riding in Marcus's car, the bass turned up so high he could feel it in his bones. Hell, he could feel it in his arteries. Blood shook by the beats. Summer break, gas miraculously cheap enough that they could spend the free days cruising. Marcus had been delivering pizzas, racking up the dough and being generous with it. They'd drive out to the western burbs, those little, quaint downtowns preserved since the fifties. He and Marcus would roll through the successive Main Streets, unabashed about their desire for attention. Marcus making eye contact with guys he thought were cute, James trying to do the same with girls but turning away real quick. "What're you scared of, man?" Marcus would say. "What is there to look away from?" He'd turn the volume up a little louder, work on his driving pose: one hand on the wheel, one out the window, devil-may-care smile. Older suburbanites would scowl, unable to keep the scorn from their faces. The younger ones seemed to look on in awe of the freedom, the cool. If they saw cop cars, Marcus would turn the volume down; they'd both try to make themselves look as young and innocent as possible.

"Okay, guesses as to what this will be?" James says to Michelle, referring to the thumping sounds.

"American Civil War reenactment?"

"Rap concert."

"Interpretive dance involving bowling balls."

James manages a real laugh at the thought.

As they get closer, the sounds of the concourse get louder, and it becomes clearer that what they are about to face is a massive party. In James, there's the desire to just skip this. He's not himself at parties. He's constantly wanting to be more social, more fun. He wants to be at ease in the large crowds, to know exactly how to party. But he doesn't, and who the fuck parties at an airport anyway? Moreover, he doesn't want to lose Michelle. In the dangers of the airport or the joys of the crowd. He doesn't want to lose any amount of time with her. How long will the airport allow them to remain together, remain safe?

Michelle, on the other hand, feels nothing but joy at the prospect of a party. Oh, to forget about all of this. For more than just a moment. To take James's hand and lose themselves on a dance floor. To sweat and drink and have time unravel unwatched. She's been painfully aware of the time this whole day, how it ticks ahead and changes nothing. At parties time is sloppy and drunk, and it has the ability to disappear, reemerge hungover in the morning.

When they turn the corner and see that it is indeed a party, they pause and smile at each other. Michelle because she's happy, James because she smiled first. Michelle hopes they have booze. Her mind flashes forward a little bit in time, envisioning a hungry, drunken make-out with James. She envisions the uninhibited way they will touch each other. A roomful of people with their minds on something other than flight delays. What a joy. She takes James's hand and leads them into the thick of it.

"We'll look for them in there," she says, both of them knowing this is just an excuse. James considers calling her out on this but then thinks about how futile it's been to search for their parents. Thinks about how futile any action has been this whole damn night, except for sticking with Michelle. Whatever the world has in store for him, he will be able to face it better with her at his side.

There appears to be a DJ booth in the middle of the concourse. Two white guys wearing big headphones in that douchey one-on, one-off DJ style are inside the booth, which was clearly a bar before. One of them looks like he's spinning some turntables, though on closer inspection, he's just pretending to do that while he chooses songs on his phone. This is Chad. He's a little embarrassed that he couldn't find real turntables for this epic party, but he's having too much fun to really care much about pretension. He also has a very low capacity for feeling embarrassment.

Around the DJ booth, it looks like there are about three hundred people. Many of them are dancing, sweating, successfully diving into a more mundane world than the one they've been presented with for the last few hours. To the right, where the duty-free store is, there are a couple of long tables littered with half-empty bottles. Michelle smiles and leads James in that direction.

At the tables, she looks around for something to pour a drink into but finds only a souvenir shot glass. So she grabs a bottle of whiskey and pours herself a shot, which she downs quickly. Her gag reflex kicks in. Never a pleasant feeling, taking shots. But there's the excitement of setting off a chemical reaction. Inside her now, there's a bunch of science-y stuff that she doesn't entirely understand but that will soon make her feel good. What a fucking wonder that is. She pours another shot and offers it to James, but he waves her off. She decides to sip at this one. Nothing different here from when people outside the airport drink: distraction from the world's frightfulness.

The booze does its job quickly. Michelle starts to forget how long she's been at Hartsfield-Jackson Atlanta. The green light stops blinking in her mind, stops prodding her with accusations, fades into a deeper fold in her brain, where she's attempting to tuck away her mamie and papi. Time blurs. The music—some easily identifiable dance-pop hit—seeps its way into her muscles, her bones, her arteries. Her shoulders start to bounce. Whoever said dancing starts in your feet had no idea what they were talking about. It starts in the shoulders, makes its way to the hips.

Michelle eyes the food court, where tables have been cleared to the side to make a dance floor. It's crowded with moving bodies, more women than men. Many older travelers fled the concourse when the music started, but the dance floor still represents a span of ages. From the group of thirteen-year-old girls shyly imitating other dancers to the elderly couple shaking and twisting in defiance of the quick beat. Michelle looks at James, wanting to drag him out to the dance floor. She imagines that he's not crazy about dancing, because most of the boys she knows are resistant. Even in Argentina, tango in their blood, the boys would flock to the walls at parties, only coming to the dance floor if they were trying to hook up with someone. In Quebec, it's as if the boys are physically repulsed by the thought of dancing. They break out into hives at the mere suggestion. Michelle and her friends usually end up dancing on their own, which suits her just fine.

Then she notices James's shoulders have a shimmy to them too. She raises an eyebrow at him. "What?" he says.

"Nothing," Michelle answers, unable to contain a smile. She wants to grab his arm, drag him out to the floor, feel his body against hers. Not yet, though. James is snapping his fingers, mouthing the words to the silly pop song.

This is how she'll always remember him. She knows that without a doubt. This image of him dancing in the dimmed lights of the E gates while music blares. For years, when her mind comes back to this night, it won't be the myriad absurd images she's seen so far. At least not initially. It'll be this American boy with the kissing skills and the soft voice, glimmer of joy and fear in his eyes. She wishes she could see him in a normal situation, on a day when there wasn't much to fear. She's never been to Chicago; maybe a visit is in order, after all of this.

Another sip of booze, her mood buoys a little further. She forgets about the vision of her grandparents in hospice care, forgets about the blame she's assigned herself for the day's events. The guilt slips mercifully away, replaced by a kind of glee that something like today is possible. She's at a party at a goddamn airport. She's witnessed gardens blooming from linoleum and snow falling from the ceiling. She has found someone she can talk with all day, someone to make out with in a janitorial closet. She's living every fantasy about an airport encounter she's ever had.

She bumps James with her shoulder. "I'm glad I met you," she says.

His smile lights her up. He looks like he wants to kiss her, but she decides now's the time for dancing. She finishes her whiskey and sets the shot glass down, then hooks her arm in his. "Let's dance."

They pass ads that line the walls, the models and actors in the photographs frozen in bright lighting, selling products that might not exist in the morning. To James's left is the interfaith chapel, near the escalators that lead to the tram. It's hidden behind a pillar, next to a recycling bin. He imagines that there must be people in there, praying to their hearts' content. Whatever you can find comfort in, James thinks. He'd rather be bound to worldly things, to people, to the joys of a dance floor.

The song changes right as they step onto it. Some people step away to the water fountains near the bathroom, or they make their way to the duty-free bar. The new tune is less pop than the ones before. It's more soulful, trumpets carrying the beat.

It starts in James's and Michelle's shoulders, moves its way down to their hips. Then their feet and finally their hands and heads. Amazing that this can exist among all the rest. Fear and confusion and worry, and still somewhere in the heart of it, the capacity for joy.

In this sweltering concourse of the Hartsfield-Jackson Atlanta International Airport, on an otherwise un-noteworthy January day, our two heroes dance their asses off.

TWENTY-ONE

\\\\\\\\\\\\\\\\\\\\\\

IT DOESN'T TAKE LONG FOR SEX TO ENTER MICHELLE'S and James's minds. The dance floor and the prospect of the world ending; how could sex possibly stay away? Their age is a factor, sure, the hormones that come with teenagedom. Pheromones too, the chemistry of attraction, whatever goes on in the body when lust awakens (we won't claim to know precisely what this chemistry entails).

Something else, though. Something James and Michelle sense, just like we do. Something that leads people to poetry and sentimentality. You know what that something is. We don't need to delve into it. Especially because of what happens next.

Easier, sometimes, to turn our heads away from joys when darkness encroaches.

\\\\\\\\

The Atlanta airport commits its most damaging act of random cruelty. When all of this is said and done, this will be the moment on which the story is always centered. In scientific studies, in news reports, in the film adaptation of one of the many books written about the evening, this will be the crux of it all. The books will get almost every part of the night wrong, except for this. If it doesn't happen, hard to know if the world would care about the rest of the events of tonight. A slew of delays at the airport, the world would tell these passengers. So what? Everyone always conflates the miseries of their travel days. Nothing interesting about exaggerated complaints and a few electrical outages.

But the world pays attention when damage is done. Maybe that's what the airport is trying to say (if we're making the inane assumption that there's a lesson in any of this, and that it was consciously unleashed by a building).

Let's take a look around the airport before it comes. James and Michelle, of course. Here at the party, pressed close together. They're dancing salsa, at least the closest version of it they can manage. James's left hand is on Michelle's lower back, his right clasped to hers. He's looking at beads of sweat dripping down her neck, smelling the sweetness of booze on her, mixed in with whatever soap or lotion is washing away. Sandalwood. Her chest is pressed against his, their whole bodies pressed together, and it makes him wonder if she can feel him start to harden.

In the interfaith chapel, a congregation gathers on their knees, whispering their prayers in a dozen languages.

The hallway garden, which will remain long after this is over, baffling scientists and delighting travelers. The woman James and Michelle saw earlier still cries, thankful for the nature that's been allowed into this godforsaken place. One of the trams headed in the direction of the D gates has turned into a contained sleepover: a traveling water polo team from Colombia has claimed a car. The coaches yell at everyone to stay quiet and get some rest.

In the F gates, the microcosm of the world keeps getting more and more accurate. After what comes next, they will mourn according to their national and cultural customs. The Irish will sing at the wakes; the Mexicans will set up ofrendas and papel picado; the Israelis will sit shiva.

In the T gates, Roger Sterlinger stifles his giggles as he army crawls through the fog. None of the men crouching and waiting to attack see him. Not that they would necessarily care. Beverly Bingham, her eyes focused on Ulf Pshyk's confounding igloo, thinks about her husband, Larry. She could have married a better man, she thinks. A smarter man, a richer man. She should have. A waste, she thinks, not knowing that she'll return to him and remain married to him for another twenty-five years, until her death catches up with her.

Joseph Flint rubs his sore finger. He's sitting on the floor at T12, covered in the fog. He keeps looking within himself to find the anger that's always there. But something has rubbed the emotion away. Now he just wants to hide, wants to cry, wants a chance to start over. What a wasted life, lugging around anger like it could protect him from anything, like it could come coupled with joy, a little carry-on suitcase rolled beside, never far behind.

Inside the igloo, Ulf beams confidence at the 114 people huddled inside. They fashioned a door for themselves so that no one can come in uninvited. Light still gets in through the ice, bathing them all in shades of blue. Every single one of them feels calm in here. They are all shocked at the warmth building up inside. They look down at their hands and marvel at the fact that they helped build it.

In the ATL Today News, Taha reads beside Rosa, who's lightly snoring. She drifted off, he's not sure at which point in the story of his life. That's just as well. It's not quite a good story yet. He told it chronologically, which is not how all stories should be told. Taha's life has been framed by his desire to create a better world. He should have started the story not with his birth in Sri Lanka, but rather with his first complete memory: his mother taking the shoes off her feet and giving them to an elderly woman shuffling down the streets barefoot.

The brown thrasher perched on the fence surrounding the airport ruffles its feathers again. Its little legs are getting tired from going so long without moving, but it's entranced by what it sees and doesn't want to leave. Beyond its fence, beyond the airport, traffic on the 285 slows, only for a little while, only for the usual reasons.

Then it happens.

A wind sweeps across the airport, a tiny stream of severely bad luck or fate or whatever you want to call it. A curse. An improbable coincidence. The shadowy monsters James saw before. Whatever it is, it stops a hundred hearts from taking another beat. In every concourse of the airport, people fall to their knees. Their eyes roll back in their heads, and they drop the book they were reading, stop chewing the chip they just popped into their mouths. Their sudden thuds and clatters alert the people around them that something's wrong, again. A lot of them—sleeping on the carpeted floor, dozing on a loved one's shoulder, curled around the armrests on a row of seats—merely stop breathing, quietly passing from this life without a bang or a whimper.

Among the dead:

Daisy Hayoon Muk, a sixteen-year-old girl from Seoul traveling to Minneapolis for a semester abroad. She is the youngest claimed by the airport, a shy and awkward girl still becoming comfortable with herself, whose biggest joy was to lie in a patch of sun-warmed grass and sleep. She had not had a full life, even if it was devoid of huge sorrows or tragedies. A quiet life that could have made an impact in the world is unceremoniously snuffed out. Her death will have its impacts too, sending her father into a tailspin of reclusiveness, from which he'll emerge in a few years with a novel. It'll be moderately well received.

Ned Carson, seventy-nine, from Harlem, New York, is the oldest person killed. He was on his way to New Orleans for the first time since he was a kid. Just as well that he didn't make it, as the place had warped in his memory. It had become something grander than real life could match, and if he had made it back to Bourbon Street, he would have been disappointed by the drunken tourists—which are a different breed than they used to be—the sheen of artifice and spectacle that's surrounded his favorite place on earth. If the airport hadn't chosen to kill him off, Ned would have lived another six years, carrying the heartbreak of the trip with him.

Six people die in Ulf's igloo, seven more in the fog of the T gates. A molecular physicist who was months away from a breakthrough in his teleportation device closes his eyes for good, and the technology disappears into the folds of history, never making it into humanity's hands. Joseph Flint passes away holding his aching finger, still searching for anger within himself.

Auzelle Stalford dies in her sleep, right in the middle of a dream where she's sleeping with her ex-boyfriend. A strange kind of rescue. Thirty-four people realize that they are dying as it happens. They experience an intense wave of fear and nausea, a panic so horrifying that they feel like the panic itself is what will kill them. They feel no pain, though, and right before the moment comes, there is relief. One woman, fifty-three-year-old Mara Spokes from Salt Lake City, has this as a final thought: The most profound moment of a person's life is their acceptance of death. Then she flits away. Her husband, Ray, sees the life drain out of her. Before his grief sets in, he imagines what the rest of his life will be like. There is a measure of excitement in the fantasy, and he is just as horrified as we are to find it there. A new life, new people. Like Taha, Ray believes in the ability of human beings to adapt, and there is a measure of curiosity about what exactly he will have to adapt to, what that life will look like. He underestimates how deeply the grief will cut.

And since the name just came up, why delay the information any longer. Taha, formerly known to us as the Peacemaker, dies with a book in his hands. It falls, narrowly missing Rosa's head as it lands between them. The noise wakes her. She stirs slowly, looking up at Taha's face, surprised to still feel desire building. Then she notices the half-open state of his eyes, the downturned corners of his mouth, and she knows he will never again beam that smile of his onto the world. A goddamn shame.

Suddenly Rosa feels more alone than she ever has before. She wants to push away the knowledge of what has happened, tries to shake him awake. Even as her body goes through these motions—nudging his side, grabbing him by both shoulders, beating her hand against his chest when a heartbeat refuses to show up—her mind is adjusting to the knowledge that she now has to deal with this alone. This motherfucking countdown on her cell phone has been driving her insane, as if she needed a push in that direction after all of what she's seen. But she's managed to keep her shit together because of Taha and his voice and his smile and his presence, all of which she no longer has. She rests her head against his chest and begins to sob, her tears soaking into his shirt.

Fifteen fast-food workers, eight active military members, three pilots. A baggage handler named Hector—who stuck around on the runway long after the rest of his coworkers looked at the parked planes and decided it was time to leave the premises—drops down onto the tarmac. His eyes remain open, an expression of shock frozen into his features, as if he can't believe that this is his reward for playing by the rules his whole life. He loved knowing what was and wasn't allowed, hated more than anything being in a situation that involved a moral quandary, no clear-cut line that showed where to stand if you wanted to be right. On this strange day, Hector stayed at work to wait for when people would need him. A trickle of blood flows from his chin to the ground, a stain on the runway that won't ever be washed away.

The E gates are hit hard. AeroMexico flight 5080 loses 10 percent of its passengers and crew, most of whom are participating in Chad and Brad's party. On the dance floor alone, nearly a dozen people die. The bodies drop around James and Michelle at almost the same time. Both of our heroes' eyes happen to be closed, their senses still so enmeshed with each other that they don't yet notice what's happening. They think it was just a well-coordinated stomp on the ground on the part of their fellow dancers. The music keeps playing for another minute.

James feels he has found the best smell in the world. Michelle's neck, right where it meets her shoulder. He's planted several kisses there while they dance, at first exploratory, then hungry. By now he's certain that she can feel his erection anytime their hips meet. Her hand dips beneath the waistband of his jeans. Bullshit fantasy, not long ago, to think he'd get laid anytime soon, especially at this airport. Now he's not so sure it's bullshit. He's ashamed of the language of this thought, but excited by it nonetheless.

Then the screams and cries start to break through James and Michelle's bubble of focus. No, no, no, thinks Michelle. Not again. Not now. James tries to ignore it as long as he can. Just a little longer, he thinks. Let me stay here for just a little while longer.

TWENTY-TWO

NOW, TO BORROW A PHRASE THAT BOTH JAMES AND Michelle might use, shit gets real.

The airport loses its collective mind. For good, some would say. The countdown on Rosa's cell phone hits the three-hour mark, and people are refusing to stay inside the confines of the airport any longer. They join that one outcast airline employee and start to bash the windows that face the outside—the only ones that have remained intact—with anything they can think of. The horde that has been moving through the airport breaks out of their weird little spell. They look at each other and then head for the nearest exit at full speed, no recollection of what they've been doing for the last few hours. In the T gates, Beverly Bingham gives the order to move in on the igloo, but the men in the fog who are still alive don't react right away, kneeling over those who have fallen beside them. "Now, goddamn it!" Beverly screams, eyeing Joseph Flint's still body and allowing herself a little smile. There's no leaving this place, she realizes, and now there's one fewer person who will try to take power from her.

James and Michelle stand in the middle of what used to be the dance floor. They're still pressed tightly against each other, but sex is no longer in the air. Soft crying all around them, manic crying too. People holding on to limp dance partners, whispering their names, begging them to respond. The music finally, mercifully cuts out when Chad realizes Brad is not just passed out from the booze. Chad does that thing you see often in movies, where someone lifts a dead person's head into their lap, hugs them close. This is not how the party was supposed to go.

Why? Everyone in the airport is asking themselves that. Why is this happening to us? Have we not endured enough senselessness tonight? Did it have to come to this? We're sorry to say, but yes. It had to come to this. Hell, we all know that everything comes to this, sooner or later. James is right in that regard, at least. Why would the airport be any different? Since when does senselessness have a limit? It is a flower girl at a wedding, remember, a little here, a little there. Sometimes it lands in one place all at once.

Clutching each other's arms, James and Michelle look around, taking in the horror of what is happening. Then they look at each other, and the recognition of the horror on the other person's face makes it really sink in. This is happening. It has come to this. They unconsciously begin to back away from the dance floor, as if that will do anything. James's heel hits something soft and limp. He's too scared to look down.

Shit, shit, shit. Mom and Pops. Ava. This whole time he's been thinking that maybe this is a day that will change everything for him. That his life will be split into before this and after this. Maybe he was more right than he thought.

Merde, mierda, ô. Maman and Papa. Her brothers elsewhere in the world without a clue as to what is happening. Michelle almost never thinks about health or safety. At least not her own. She sure as shit is thinking about it now. She tries to check if anything within her feels wrong, if she's been affected by whatever this is too. Food poisoning, a gas in the air, another virus.

More mayhem explodes around them. A fistfight near the DJ booth. The bottles of booze start to smash down around them. Only the TSA's lighter policy prevents Molotov cocktails from flying around. One man is using two forks to try to cause a spark, but the forks are plastic and that's clearly never going to work. Chad, unsure of how else to process something of this magnitude, sets down his buddy's corpse and resumes his looting from earlier in the night. It certainly fits in with a lot of what's happening around him. Destruction, his only remaining friend.

In the other instances of sudden mayhem, James and Michelle chose to run. But the destruction is spreading all around them, and there's no clear direction that will take them away from this. Who knows if it'll even make a difference? They both think of the janitorial closet again, and Michelle wishes deeply that she hadn't ever pulled them away from it. Her list of tasks was so intensely misguided. They should have stayed in the safety of that darkness until starvation or thirst or normalcy forced them out.

James isn't quite on board this same train of thought. Michelle's list of tasks is the only thing keeping him from breaking down. Find their parents, reunite with Rosa and Taha, destroy the green light. Steps that they can take that might lead to something else. He has made it this far and survived. The fear will be there whether or not he acts. So he decides to act.

His hand finds its way to hers so easily now. "Come on," he says quietly. "Let's go." She turns to look at him, those lips that would make him fail a semester, the nose ring she can't stop fiddling with. His senses aren't screaming out *Girl!* anymore. The wonder of her proximity to him is still there, just hidden beneath so much now. He wants her to be safe.

Michelle gulps for air. She pulls the breath in deep and long, trying to get the oxygen inside her to calm her nerves. The breath comes out shakily, and she's not sure it helped at all. She can't stop looking around at the floor, at all those still bodies. As if they're all just in some TV show and half of them have been paused. She keeps thinking of how deeply all those lives go, all the thoughts that have been put on hold, all the threads of humanity that have been snipped. She is an idiot for wasting her goodbye with her grandparents.

She thinks of one of her favorite songs: "This Bitter Earth" by Dinah Washington. That opening swell of strings, the pause for Dinah to sing out the opening lines to silence. Michelle wants to lie in a bed with James at some point in the future and play this song and tell him about how she was afraid she'd never hear it again. She allows James to lead her away.

A loud hiss erupts nearby. Someone has found a fire extinguisher and is spraying continuously as they walk through the terminal. The fistfights have started to merge, an almost cartoonlike cloud of punches and kicks and curses. James spots a relatively calm area nearby and leads Michelle away from the dance floor. They skip over fallen bodies, evade groups of men shoving each other, duck every time they hear glass smashing. They reach a wall and press themselves as flat against it as they can. Someone comes running past them with what looks like another javelin. James watches the man scream his way to the nearest window and attempt to throw the javelin straight through. When it reaches the glass, it stops and clangs to the floor harmlessly. The man falls to his knees and lets out a blood-curdling scream.

"You might be right," James says. "About the light. When we pressed it again, it got worse."

"There's no plan we can come up with, James. None of this makes sense. There is no logic."

"There is; we just don't know what it is. Maybe pressing it was the wrong thing to do. We should destroy it. Just rip it off the wall."

Michelle thinks of her grandparents, how pretending it wasn't a goodbye didn't make the goodbye any less real. If the green light did this, if she did this by pressing it, bashing it to hell sounds exactly like what she wants to do. A plan, even if it's a stupid one, is at least a distraction to keep them busy.

"Okay," she says, squeezing his hand, thankful for its warmth.

James and Michelle slowly make their way away from the madness. They pass by the interfaith chapel, where the prayers have quickly transitioned into the funereal. Several inside pray for rapture, or they accept that it has arrived.

James and Michelle descend toward the tram. James wants to get them to the T terminal as quickly as possible. He's just going to assume for the moment that his family and Michelle's parents stumbled their way to the snow and are now waiting for them beside Taha and Rosa. Once they're all together, then they'll destroy that green light and escape this nightmare.

Somehow, the tram arrives. The Colombian water polo team is not on this one, but one of their jackets has been left behind. James picks it up from the floor as they step in, and he wraps it over Michelle's shoulders. She almost shrugs it off, but James says, "We're gonna go back to the snow. You left your sweatshirt at the party."

Michelle will keep this jacket for years. She'll never wear it again, but it'll remain in her various closets over the years, always buried in the back yet always making the transition into a new resting place. Every now and then—while moving, maybe, or just when she's feeling particularly wistful—Michelle will see its bright yellow cloth and be drawn to it. She'll take a sleeve between her index finger and thumb and give it a gentle rub, as if drawing memories from the fabric.

The tram kicks into motion. Blind luck that there's no one dead in here. Michelle and James stand there, panting, hands clasped tighter than comfort would allow, as if they could care about comfort right now. The robotic overhead voice announces their stops. Shockingly, no one joins them. It seems everyone is grieving or destroying or fleeing on foot. At every stop, actually, James sees the same family sprinting past the tram, keeping pace with it. A man in a tan suit and a red tie holding a young girl to his chest as he runs, a woman holding hands with a ten-year-old boy. They look like they're just running late for a flight.

Michelle rests her head on James's shoulder, even if the bumpy ride makes it less than ideal. "This is for sure the weirdest date I've ever been on."

James barks out a laugh. "This is a date?"

"Dinner, good conversation, closet make-out. That feels like a date to me."

He brings their interlocked fingers up to his mouth, kisses the back of her hand. The tram rumbles on to the T gates. It's hard to tell in this little box of glass and metal how much of the world has unraveled. There's a screen that shows restaurants and attractions at the upcoming gate. The chicken wing sports bar they passed by at some point, a sushi spot, a place that offers private beds and rooms within the terminal by the hour. "That means this was my first date ever, then. So I'm not sure if this is really that weird. I have nothing to measure it against."

"Eh, most of them don't go quite this well," Michelle says.

"Guess it's all downhill from here, then."

The train rumbles to a halt. The automated overhead announcement says, "Concourse T. Domestic baggage claim and access to ground transportation, short-term and long-term parking." The family of four sprints past the opening tram doors, racing up the escalators. Even from here, James can hear a commotion at the T gates above. James and Michelle disembark, hands held, one tiny step in front of the other.

The escalators, at least, aren't crowded. They stand, listening to the whir of the mechanical stairs that move them back up to the snow. James reaches for his backpack to get his sweatshirt but realizes he left the pack behind in the E gates. His headphones are maybe his favorite material possession. Normally he can hardly fathom the idea of walking somewhere without having them on, piping in music or an audiobook. A few times a week, he thinks he's lost them, or they get disconnected and he fears that they've stopped working. So he's surprised now by his relative calm in the realization that they've been left behind. Ah, the hierarchy of worries.

At the top of the escalators, the first thing James sees is a window. The forsaken planes out on the tarmac, their windows dark now, those emergency exits popped open and the yellow slides already starting to deflate. James wonders when the people got out, if they made it to safety. He hopes they did.

The runway lights are still on. Eerie to see the lack of movement out there, none of the usual vehicular activity, no orange vests waving people through. It won't be long now until the sun comes within view again. The beautiful soft bruising of the horizon will start right beyond the tree line surrounding the runway. Sunbeams will poke through the leaves, casting the passengers in a bright orange glow. Not yet, though.

At the TSA checkpoint, a manic crowd beats on the invisible barrier keeping them from the outside world. Beyond the barrier, an empty security checkpoint, stairs leading to baggage claim. Beverly Bingham is not a fan of this development, but she'd rather focus her efforts on the damn igloo. She isn't even concerned about the brown fellow anymore. The igloo implicates the Russian [sic] beyond the shadow of a doubt. She's sure no one in his little group was felled by whatever it was that killed dozens out here. Traitors, all of them.

Her bevy of goons beat on the walls of the structure with their fists, with books, anything they can. A few of the stronger ones heave abandoned suitcases at the igloo. They barely inflict any damage. A few flakes of snow stick to their hands, and one block of makeshift ice cracks. But they can't seem to make their way inside.

More and more people are finding their way into this

terminal. James and Michelle clear out from the top of the escalator and wordlessly head toward the ATL Today News. James is thinking that Rosa probably knows some secret way out of here. She's got to. They have to push their way past a few people to clear the crowd. Neither one of them comments on the fog, not remembering if it was there before they left. Roger Sterlinger does a barrel roll on the ground in front of them, giggling to himself as he does it. They only hear the giggle, pausing midstep to try to figure out where it came from. A shared look of confusion. Roger giggles again. He can sense the end of this light-heartedness coming. As the crowd grows, a part of him stirs with the memory of what having this many people near him usually feels like.

Entering the ATL Today News, James gets that same feeling. That this is all so close to ending. That he has made it this far, and that whatever else is to come, he will survive that too. Then he sees Rosa sitting on the floor. She's got her knees up, hugging them to her chest. Her eyes are red and swollen, and her jaw is set so rigidly that James thinks maybe the airport got to it. None of them say anything for what feels like a long time. Rosa barely even seems to notice them. Finally Michelle's voice croaks out, "Where is Taha?"

TWENTY-THREE

\\\\\\\\\\\\\\\\\\\\\\\\\\\\\\\\\\\

JAMES STEPS CAUTIOUSLY BEHIND THE COUNTER TO where Rosa dragged Taha's body. None of the other corpses have gotten to him so far. On the dance floor, slumped over seats, in the hallway. Amazing how easy it is for the mind to shut itself off from processing what it's not ready to.

But the sight of Taha hits him full force. He staggers backward into Michelle, wanting to turn away but unable to. She holds him, and he feels like running with her back to the closet but remains frozen in place. He would have thought he'd cry in this situation. A panic attack, maybe. But all that hits him is sadness, deep, not showy. The final sinking in that it's not a lie. That this really is what happens to us. "I've never seen a dead person before," James says, so softly we shouldn't be able to hear him.

Michelle has, once, on a freeway in Bangkok, mangled legs poking out from beneath a makeshift blanket, dancing police lights on the asphalt. She doesn't say that, though.

Taha's eyes are still half-open, James notices. Movies always show people closing dead people's eyes for them. Rosa must have forgotten. Or maybe that's not a thing that happens in real life.

It really can come to this, he realizes. All this time, a part of him has felt that everything happening has been just for him: that the airport has been symbolically acting out how James feels about growing old. The fears and absurdities therein. But no. It's real, and consequential.

"Come on," Michelle says, a hand on his shoulder. She has to physically spin him away from the body, and she leads them back toward Rosa. James takes one last look at Taha, surprised that his fear isn't increasing. Rather, he's starting to question what this fear is good for. Absurd or not, there are events in the world that James will simply have to live through. The joy's nestled in among it.

Beyond the store, the sounds of mayhem. People beating on the invisible barrier, which makes a sound as if they were hitting solid steel. Beverly yelling at her cronies to keep it up. Shouts and cries. Michelle thinks about the sound Taha's head made when it hit the ground after he got punched. She's afraid for the violence that'll come, and she's right to be.

The obvious absence of guns in the terminal probably saves dozens of lives, but that doesn't mean people are spared. When the barrier to the outside world refuses to budge, to crack, to open, to release them from this nightmare, people finally take their frustrations out on each other.

All around the airport, people are feeling an urge to punch anyone, and too few of them resist.

"Jesus," Michelle says. "It sounds like hell is breaking loose out there."

"It sounds like rain," Rosa says quietly.

They fall quiet, listening. James doesn't hear rain, just fists. When he's had enough of that, he kneels next to Rosa. "Do you know about a green light? Or a button, maybe. In the B gates, by the bookstore?"

Rosa squints in thought, then shakes her head.

"We think it started all of this. We want to go destroy it." The words are absurd. James knows that. Michelle probably does too. But they live in an absurd world, and this is hardly the most ridiculous thing that could be said today. "Come with us."

"I think my phone's doing it," Rosa says. Her phone's in her hand, and she turns it to show James the screen. "It's been count-ing down since this all started. I don't think we can do anything to stop it. The airport's gonna kill us all."

2:27:24. Rosa tries to swipe the countdown away one last time, to no avail. She wishes she could send Micki a message. She's imagining everyone around the airport is sending last goodbyes to loved ones, and she thinks it's a shame that she can't do the same. (What she imagines is not quite true. Very few people are willing to accept that this will end in their death. Some death, sure. But not their own.) She's not sure what she would say. She doesn't even know if Micki's given her another thought since that night, if the message might be met with dismissal, whatever it said. Micki might laugh off the sentimentality. Still, worth it to reach out before getting erased. *You made my life better, even if only for one night.*

James kneels down next to her. "That's not gonna happen. We're gonna be okay." He's saying the words to reassure her but finds that he believes them. He's tired of fear reigning supreme within him.

Rosa blinks away from her thoughts. "Okay," she says. She relaxes a little, looking at this kid's eyes. She notices the way Michelle is looking at him, and she feels herself smiling. "You two hooked up."

Michelle blushes, and both of them break out into similar grins.

"At least that's something," Rosa says. Then she sighs and unclenches entirely. "Fuck this cold." She stands up slowly, joints stiff and aching. If death is coming, might as well move around a little before. Try something, not go gently. "You lead the way," she says.

They poke their heads out the doorway. James and Michelle look for their parents' faces among the fog and the violence. Rosa tries to empty her mind of thoughts. She buries her phone deep in her pocket. The snow in the hallway has turned into brown-and-gray slush. People in the growing crowd at the invisible barrier are slipping and sliding around, a few of them falling on their backs and looking about to make sure no one noticed it happening. At the front of the crowd, three sisters in their seventies kneel at the invisible barrier and pray for it to come down.

"I think we can go out safely this way," Michelle says, stepping into the hallway. James and Rosa follow and immediately trip over something large that's on the ground. On his way down, James is sure that it's a body, and he hopes he doesn't land on top of it.

It's all snow and tile, though. A bruise starts forming on Rosa's hip. A giggle sounds out, and Roger Sterlinger rises from the fog. "Sorry, friends!" He immediately holds out a hand to help Rosa and James up. "I've been rolling around all day; it was a matter of time." He shrugs and offers a smile. Without the fog, James would notice Roger's pant leg tucked into his sock and remember the conversation he and Michelle had about adulthood done right. But that doesn't happen, and instead the four of them stand awkwardly for a moment, James and Rosa brushing themselves off.

"So," Roger says, breaking the ice, "what's everyone been up to? Staying safe, I hope."

James, Michelle, and Rosa exchange raised eyebrows. Michelle half smiles. James thinks they should probably get away from this guy. Then Rosa says, "We're gonna try to destroy a light that's causing all of this before it kills everyone. I think."

She says this with the same weight of someone announcing they're going down to the store to pick up some milk.

"Great!" Roger says with a punctuating clap. "I'm in."

"Um," James says. "That's it? You've got no follow-up questions? You're just down for this?"

"Sounds like a mission for good." Roger shrugs.

James finds himself smiling, at least for a moment, before the image of Taha's empty eyes comes back to him. He reaches out and puts his hand on Michelle's back, to comfort her in case she's got the same image in mind. Though the truth is, he's just comforting himself.

"I just want to say, none of you have to come," Michelle says. "It's just a notion I have, and who knows if it'll accomplish anything. So if you want to lie low somewhere instead of traipsing through this hell, that's probably the more reasonable thing to do."

Just then a cold wind blows through the hallway. Snow that's built up on various surfaces around the concourse—on top of freestanding posters and on the many monitors still flashing DELAYED—flurries around, sticking to their exposed faces.

"Reasonable shmeasonable," Roger says.

"I'm not staying here," Rosa adds. "I'm cold."

Michelle turns to look at James. "You sure you want to keep following me around?"

"That depends. We gonna pass by any broom closets?"

She smacks him playfully across the chest and then they make their way down the hall.

Our four heroes stand in front of the tram doors, waiting for the automated announcement that will tell them the train is approaching. It's a scene right out of a nightmare, or at least a calm beat in a horror movie. Dead bodies are strewn about within view of the group. They all try to ignore the sight, but our particular camera angle clues us in. We can even zoom out a little and see the bodies on the staircase, see them dotting the entire stretch of the hallway, forever felled by something we don't understand. Arms pinned beneath their torsos, legs akimbo, eyes half-open but blind to the world around them. Loved ones weeping at their sides, or draping over them, or staring emptily in their own ways.

Roger tries to whistle a tune while they wait, but the sound fails to emanate from his lips. The tram, too, does not make an appearance, despite the fact that only twenty minutes have gone by since James and Michelle took it last. James wishes there were a button he could press, like with elevators, just for the comfort of knowing he's doing everything within his power to summon the machine.

After a couple of minutes, Michelle sighs, her breath a puff of white in the cold air. She shoves her hands into the pockets of her Colombian water polo jacket. "I guess we're walking."

"My step counter is going to be off the charts today," Roger says cheerfully.

They all sigh in unison, then turn down the hallway, James and Michelle leading the way. They reach for each other's hands at the same time, despite the cold.

"That's adorable," Rosa says quietly.

Roger nods and smiles. "You have to admire life's ability to provide joy amidst heartache. I'm so often blind to that. Of course, that's because of a chemical imbalance in my brain, or whatever deep-seated childhood trauma causes my social anxiety." The words out loud make him realize that, if normalcy ever does return, his specific version of what is normal might too. And just that realization makes him almost lose this newfound calm and joy. He pushes the fear down, since he still can.

"I guess," Rosa says, kicking away some dirty snow from her shoe. She only agrees because she thinks Taha would too. Fuck, Taha. Lying dead in a ATL Today News at the Atlanta fucking airport. What a way to go.

Meanwhile, James is doing some fairly hard-core staring at Michelle.

"Dude, you are doing some fairly hard-core staring right now," Michelle confirms.

"People look at each other. It's a thing we do."

This gets a smirk out of Michelle. "Touché."

"I'm sorry. You're pretty. I'd rather look at you than anywhere else. Is that okay?"

"Sure," Michelle says. She likes the thought of him looking at her, his attachment to her growing deeper. Actually being under his gaze, though, is a little nerve-racking. She doesn't know how couples stare into each other's eyes all the time. She's not sure she believes anyone really enjoys that.

They hit the A gates, which are eerily quiet. James doesn't want to think about why that might be. "Do you think we'll ever see each other again?" he asks.

Michelle takes a moment to respond. Her grip on his fingers tightens. "Don't start thinking about that." She starts walking a little faster, as if wanting to run away from this conversation. James doesn't notice, though.

"What do you mean?"

"There's no good answer to that question," Michelle explains. "We don't make it out of here, or we do, to our respective homes. Our respective lives."

"So? Life is long. The world is small now. We've got these things in our pockets that can get us closer to almost anyone on the planet. Travel is relatively affordable. You saying we can't figure out a way to see each other again?"

Michelle sighs, unravels her fingers from his. She doesn't mean it as a symbolic gesture, but James has no way of knowing that. His heart sinks a little. "I'm not saying we're, like, a thing now. I'm not saying we should be in a long-distance relationship." He adds a little chuckle here, as if that thought is completely ridiculous and had not occurred to him at all. He looks over his shoulder at Rosa and Roger, who are walking close enough to hear the conversation but far enough away that it's believable when they pretend they can't.

"I'm just saying that it's not unreasonable to think we might see each other again. All we have to do is exchange names, numbers, email addresses. Something. A summer road trip to halfway between Chicago and Quebec, wherever that is. We end up going to the same college somehow. Or I get a job and save up money and buy a ticket to come see you. Maybe not immediately, maybe not even at the first chance that I get. But at some point, when everything feels right."

Now James is falling into the line of thinking Michelle didn't want to encourage. She's still trying to resist, but there's no doubt that she feels joy at the rant, and she stays quiet, wanting it to continue. She cannot find it within her to deny someone's idyllic plan, not again.

"Or maybe not even then. Maybe I like every picture you post on social media for a few months, then I meet a girl back in Chicago, and I start to give it a rest, feeling unfaithful to this new girl. We lose touch for a few years, only thinking about each other every now and then, when we're at airports, or making out with someone in a closet." Michelle rolls her eyes at this, but James spots the smile she tries to suppress. "Then one day we're full-on adults. We still don't know what the fuck we're doing, but we've gotten pretty good at pretending. We've each had successful romances that have since ended, and we've told the story of tonight more times than we care to remember.

We've managed to move beyond all the trauma it's caused us, but we still hang on to the lesson it taught us about magic in the world. How it can come to us in the weirdest moments, when we're least expecting it. Shit, we're both having the same exact thought one day. We're living in . . ." He strains his mind for a random place in the world, somewhere that seems likely and romantic and a little ridiculous. They pass by a flight monitor, all those yellow DELAYED labels that seemed so ominous at the start of this narration and have now faded from importance. James scans the list of city names, somehow settles on Fort Lauderdale, even though it seems not to meet any of his criteria. "We're living in Fort Lauderdale, and we run into each other at the beach. We've both been in town for a while, so we're there with friends, but we take a walk along the shore together and catch up. We fall into a conversation like we've had today, and we think about all the fucking laps we took around this place. Something comes back. The ease with which we've been able to shoot the shit and delve into real talk. The overwhelming desire to jump each other's bones."

Michelle laughs, and she pulls her hand from her pocket and returns it into James's grip. Again, she doesn't mean this as a gesture of any sort, but James thinks she does. "The only problem here is that I would never live in fucking Fort Lauderdale. I'm not even sure it has a beach," Michelle says.

"Of course it does," James says. "Florida's one big beach. Even if it's not on the coast—which I'm kind of embarrassed to admit I don't know, since I was just in Florida—we'll walk to the beach in order to have our brilliant, romance-rekindling talk."

They enter the hallway from the A gates to the B gates, the group's combined gait slowing at the sight of jungle foliage coming down the escalators.

"Well, that's lovely," Roger says.

"Shit doesn't even make sense," Rosa counters. "We're on the cold side of this goddamn place. The jungle should be where it's hot." Complaining about the logic of the airport's decisions feels useless, exhausting, and absolutely necessary for her sanity.

A canopy of trees stretches out overhead. Vines cover the myriad tree trunks as well as the walls and the floors. There's the sound of insects and wildlife, but unlike before, when it was clearly a recording, this time there's a thickness to the noise that feels real. A loud roar erupts from somewhere within the trees, like a stadium full of people cheering. James prepares for the horde to come tearing through again, but Michelle knows what the noise is. "Howler monkeys," she says. Everyone else looks at her like she just suggested the noise was coming from soup. "Crazy, right?"

She leads James and the others into the jungle, swatting away the wall of insects that greets them at the edge. On the ground there's dirt and fallen leaves, roots that look like they've been growing for decades. They'll fade soon enough, disappear back into the senselessness that spawned them. Few outside the airport will believe any of this happened, but the layers of dead mosquitoes will litter the floors of this particular hallway for a few days.

The howler monkeys roar again, the sound echoing off the walls. "Those are *monkeys*?" Roger asks. "Like, a thousand of them, right?"

"Probably just a couple," Michelle says.

"Nature is so fascinating." He starts walking with his hands behind his back, still trying to whistle. "They don't attack or anything, do they?"

"Not that I know of," Michelle answers. "But I'm not really an expert."

"You don't think there're snakes and shit in here, do you?" James says, now checking before he puts a foot down. All the roots and vines on the ground look like snakes now, his mind playing tricks on him.

They all start to pick up the pace, rushing through the trees as quickly as they can. The buzz of insects gets so loud they can barely hear anything else. Not their footsteps or each other's breathing, not the swish of Michelle's Colombian jacket.

Michelle and James strut forward, fingers interlocked. Little electrical reactions spark where their skin touches. Well, maybe not electrical. Again, we're not all that versed in science. But something's happening there.

The group is nearing the end of the hallway, almost at the B gates, where the jungle disappears and gives way to typical airport decor. Michelle gets her first look at the artificial lighting beyond the trees. She sees tram doors, escalators, a group of flight attendants huddled on the floor with their suitcases and crumpled uniforms, eating sandwiches with only a slight look of horror on their faces. Somewhere in there, hope. Michelle can spot it from here. The undying human hope that things will be okay, even in the face of too much evidence to the contrary. Just a little longer, she thinks. Keep moving forward. Persevere. It'll all be okay so soon.

TWENTY-FOUR

\\

THIS IS WHEN THE SHAKING BEGINS.

If you've never been in an earthquake, it's less washing-machine-hard-at-work and more like something you feel in your gut. Okay, maybe it's both. It's your whole world swaying, rumbling, threatening to topple over.

Which, incidentally, is what several things in the airport do. The flight attendants' suitcases clatter to the ground. A couple of overhead signs directing passengers to the bathrooms and other concourses come crashing down, the bangs startling everyone in the vicinity. Our heroes all simultaneously decide that it's a good idea to run away from the direction the noise came from.

James and Michelle keep looking over their shoulders, wondering what caused the noise. Rosa and Roger are right behind them, panting. They haven't yet noticed the shaking. All around the airport, others do. They instinctively clutch at their chests, their throats, their heads. They wonder how it's going to happen to them, or if they'll survive again. Deep down, they don't want to believe doom is coming, but that's gotta be what the shaking means.

The igloo at T8 releases a light shower of snow on its temporary inhabitants. Ulf furrows his brow. He made this refuge as strong as he knew how to, but he couldn't have foreseen this. He wishes he could expand himself into a second layer of protection for the people in here with him. If the igloo crumbles, he wants to take the full force of the impact on his own back.

At the E gates, the few bottles of booze left on the shelves of the duty-free store come crashing down. Forgotten half cups of liquor fall off the edges of counters, spilling onto the tile, streams weaving among the bodies on the dance floor.

At the bookstore that consistently miscategorizes its books, relative calm. The books hang on to their places on the shelves. The signs that categorize the books do get rattled loose, but not much harm is caused. Food, somehow still in plentiful supply, continues to emanate from the kitchen, crowding the minuscule tables.

Our four heroes make it to the escalator leading up to the B gates. They pause before getting on in order to catch their breath. Now they all start to feel the airport's quaking. They exchange meaningful looks, but no one wants to really acknowledge what's happening.

"We're almost there," Michelle says, steadying herself on the escalator's rubber handrail.

"Yeah," James responds, a hand on her back. His stomach feels hollowed out by this shaking. He feels it's a miracle that he can even stand still. "Almost."

They start heading up the stairs, holding themselves steady. Rosa and Roger barely understand what they're headed to, but they're both happy to have some sort of mission to keep their minds off things. The countdown on Rosa's phone continues to tick away, unseen by anyone affected by it. 1:20:48.

Initially, the nearest seismographs record a sustained 5.0 on the Richter scale for the first two minutes of the shaking, despite their distance from Hartsfield-Jackson Atlanta, where there are no fault lines. Then it quickly intensifies, in perfect synchronization with the steps our heroes take toward the B gates. Halfway up the escalator, the seismographs measure a 6.3. Moments later, a 6.7. Jonah Friedrichs at a science center in Gainesville, Georgia, looks at the monitor displaying the event and comically taps at the screen to correct what he believes has to be a mistake. It immediately shoots up to 7.3, which would be the second most intense seismographic event ever in the eastern half of the United States, if it counted. Experts will disagree on whether it should. Jonah looks down at the cup of tea cooling next to his computer, searching for the ripples that will confirm the quake. But the surface of the tea is calm, as are the overhead lights. 8.2. "Well, ain't this some shit," he says.

The Atlanta airport is certainly not built to resist earthquakes of this magnitude, and the very foundation of the building should be cracking (literally, if it hasn't already been pushed to its figurative limits by the day's events). By the time James and Michelle reach the top of the escalators, the earthquake has reached a 10.3. The airport feels like it's attached to a particularly violent roller coaster. A few more people die, crushed under signs and fallen TVs. Two more are felled by heart attacks. But the building holds its ground, even if certain concepts of physics do not, so the damage is contained to a few particularly unfortunate passengers. Mercy from the airport, perhaps?

James and Michelle stand for a moment at the top of the escalator, knees slightly bent. They look out at the concourse. By now they know it so well. A pizza place on their right, along with one of those places that sell prepackaged salads and sandwiches labeled as "fresh." Across the hallway, the bookstore and the franchise restaurant with the happy employees. Right between them: the green light. James can see it blinking, exactly how it was when all of this started.

He had just been walking past it, killing time. The song he was listening to was Bobby Womack's "The Bravest Man in the Universe." It's funny how strongly a certain song can be linked to one specific memory, even though he's been digging this album for months now and has probably heard the song a hundred times, easy. He tries to remember another instance when he listened to it, but the only thing he can recall is the moment right before he met Michelle.

Then the shaking escalates, knocking people to the ground, making everyone reach out to steady themselves, but even the walls are swaying. Cracks appear in the floor, and it's hard for James to stay focused on anything but the flimsiness of his footing. God, what a feeling, to realize the world is not as solid as you always thought it was. He reaches out to Michelle, brings her close to him. He barely knows Rosa and Roger but turns over his shoulder to make sure they're okay too. They're both crouching like they're expecting the ceiling to cave. Rosa's eyes are full of fear and Roger looks like he's merely bearing witness to it all. A gift, that. Treating everything a step removed, like you're nothing but a scribe.

James steps forward toward the hallway. Time to make all of this stop. As soon as his sole hits the floor, though, a crack appears in the tile. Whether this is a logical consequence of the intense shaking or another absurdity on behalf of the airport is hard to tell. The crack spreads rapidly, turning quickly from a mere crack into a gaping chasm. The entire hallway, from B1 to B36, splits in two. Instead of wiring and plumbing, steel rods that help keep the foundation in place, there is only darkness. An extended black hole in the middle of the airport.

The shaking continues, and even though he's a few steps away, James finds himself backing up for safety. The group is marooned on one side of the chasm. The green light continues blinking on the other side.

Shrieks fill the air. A handful of the most unfortunate people, who are in the wrong place at the wrong time (well, extreme versions of wrong-place-wrong-time, we suppose, since everyone in the airport can be said to exist in that category), slip into the chasm, disappearing into it without a trace. There's a TGI Fridays To-Go kiosk that falls directly into the crack, and it, too, gets sucked into the void in its entirety. Somehow, everyone in the B gates finds themselves on the same side of the chasm. Even those who were in the bookstore/café were shaken loose from their seats and sent sprawling across the hall before the crack appeared. Several plates of food did not make the journey safely.

James's arm shoots out to hold Michelle back from falling into nothingness. Rosa just kind of nods her head and shrugs. They stand back from the chasm, looking left and right to see if it extends the entire way. They hold themselves steady against the wall, which somehow remains standing for the next two minutes, until the shaking stops.

Like everything that has happened already, once the shaking is over, it's hard to believe it ever happened. A growing murmur in the airport, whispered prayers, the increasingly uncertain assurances of parents telling their kids everything will be okay.

Once she catches her breath, Michelle leans down to untie her shoelaces. She takes both shoes off, then starts moving toward the chasm. James wants to reach out to her shoulder and hold her back, but she advances quickly, and then she lets loose with a soul-emptying scream that causes James to retreat. As she screams, she chucks one of her shoes across the expanse, clearly aiming for the green light. "Why won't you stop fucking with us? I'm sorry, okay?! I'm sorry I pressed you! I'm sorry I'm a terrible granddaughter." The shoe lands well short of the green light, rolling on its side a few times before coming to a full stop ten feet from the wall. Michelle shouts a few more curses in French and then tosses the other shoe, which hits the green light dead-on but nevertheless falls harmlessly to the floor. The chasm remains. She waits for someone to come pick up the shoe and maybe toss it back, but that side of the hallway seems to be completely devoid of people.

She breathes in and out. In the shaky way air leaves her body, James can hear everything he's feeling too. Michelle looks left, then looks right. She's trying to get a sense of some logical step forward, some way to advance with their stupid, simple plan, even if nothing will come of it. There's the far-off sound of wailing somewhere in the terminal, the pounding of her heart reverberating in her ears. Her lips still feel recently kissed; her hair is still tousled from James's fingers. She can't believe that earlier today—or yesterday, or whatever day it is in this other version of life—she was saying goodbye to her grandparents.

It was twenty-two hours ago, give or take. Her grandparents insisted on coming with them to the airport, even though the week's events had visibly drained their energies. The living funeral itself had happened the night before, and Michelle had spent it drinking, wandering the house from room to room, avoiding her family, soaking up the memories of her grandparents and her summers in Bordeaux instead of actually spending time with them. In the morning, everyone emerged hungover from wine and the weight of the looming farewell.

They were silent in line to check their bags, Mamie and Papi too, their lighthearted chatter exhausted after all. Every now and then Michelle's mom would blow her nose in a hand-kerchief. Michelle tried to keep her mind off things by people-watching, and when that failed, she watched the rain come down on the glass ceiling in the terminal. She wanted to put her earphones in too, shut herself away from sensing anything about the morning.

They arrived at the security line, and the long hugs began. She watched her dad hold on to both his parents at the same time, watched his back rise and fall beneath their wrinkled hands. His demeanor was calm, but she didn't want to overhear a single word of what they said to each other in that embrace. The smell of garlic on her grandfather's skin was wafting over, impossible to escape. When the time came for her to embrace them, Michelle longed to be in the air already, surrounded by the whir of the jet engines, sweet sensory deprivation. Instead, Papi's gruff voice, unbroken by tears. "L'adieu n'est pas ce qui importe." Mamie's hand on the back of her neck, warm to the touch.

Is there a stranger feeling than recalling where you were ear-lier in the day and feeling completely removed from that scene? Probably, Michelle thinks. She wipes at her eyes with the back of her hand.

James moves forward to put a hand on her back. "We'll find another way to cross," he says.

She nods but can't bring herself to say anything, her thoughts still back in Bordeaux.

"You okay?" James asks.

Michelle keeps her eyes on the other side of the chasm, looking up and down for something else to focus on. "It's hard to know how to say goodbye, you know?"

James knows she's talking about her grandparents, even if he still doesn't really know what happened. And he can guess at her feelings, put himself in her shoes. But that doesn't mean he knows what to say, how to tell her that she'll still get a chance. He's not sure if he believes that she will. So instead he keeps his hand on her back and steps closer to her, tries to provide comfort with his presence alone.

Michelle, still looking for some way across the chasm, sees a restaurant up ahead decorated with lots of wood. She imagines they can build themselves a little bridge across. Somehow.

Just as she's about to step in that direction, though, a blinding light shines throughout the airport. No one is surprised anymore. They shield their eyes, duck their heads, wait for it to pass. When it does, the 352 people who previously blinked out of existence at the airport now reappear.

TWENTY-FIVE

\\\\\\\\\\\\\\\\\\\

BEFORE YOU GO THINKING THAT THIS IS SOME DEUS ex machina coming into play, rest assured that the reappearance of the missing people, among them James's and Michelle's parents, is the only thing the airport decides to un-fuck. Cartoon-like tornadoes of fighting still rage through the airport, more snow falls in the T gates, a handful of other people die in the unspoken battles of the A gates. Fear courses unchecked through the passengers' bloodstreams. Those who don't hide away succumb to their biases. They blame the people they know the least about: Muslims, Black people, Latinx people, Jews. Physical and verbal assaults only increase after the reappearance of loved ones, because people left behind want someone to blame. In the F gates, what began as a fun re-creation of the world now takes a sadly realistic turn, and borders harden. Visa applications among certain countries get denied. Hope, unquantifiable and inexhaustible though it may be, weakens.

For James, though, a glimmer of it. As he, Michelle, Rosa, and Roger walk through the concourse, trying to find a point to get across, James sees his family splayed out on their chairs as if nothing has happened. He immediately sprints to them before they can disappear again.

Ava is napping on the floor, head resting on a pile of sweatshirts. Mom's still flipping through that same magazine; Pops is working on his crossword and a cup of coffee. He's got earbuds in, stolen from Ava. When they see James coming, they don't freak out or rise to their feet to welcome him into their arms. His dad rolls his eyes and gives a little hand shrug, as if all that can come to mind right now is, Can you believe we're still delayed? Mom's got a little scowl going, like she's pissed he's been gone all this time.

Turns out, that's exactly what they're thinking. When James comes crashing into them, throwing his arms around their necks, breathing in their smells, Pops chuckles and says, "This layover making you go crazy or something? You haven't hugged your dad like that since you were ten, son."

Mom says, "C'mon, don't fall for this. Don't you see he's just trying to apologize because he's kept us worrying? Where've you been, James? I know we're probably not taking off anytime soon, but you gotta keep us posted on what's going on. We can't have you running around, not knowing where the hell to find you if something happens."

James stays nestled between them, eyes closed to everything

else but their presence. He stays quiet, hugging them hard, to the point where his parents both shift uncomfortably and share puzzled looks. Then they notice the three people who have followed James and are standing awkwardly nearby. "Who's this?"

Not quite ready to step away, James hugs his parents even tighter. He's always been close to his family and held the unexamined belief that family is important. But this reunion will shape how he views them for the rest of his life. In a few years, when he earns his first paycheck while working a part-time job during college, he will not spend it on a flight to visit Michelle, but rather on gas money to go back home and surprise his parents.

Finally he pulls away, wiping a tear from the corner of his eye. "Are you guys okay?"

Another quizzical look passes between his parents. His dad sits up a little straighter. "You get a concussion or something? What's going on?"

James shakes his head. "Never mind." He kneels down and gives his sister a little rub on the shoulder. She groans a sleepy complaint, waving his hand away. James laughs, then looks back at Michelle and the others. He introduces everyone, though he has to pause and ask for Roger's name.

His parents say hi with handshakes and smiles, though it's clear to everyone how confused they are by the situation. James can tell that they have no idea what's been going on at the airport in their absence. He wonders if they even know they've been gone for hours. If they remember the rain, which has stopped, though several puddles still shimmer in the overhead lights. As they finish their hellos, they start looking around at the scenes of mayhem left behind, at the body someone has dragged into the corner of the gate.

James motions to the big-ass chasm that separates the two sides of the terminal. "We gotta . . . ," he starts, but trails off, not knowing how to fill them in on everything.

"What, they decided to start construction in the middle of the night?" Pops asks, scratching his head. "How'd we miss that?"

"Don't be a fool," James's mom says. She makes eye contact with her son. She feels the gaps of understanding in her mind, knows something is askew, even if she can't quite put her finger on it. It's like she's in a dream. Jaquelyn Herrera often has lucid dreams, that incredible ability of the mind to recognize its own subconscious and yet remain in it. In these dreams, Jaquelyn has discovered that she prefers not to take the reins. She likes letting the other parts of her mind determine where the dream will go. And though something tells her this is still reality, Jaquelyn feels the same desire to relinquish control. "You need us to do something, baby?"

Stay safe, he thinks. Which makes him feel old as fuck. He shrugs and looks back at Michelle. "What do you think?"

James looks so relieved. Michelle wants to be happy for him, wants to assume that his family's reappearance means hers is safe as well. But that thought is just a reminder of their absence, and seeing James's family only adds to her weariness. In another life she'd be trying to make a good impression. In another life she'd be thrilled at adding another little bit of knowledge about James to the stack that's been assembling all day. A little pillow of James factoids, anecdotes, and details on which she can rest her head and sleep. This is what it feels like to know another person, Michelle thinks.

But this is some other life, in which the more she knows about James, the less okay any of it feels. Destroying the green light will accomplish nothing. The TSA agent is probably right. Time will expire, and they will be snuffed out of existence. She has seen her grandparents for the last time, and her parents too. She puts on a smile for James's benefit, decides to crack a joke, for her own sake more than anything else. "Depends. Do you know how to build a bridge?"

The Herreras (except for Ava, who is right now dreaming that she is flying a kite on a beach in Florida and that the wind is carrying her away into the sky) all smile.

\\\\\\\

James does most of the talking. He explains to his parents the things that can be understood, every now and then looking to Michelle to make sure he hasn't left anything out. He senses something off with her and tries to offer little touches of reassurance, but he can't tell if these are helping at all or if they're just further annoying her.

His parents have their misgivings about the green light's responsibility for the events at the airport, but his mom stifles his dad's loudest doubts and says that both of them will help. They accept the mission at hand, and Jaquelyn Herrera decides she will build the bridge that will get them across the chasm.

To do this, they first have to collect some information. As a mechanical engineer, Jaquelyn is first and foremost a scientist. And as a scientist, she knows that the best chance at success in building a bridge here is to understand all the factors at play. Usually a twelve-foot gap in an airport hallway would be relatively easy to fix: just twelve solid feet of some sturdy material secured end to end that can allow people to cross.

But from what James has explained, there are plenty of unknown factors. The possibility of earthquakes and random acts of violence need to be accounted for. The laws of physics are not a given. First and foremost, they have to investigate the chasm itself. Without fancy equipment around, Jaquelyn determines that the best way to do this is to basically throw shit at it and see what happens. This is the essence of science.

First up: objects. This is the fun stage. Roger volunteers gleefully, tossing bag after bag of potato chips commandeered from nearby stores while Jaquelyn takes notes on her husband's tablet. James, Michelle, and Rosa stand at different points along the chasm, shouting out their observations. James watches a bag of Lay's sail harmlessly into the void, disappearing into darkness almost as soon as it enters. "It's not like a bottomless well," he calls out to his mom. "It's sudden. The bag didn't fade from sight; it blinked out."

Many others bearing witness join in on the fun, eager to work out their frustrations by throwing whatever is nearby: empty water bottles, napkin dispensers from a nearby fast-food restaurant, their own luggage with the fucked-up wheel that's been driving them nuts for years.

Rosa and Michelle have to be prodded by Jaquelyn to offer anything. Michelle stretches her toes on the ground, kind of wanting to feel her bare feet on the tile. Then she realizes nothing is holding her back, and she peels her socks off with her feet and kicks them into the void in front of her.

"Observations, Michelle?" Jaquelyn calls out.

"I don't know. They fell kind of slower than you'd expect, I guess," Michelle says, not enough energy in her to really project her voice down to James's mom. "I really don't know."

They throw progressively larger items in. A plastic foldout chair that was knocked over in the middle of the hallway, who knows where it came from originally. An abandoned duffel bag, emptied of its contents in case its owner came back for it. The rack where all the bags of potato chips were resting.

Eventually a crowd starts to gather. At first it's just people looking for a distraction. When life tosses so much at you, you start looking for little things that will simply take your mind off the sources of your anxiety. Can't blame them, really, for flocking to a distraction. It builds to honest curiosity when Jaquelyn announces that the next stage of the scientific process is to lob words at the chasm.

"Mom, I don't mean to be rude, but what the hell did you just say?" James asks.

"If you don't mean to be rude, you'd better stop opening your mouth when you're thinking rude," Jaquelyn says calmly. Michelle cracks a smile, then tries to suppress it. She looks beyond James's mom at the floor-to-ceiling windows of the airport. They are smeared with fingerprints, with greasy spots where someone rested a forehead to try to get some sleep. There are a few streaks where people tried to smash the glass in order to escape.

"You heard me," Jaquelyn says. "Speak to it."

"What makes you think that it's listening?" Rosa asks.

"Butthole!" Roger shouts, following up with a mad cackle. He hopes he can remember this feeling. Better yet, he hopes his body remembers what it's like to feel okay, and he hangs on to the memory like a flotation device.

Everyone laughs and wrinkles their foreheads in confusion, but they all lean toward the chasm and wait for a response. They train their eyes upon the darkness, which moments ago felt like it could suck the life out of them. It made them too self-aware, made them remember things about themselves they try to keep buried. It felt exactly like looking at nothingness. But now they train their sights with a scientist's eye—curious, rapt with attention, fine-tuned to detail.

"I'm simply not convinced that it isn't listening," Jaquelyn says, and she makes a note in her tablet next to the word "butthole."

Nothing happens. Then Rosa speaks up. "Fear," she says, barely a whimper, but an audible one. Michelle hears the quiver in the word, and she wants to come up to the girl and hug her. She doesn't, but since other people are starting to fill the gaps in between the observational posts Jaquelyn has set up, Michelle feels it's okay to move a little closer to Rosa. On her phone, the countdown has just hit an hour. A few dozen people look into the darkness in the hallway, and they wait. They don't really believe anything will happen. Not on the surface anyway. But murmurs about the mission have begun to spread through the assembled crowd, and they want to bear witness.

They wait with bated breath to see what will happen. No one really questions the act of lobbing words at this enigmatic threat; they just wonder about the result. If the chasm will react at all, and how. Will it laugh off their attempts to understand and conquer it? Will it rage at their insolence? Or rage at random, with no clear purpose to its mayhem, the damage it inflicts inflicted with thoughtlessness? Will it listen, absorb their words, feel for them? What is it down there that they're facing, and does it mean them harm? If so, can it be talked out of it?

"Fear," James mimics, a similar quiver to his voice. He moves toward Rosa too, driven by the same urge to hug her, stopped by the same reservations. He's thinking of so much when the word passes his lips. Of never seeing Michelle again. He's afraid of having the option exist and life leading him in a different direction, one where they never get another try. He's afraid of them never having the option, that this is where his story ends. Where so many stories end. He's afraid that he won't know how to be grown up, how to be on his own in the world, having to maneuver through obstacles and catch all that life throws at him with just his two hands and his weary heart. He's afraid that if he wants or needs help when he's older, he'll have to seek out someone to help him, and that he might be bad at reaching out. He's afraid of fires, of violence, of the sound a head makes when it hits the floor. He's afraid of senselessness and of the lack of magic. He's afraid of order, absurdity, small people who want to have their way and are fine hurting those who don't succumb.

But if there's anything the airport has taught him, it's that he can survive this fear. He can find joys while the fear presses in around him. Joys that will help him push back.

The word doesn't echo in the chasm, or in the now-mostly-quiet walls of the B concourse. It does seem to spread from mouth to mouth, everyone speaking it in their own way, a thousand different inflections carrying the word, shaping it with their own individual nuances, and we simply don't have the time to capture all its usages. The word floats across the Hartsfield-Jackson Atlanta International Airport, lingering between people, getting stomped down by others. It sinks into the chasm, as if getting swallowed up by the building itself. Outside, the night sky starts to lighten. Barely, as if by accident, like it's been caught doing something embarrassing and can't control the blush of color that floods its horizon.

TWENTY-SIX

WHO KNOWS WHY THE PEOPLE AT THE B GATES KEEP going. They start shouting their specific fears into the chasm. It's not just James, Michelle, Rosa, and Roger, but everyone gathered at the terminal. Single words at first, like "death" and "disease" and "loneliness." A seven-year-old named Max Saltzman creeps up to the edge of the chasm, and he whispers, "Mr. Fluffs-a-Lot," so that his sister, Clarice, whose hand he's holding, won't know he's afraid of their cat.

Then they start telling it stories.

Clarice, fifteen, tells the chasm how scared she is that the world might not be good. "There's a lot that I'd be okay with. Not finding love or whatever. My parents getting divorced." She looks down at Max to make sure he didn't hear that. She gets the urge to ruffle his mop of dark curls but resists. "I'd be okay with living a much worse life than what I have. Just as long as I could keep believing that the world is more good than bad.

That people are that way too." Clarice fiddles with the strap of the lanyard the airport employees gave her and Max marking them as unaccompanied minors. She's been in touch with her parents via text this whole time but hasn't had the heart to tell them exactly what she's seen (though she doesn't know that the airport would not have allowed her to describe any of it to the outside world anyway). Her parents still believe that she and Max are safely in a hotel right now, waiting out the delays until morning.

Two blind women stand among the crowd, holding on to each other lightly. Seema Laghari, the taller of the two, moves her hand back and forth in order to jiggle the gold bracelet on her wrist. The turquoise charms clink together in that pleasant way she's familiar with, a noise she can unreasonably hear at all times. Seema is not particularly afraid at the moment, so instead she tells the chasm the story of the bracelet. She found it on a beach in Goa when she was nineteen and still had her sight. It was almost entirely hidden in the sand, but a glint of the sun alerted Seema to its presence. At the moment she reached for it, a boy running after a football barreled into her. They were both there with their families, and they snuck away to meet each other in the middle of the night on the rooftop of Seema's hotel. The bracelet jingled in the wind, and every time she moved to nervously comb her hair back behind her ear. When Raja moved his hand to her hip and asked to kiss her, the bracelet jingled again, those turquoise charms reflecting

the moonlight. A soundtrack that she didn't know would follow her the rest of her life. A miracle that she's managed to keep
it with her all these years. Every now and then, during sex,
she'll still picture Raja's face instead of her husband's, which
she's only ever felt.

Six feet away from Seema, Rosa wipes her nose with the
sleeve of her work shirt, the back of which is stained muck
brown with Taha's blood. She wishes she could have had one
more night with her friends. Just one more night, knowing
it would be the last one, so she could have gotten her fill of
the small joys to be found there. She wishes her phone were
still working so that she could tell her stepdad, Steve, that
she appreciates the rides to work every day. More than that,
she wants to thank him for trying to make her mom be cool
with this whole non-college path to her life. It turns out
Mom was pretty wise about the airport job being a bad
idea. Instead of all of that, though, Rosa tells the chasm about
Micki.

Slowly the chasm does start to react. It's hard to pin down
exactly how. Some people think that it's expanding. How could
it not, absorbing so much of all these people's lives? You can't
take in all that life and not grow from it. Other people think that
the darkness is waning. A bottom is visible, they insist. Their
fears taking a toll on it, perhaps. They shine their phones into
the darkness, not noticing that for the first time in hours, their
batteries are starting to drain.

Jaquelyn tries to keep up with the observations. Part of her scientific mind is confused by all of this, thinking that all that matters is measuring the gap and constructing a passageway to the other side. She tells her husband to get Ava, who woke up as the commotion in the B gates grew, and to look for materials that could be constructed for that purpose, assigning a few others to accompany them and help carry as much back as they can. Wood, sheets of metal and plastic, tile pulled from the floor itself. Anything, really. The other part of Jaquelyn's scientific mind knows that this storytelling matters too, just in a way that she can't quantify.

Within fifteen minutes, every single one of the passengers at the B gates is gathered by the chasm, speaking into it. Unlike everywhere else in the airport, here there is absolutely no violence. No one is begging to escape or trying to find someone in uniform to complain to. James and Michelle's mission is the sole focus, somehow uniting the wide hodgepodge of travelers.

Taking advantage of the assembled crowd, James moves closer to Michelle. If this is almost over, he wants to spend as much of the remaining time as he can by her side. "You think we should say something?" James says.

Michelle turns to him and smirks, remembering their initial interaction. Then she rests her head on his shoulder, slips her hand into his. No way does anyone ever tire of hand-holding. "I'm gonna miss you," she says softly. God, he loves her accent, how indefinable it is. The soft imprint her mouth leaves on words.

"You are? But we just met." He squeezes her hand so she knows he's teasing, draws her a little closer. He looks over at his mom to see if she's noticed, but if she has she doesn't show it. She's sketching something on the tablet with her fingernail, showing the sketch to a nerdy-looking South Asian dude in a checkered shirt.

"So? I'm allowed to miss whoever the hell I want to miss. You've worked your way into my . . ." She gestures with her hands, reaching for the word. Then she fiddles with her nose ring, keeping her head firmly set on his shoulder. ". . . heart? I don't know. That sounds cheesy. Whichever part of the brain is responsible for missing someone. You worked your way into that." She glances up at him and offers a smile. It's a sad one, which makes plenty of sense, all things considered. Then she looks back at the hole in the ground. "I keep looking at it, thinking I can jump across."

"Yeah? You've got hops?"

Michelle laughs. "No. Probably not. Even if I did, maybe there's a monster in there, just waiting for us to try, and it'll snatch us when we do. Or it's a black hole, and it'll suck us in any moment now. That's my best theory. Based on what it looked like when we were throwing things into it. What's your theory?"

"I haven't really thought about it," he says. He glances down at the chasm, even though he doesn't like looking into it. He looks up and out the window instead, sees that the sky is lightening. He wants to believe that it's a symbolic sunrise, that all will return to light and normalcy soon. Just the thought gives him hope. Plus, there's his mom, who's the smartest person he knows, taking charge and believing that destroying the light will undo the madness. There are all these people who're spellbound and peaceful. On their faces he can sense the fatigue and the hope combined. No one here will ever complain about travel ever again. "Maybe it's just a blip, you know. A bout of darkness that the world is always susceptible to. Just random dark shit happening, which will pass, just like random good shit passes."

Michelle kisses his jawline. "I don't know if we deserve for dark shit to pass," she says. "All that we've seen today. It's a reflection of all of humanity, no? This happens everywhere, all the time. This is the world. Outside of the airport, the same shit happens. Maybe it makes a little more sense, but not really."

At that moment a group of three men in military garb come through the crowd, carrying what appears to be a replica of Atlanta's Peachtree Street Bridge. They shuffle over toward James's mom. She looks up from the tablet, eyebrow raised. "Uh," she says.

"We heard you were looking for a bridge, ma'am," one of the men says. This is Sergeant Ryan Hill from Little Rock, Arkansas.

He's on his way to his second deployment and eager to provide service to others.

Jaquelyn laughs but then remembers that she's treating this like a lucid dream. "How long is that?" she asks.

"My guess is about fifteen feet, ma'am." He and the others set it down gently on the floor in front of Jaquelyn. "I've been to the real one, and it doesn't seem to be to perfect scale. But maybe it'll do for our purposes. We got it from a display case in the F gates."

James watches as the man and his mom talk for a little while. He holds Michelle close, wanting his touch to ease her mind. Michelle is still staring into the abyss in the terminal when Ryan Hill follows Jaquelyn's orders and confidently steps onto the bridge. It seems to support his weight at first, but when he takes another step forward, his boot goes entirely through the model, sending shards of plastic shooting outward. The other men in military garb laugh at Ryan, who tries to free his foot from the model.

James looks down at Michelle to see if she's cheered up at all by this exchange, but now her eyes are closed and she's breathing in a slow, controlled way. "Just zoom in," James whispers. "Shit gets scary when you look at the big picture. But if you zoom in to individual people, I think you're more likely to feel better about the world." The earth rotates a little more, bringing the sun closer to the horizon in Atlanta. Gold appears over the tree line. Not the sun itself yet. Just a hint of it for now. But it's coming. "Zoom in, and you can see the good."

\\\\\\\\\

In the T gates, Beverly Bingham watches the igloo withstand her attacks, even after the earthquake weakened it. She watches the men at her command grow tired and weary. They're shooting her angry looks. "Keep going," she yells in her best volunteer-during-recess voice. Not as forceful as she'd like, though.

Corey Walford, tired of pounding his fists against the igloo, rests his back against its wall and slides down to the ground. He wheezes, not used to this much cardio. "Lady, if you want to tear down the igloo, be my guest." He gestures toward it. "I'm done." He wipes some freezing sweat from his brow and then gets up, feeling a strangely specific urge to go to the B gates.

Right before he disappears down the escalators, Beverly decides to scream "You'll be sorry!" at him. It's deeply unsatisfying, but at least she gets the final word.

Inside the igloo, Ulf sighs in relief. Thank God, he thinks. They've given up. He offers his housemates a smile. "They've stopped, maybe." He looks up, waiting for the pounding to resume on cue. When it doesn't, his smile spreads. He wants to suggest they play a game, but there is a somber tone in the blue light of the igloo. He hates the pragmatism of the thought, but at least with fewer people inside, the oxygen will last longer.

Throughout the airport, amidst the violence and mourning, amidst the confusion and claustrophobia, the complacency, the despair, the hope, people feel this strange urge to stop what they are doing and move on. Those who succumb to this urge walk almost zombie-like, not knowing exactly where they're headed until they see a sign for Concourse B.

TWENTY-SEVEN

\\\\\\\\\\\\\\\\\\\\\\\\\\\\\\\\

AT THE 35:00 MARK ON ROSA'S PHONE, MICHELLE feels a panic rising inside her. This is not how she wants it all to end. She doesn't know what ending she'd be okay with, but it's not like this. Please not like this. She presses herself as close as she can to James, slips her hand beneath his T-shirt for the comfort of his flesh. Just when the panic is about to hit the surface and break her, she feels a hand on her shoulder.

Her parents appeared in the F gates, floating in the stretch of tile meant to represent the Pacific Ocean, holding hands the way otters do when they sleep, so that they don't drift away from each other. Then they felt the urge, like so many others, and when they arrived in the B gates, they immediately spotted their daughter with the American boy.

Michelle steps away from James and into their arms, tears coming, much different from the ones she was expecting only moments ago. She's always thought her dad smelled a little too much of sweat and garlic, but right now the scent brings her joy. It reminds her of being a kid, getting tucked in every night before bed, his smell wafting over when he'd bring her a glass of water. In the other room, she could hear her brothers playing video games, all the accompanying chatter.

"Où étais-tu?" her father asks.

She pulls herself closer into his chest, reaches out to yank her mom into the hug too. "I'm sorry," she says, in English only because it's been the language of the evening, because it's easier to say the words in a tongue that doesn't feel entirely her own. "I'm going to miss them, and I fucked up the chance to say goodbye. I fucked it all up."

Her father stammers, "Qu'est-ce que tu dit?" Then he remembers, through the fog of the past few hours, her moodiness after the goodbye with his parents, her unusually quiet demeanor. He connects the dots and hugs his daughter tighter. "You didn't fuck up anything," he says, and plants a kiss on the top of her head.

And Michelle knows that. She knows none of this is her fault. She knows the past is so often just a story we tell ourselves, knows her grandparents love her, and that if all this passes, as most things do, she will be able to call them and give them a proper goodbye. She knows that regret—like fear—is something she can overcome. As long as she survives.

The terminal has flooded with people straggling in, unsure why, finding the crowd, then somehow picking up on the plan to speak into the chasm and quickly getting on board with that plan. Stories, confessions, jokes. They all get lobbed into the chasm in a dozen different languages.

Then, an interruption. Jaquelyn Herrera's voice rings out. "All right, everyone," she says. The voices quickly fall silent. "I've got a plan."

\\\\\\\\

James stands back by the wall with Ava. She's still texting her friends, the messages leaving unobstructed as long as they don't mention anything about the airport. He tries opening up with her a few times, telling her that he's glad he's got a little sis, glad that she's okay. But she looks at him like he's had a stroke or two, so he drops it. Pops, who's good with his hands, is helping a few other men assemble the bridge Mom designed. The old model has been cast into the chasm. The airport is a flurry of activity, people pulling nails, screws, and bolts from wherever they can. A human chain passes off wood, cinder blocks, and steel plates pilfered from a construction zone all the way in the T gates. Gold is now undeniably visible in the morning sky, along with the silhouettes of a few dark gray clouds.

Michelle is about fifty feet away, tearfully, happily talking to her parents. It felt a little weird to stand by while they hugged, and even more so when they started up with the French-and-Thai combo. Michelle was speaking so fast and didn't switch over into English, so James kind of backed away. Then his mom told him to stand with Ava, and he thought, Yeah, this makes sense. Family.

With no other assigned job but to keep Ava company, James looks from Michelle to the brightening sky; to Rosa, still standing at the edge of the chasm; back to Michelle. He wonders how much time is left on the countdown. He wonders what happened to the PA guys, if they're standing somewhere in this assembled crowd.

When he looks around again, he's surprised by how many people he sees. Definitely more than were there a minute ago. Some people he recognizes from earlier in the day. The woman who was sobbing in the flower garden is here with her two daughters, holding their hands. That dickhead whose errant punch hit Taha is here too, bleeding from his eyebrow, his clothes tattered, missing a shoe, the light gone from his eyes. Helping because he can no longer think of who to fight.

At airports, James is always wondering if he'll cross paths with anyone around him again, even if neither of them knows it. Now he thinks about this, and he wonders if he's automatically connected to the people who've experienced this layover the way he has. Like, if he runs into Dickhead in another facet of life, will they share a knowing look? Has this experience marked them in some way, or will the connection fade? It's weird how a person's experiences aren't reflected anywhere on the surface. Maybe in the eyes. You have no way of knowing what a person has survived. James yawns, the night catching up with him. He leans his head back against the wall but fights to stay awake.

The concourse fills with the sounds of hammering, people talking to each other instead of to the crack in the ground. Every now and then someone will throw a physical object inside. A shoe, a book, a busted pair of earphones. The laces, the pages, the wires, they all flutter and float for a moment, almost beautiful, like still life, before fading into the dark. Some guy clears the crowd and takes a running start, his arms pumping fiercely, preparing for the jump. But he changes his mind at the last second, skidding to a halt that nearly fails, his toes over the edge when momentum stops. A few artists in the crowd try to sketch the scene into their notebooks, drawing and erasing and redrawing because they can't quite capture the depth of the chasm. The literarily inclined passengers type out story ideas and poems into their phones, wanting to capture this moment for posterity.

A waste of energy, Rosa thinks. 27:27 to go. Her best guess is that the airport will be completely wiped out. She's not thinking an explosion, exactly. This is obviously not terrorism. Her time at the TSA has taught her that it's never a bomb. It's usually something weird, a bunch of shredded wires kept in a ball, a sex toy. Lotion. It's always lotion. She'd love it if that were the case here, just a big splash of lotion over everything, then the doors open to the world.

She sighs and notices James standing off to the side. She walks over to him with a little nod.

"Hey," he says. "How much time is left?"

"You think it means something?"

James shrugs. "Probably not. Just curious."

They both look out at the terminal. There are so many people working on the project that it's hard to tell what stage they're at, if they'll manage to get across. "I was supposed to be home by now," Rosa says, a quiver in her voice.

"Yeah, me too," James says softly. His eyes flit back over to Michelle, as if he can feel the time with her ticking away. Three guys carrying a picnic table pass by, taking quick, short, shuffling steps and sweating. "You ever had a day like today?"

Rosa scoffs. "C'mon, bro. You serious?"

"I dunno. I've been checking my phone all day, and there's been nothing about us in the news or anything. It's like we're in some secret dimension. Which makes me think this could have happened before. Maybe all over the world, every day, crazy shit is happening that gets kept secret."

"Wouldn't all those people be talking about it, though? We'd hear about it."

"I guess," James says. He makes himself look away from Michelle. Ava's still busy on her phone, chill as hell. Chiller than everyone else here. He's happy she got spared the worst of it. His mom's now walking over to where the hammering is happening. She looks down at her schematics, then says something to a woman in a tank top. The woman listens, then nods and returns to whatever it is she's doing. Something that sounds suspiciously like a drill rings out. "I just like the idea that this isn't the craziest thing that's ever happened, you know? That it's a lot more normal than it feels."

Rosa sighs, and she runs a hand through her hair, tugging surreptitiously at the roots. She wants to feel something superficial, not this gaping emptiness that's threatening to overrun her. "Weird how that happens, right? Feeling a fear on your own is a lot scarier than if you've got someone with you."

"For sure . . . ," James says, his voice trailing off. Michelle is hugging her parents again, her head resting on her mom's shoulder, eyes closed, soft smile. His heart flutters with joy, and then a part of his brain goes: Shit.

"Hey, do me a favor?" Rosa says.

James turns to her, forgetting what they were talking about. "Hmm?"

She pulls her phone out of her pocket, making sure to keep it facedown. "Hang on to this. I'm sick of looking at it."

\\\\\\\\

At the fourteen-minute mark, Jaquelyn calls out, "I think we've got it," and the entire concourse bursts into cheers and applause. Most people aren't exactly sure what it is they're applauding, but it feels good to cheer. About 50 percent of the survivors in the airport are now in this concourse, crowding the hallways and the gates, the restaurants, the bathrooms even. They clap their hands together and whoop. They have vague notions of the mission and the timer, have no idea that all of this is to get to a light that may not have anything to do with the day's events; they're just glad to be a part of something that is not destructive, something that is not clearly motivated by fear and worry.

The crowd moves aside to let the crew of workers lift up Jaquelyn's creation. James tries to get a closer look, dragging Ava with him, but most of the people around him are moving in too. He can see about fifteen people hauling something massive but can't make out the details. He's afraid the crowd will turn into another mob and rush the creation, destroying their only hope. Elbows keep digging into his ribs, slight shoves move him aside. The crew moves the slab of materials that'll serve as their bridge toward the edge. He can hear his mom's voice calling out further instructions, but no matter how many "excuse me"s he mutters, no one lets him through. He's lost sight of Rosa already, which makes him whip his head around, looking for Michelle.

All he sees are strangers. He holds Ava tighter by the wrist, and she complains loudly but makes no motion to pry her hand away. James stands on his tiptoes, but he can't catch sight of anyone. Fuck, fuck, fuck. He checks Rosa's phone. Twelve minutes to go. What if he won't ever see Michelle again? What if this crowd doesn't disperse in time? What if none of what they're doing matters at all, and all that has mattered is the countdown? What if this is it? James's last moments alive?

He hears a massive thud, and the crowd erupts in more

cheers. He tries to focus on his breathing, but his lungs ignore him. They suck in air, quick and shallow, and James soon feels his head start to spin. There are too many people here, there's too much noise. He can hear every instance of clapping, can hear every individual voice that's adding to this cacophony of human noise. He can't hear Michelle at all, can't hear the sirens of fire trucks and ambulances coming to the rescue. Dread claws its way down his throat, into his stomach. A pain shoots across his ribs.

Then, silence. James is sure it's the airport fucking with him again. If not that, then it's his panic attack intensifying. What a way to spend your last twelve minutes alive. He begs his lungs to work like they usually do, begs the despair to leave his insides, begs the thoughts he's having to banish themselves from his head.

Among all this despair, one other thought—quieter than the others, but still there. He's glad to have met Michelle.

Then everyone in the concourse turns to look in his direction, and one by one they step aside. James furrows his brow in confusion. Ava looks up at him and whispers, "What's going on?"

"I don't know," he manages to say, though his mouth is completely dry, and it feels like he hasn't spoken since they got off the plane from Tampa.

The human sea eventually parts and reveals his parents. They're standing side by side, their arms around each other.

They beckon him over with a gentle wave of the hand, and James starts walking toward them. He checks the countdown. Ten minutes.

A few feet before he reaches his parents, they step to the side too. Behind them is Michelle, fiddling with her nose ring. In a daze, he walks toward her. She takes his hand, and he instantly relaxes. At least he's had this.

They face forward. He can see his mom's creation now, a simple bridge that stretches up and over the chasm. It's made up of dozens of materials, surprisingly sturdy but also obviously a last-minute collaboration between desperate strangers. All around James and Michelle, smiles flashing, thumbs up in the air, strangers with hope in their eyes.

"What are we doing?" James asks.

"It's time, I think," Michelle says. "It's time for this to be over."

TWENTY-EIGHT

TAKING THE FIRST STEPS ONTO THE BRIDGE FEELS LIKE boarding a rocket ship. A certain amount of pride and hope, with equal parts fear and what the fuck am I doing? It almost feels like James should be wearing a space suit, one of those huge astronaut helmets that make breathing sound very dramatic.

Michelle squeezes James's hand. It's so easy to tell when he's nervous, or rattled. It's like they've been trading off this feeling back and forth between them. "Hey, we're gonna be okay," she says. They step forward, the makeshift bridge sturdy beneath them.

"You think so?"

Michelle shrugs. "Sure, why not?" James laughs nervously and rubs his thumb along Michelle's. "How much time do we have?"

"Nine minutes," James says. He's got the phone in his hand

as they walk. Michelle is holding a metal rod she grabbed from the construction crew, who have no idea why these two kids are at the forefront of the plan but still feel proud to have helped. "We should be good," he says. Which is a stupid thing to say in this particular hellscape, on this particular day.

Here comes the aftershock.

Jonah Friedrichs in Gainesville, Georgia, looks at the seismograph and shakes his head, completely unaware of the events unfolding in Atlanta. He blows on his tea and takes a sip, wondering which machine is malfunctioning.

Due to the time constraints, the makeshift bridge was not built with any sort of handrails. James's mom had enough foresight to predict that another quake could conceivably happen, so the bridge itself holds. But it does start to rock, and James and Michelle get hit with a dangerous bout of vertigo. They have to fall to their knees to avoid toppling over the edge. Michelle looks backward and sees many in the crowd do the same. For the umpteenth time during this layover, screams fill the air. Children and adults alike wail and weep, unsure of what else to do. The desire to flee, again, takes hold in several passengers. They resist for a moment, until someone shouts out, "The chasm! It's growing."

Michelle peers over the edge of the bridge and sees that it's true. The rift between the two halves of the hallway is spreading. They're about halfway across the bridge. Behind them, the anonymous yell has unleashed what appears to be a full-on stampede. Those unfortunate enough to take to the ground brace themselves for uncaring boots. They curl up into balls and protect their heads.

But the people in the B concourse have had enough of trampling. They've had enough of the airport turning them against each other, have had enough of concern for only their own safety. They can't stand to see another person hurt, can't stand to see any more pain in this goddamn world. Those who want to flee help people up on their way, strangers' hands reaching out to each other. Aside from a couple of bruises and the occasional sprained ankle, the stampede causes no harm.

The chasm, however, keeps spreading.

"We have to move!" Michelle says to James.

"Let's wait for it to stop."

"No," Michelle says. "We don't have time." She starts crawling her way forward, keeping her eyes on the green light. Behind them, a section of the floor gives way, causing the bridge to jolt violently. James's body gets shifted out of balance, and his legs go sprawling over the edge. Everyone in the crowd who is still watching gasps. Jaquelyn Herrera holds her breath, and Ava whimpers. She's been keeping all her fear at bay with her phone, but seeing her brother dangle over an abyss brings it all into her gut. Roger Sterlinger, who in this situation would normally be curled up into the tightest ball possible, in the most remote corner possible, stands calmly in the middle of the mayhem. He speaks, mostly to himself: "They're going to make it."

James screams out in fear but manages to hang on to a crack

in the bridge, the minuscule space between two pieces of plastic. Michelle scrambles to him, holding his arms. "I've got you," she says, not sure how true it is. "I've got you. Come on."

James tries to swing his legs back onto the bridge. He can't quite get them over, though, and the momentum of them falling back makes his grip weaken. "Michelle, I don't think I can." He grunts, this time trying to lift himself up with his arm strength. But the night's been so long, his body is tired. His knuckles tighten with pain. "I don't want it to be over."

"Try again," Michelle says calmly. "This isn't how it ends."

James looks into her eyes. Amazing how, even now, there's a part of him that sees her and feels nervous. Maybe he should just let himself slip right now. Let her face be the last thing he sees, instead of whatever destruction the airport has planned for them, whatever other horrors life has planned for him. Immediately after this thought, his brain shoots back that he hasn't lived long enough. So much he hasn't done. There's been plenty of good too. But it's hard to think of that side of the equation. Hard to add up all the joy in a life and think: Okay, that was enough. Hard to think he's had enough time with Michelle.

"James," Michelle says, more firmly. "This isn't how it ends. This isn't how we say goodbye."

He takes a breath and remembers: he is tired of fear. It is not all that useful, and it wants him to ignore all the control that rests in his hands. It ignores all the beauty and goodness that can exist in an absurd, scary world.

He nods at Michelle, then tries again. On this attempt, she

pulls at the same time, and despite the fact that the shaking is still happening, he manages to bring himself back over the edge. Michelle takes him into her arms, and they embrace. Behind them, the portion of the crowd that has not sprinted away in terror feels a lightness in their chests. At least this, they think. Small proof of our capacity for good. If any of the day's events are remembered, let it be this embrace between two young people.

The bridge jolts again. They look at each other, understanding. Then they clamor toward the other side of the hallway, the bridge groaning beneath them, scraping horribly against the floor. James and Michelle spill onto the tile moments before the chasm expands beyond the bridge's length and the entire thing disappears into nothingness.

The crowd strains to see if James and Michelle made it. No one wants to cheer, but the relief is palpable in the concourse. The Herreras all breathe easy.

Panting, Michelle turns to James. "You okay?" When he nods, she starts to stand, brushing herself off. "How much time do we have?"

James slides his hand into his pocket, feels nothing. He stands up and feels in his other pocket. Nothing. He does that thing where he taps at every single one of his pockets, even though he knows damn well there's nothing in there. In the abyss, the phone continues to count down. Three minutes to go.

Michelle picks up on the act. "Doesn't matter," she says. She bends over to grab the metal rod and starts walking toward the green light. "Let's hurry."

James trots to catch up to her, still patting at his pockets like he can't believe the phone is gone. Within a few seconds, they're standing in front of the light again. They're wearing some different clothing items than they were when they met, and James is missing his backpack. There are a few bumps and bruises on their bodies and about fifteen hours' worth of shared experiences between them.

Michelle raises the metal rod to bash the damn thing into oblivion right away. Mid-swing, she has sudden doubts that it's to blame for anything at all. It is not the embodiment of her regret, is not the universe lashing out at her for being cruel to her grandparents. Maybe it is just a camera looking out at them, something simple and boring, not nefarious and otherworldly. A smoke detector that's perfectly functional, a light meant to guide passengers to an exit in case of an emergency. Either way, she means to bash it to hell.

Across the hallway, people start to look at their own phones to check the time. Or anxiety tightens their chests until they feel like they can no longer breathe. Roger Sterlinger can still breathe, but he feels that old anxiety returning to him, and he bows his head in acceptance, tears in his eyes, knowing he'll have to live with it again, fight through it every day again.

All around the airport, muscles twitch in anticipation. Even the people who aren't around to witness the moment feel that something is about to happen. They're not sure if it's good or bad, but their bodies seem to sense the significance.

For Ulf Pshyk it's a leg twitch, something that hasn't happened to him since he was a child, sitting for long hours in a classroom. As he's remembering this, water from above starts dripping down on him. For Beverly Bingham, it's her eyelid. She practically growls at it, as if it's nothing but a misbehaving child. Then she tries to rub it away, almost on the verge of tears when it refuses.

A Japanese businessman known to his friends as Carrots feels the twitch in his tongue, almost a tingling, like tasting something sweet first thing in the morning. Carrots has been at a sports bar the whole night with a group of other travelers, mostly American businessmen. It's felt a little like a marathon of *Cheers,* a show he loves deeply. The twitch in his tongue makes him fear the night is over.

Sonja Kersenovich, a Serbian surgeon who built herself a fort out of her clothes in the D gates, feels it in her abdomen, a little pulse of tension that feels almost like indigestion. Indigestion is, in fact, her initial assumption, until she realizes the twitch runs a little deeper, at which point she assumes it is her soul chastising her for cowering away all night when there could have been a need for surgeons in the airport. Certainly some of the screams she's heard indicated conditions that could have been treated by a medic.

And so on and so forth, the thousands of human lives in the

airport feel . . . something. Outside, millions of human lives in Atlanta and around the world also feel something, but that something is more varied than a muscle twitch. It's a whole array of somethings. Fear that the world is getting worse and worse and that human beings are irredeemable. A craving for carrot cake. A sharp pain in the tendon that connects the shin to the front of the foot, and slight concern that it seems to have come from nowhere, slight concern at the aches and pains of having a body. They feel an indecisiveness about how to spend the day. A deep appreciation that nature or God or the universe made it so that the simple spinning of the world around the sun creates the beauty of the sunrise. A wonder for the gift of flight, the ability to traverse great distances in a single day. An intense frustration that a goddamn mosquito attacked again last night, and now there'll be an itchy arm to deal with for at least the day ahead.

The sun pokes out from above the tree line surrounding Hartsfield-Jackson Atlanta International Airport. Michelle swings the rod forward.

TWENTY-NINE

\\\\\\\\\\\\\\\\\\\\\\\\\\\\\\

IT'S HARD TO TELL EXACTLY IN WHICH ORDER THESE things happen, but here's what happens next:

Michelle perfectly hits the green light with the metal rod. The light shatters, and the fixture itself comes cleanly off the wall. It leaves no mark behind, no exposed wires, no evidence that it's connected to anything else in the airport, no evidence that it ever was. It shoulders the blame for the day's events, as something must. People do not like the inexplicable or the tragic to get away without a scapegoat.

Rosa's phone, previously suspended somewhere in nothingness, now clatters to the floor at her feet. The timer is gone, her usual home screen returned. The background is a picture of her cat, Justin, obscured now by dozens of notifications from her friends, her mom, Steve. The time reads 7:43 a.m.

Flight monitors across the terminal update, providing new departure times for every flight scheduled. The chasm disappears; the control tower outside reappears. The temperature across the concourses regulates. All invisible barriers to exit the airport disappear, as do any tunnels and creatures that shouldn't technically exist but did for a while there. The brown thrasher perched on the fence surrounding the airport opens its eyes, flutters its wings, and takes off.

Michelle drops the rod, which hits the floor with a clang. This is the sound that lets James know he's still alive. He didn't mean to close his eyes, and it's only when he opens them that he realizes how tightly shut they were. He surveys the scene, waits for the next insane thing to happen. A cartoon Tasmanian devil tearing through the hallway. A dragon, or something. Instead, it looks rather . . . normal. Everyone in the airport kind of has the same expression on their faces, like they're bracing for something. There's still broken glass shimmering in the hallways, rows of seats where they shouldn't be, a complete absence of garbage cans, since they were all tossed into the chasm. But other than that, nothing. The sun is beaming now, bright rays dipping into the terminal, turning everything golden. The bridge his mom designed is in the middle of the hallway, tipped on its side, clearly damaged. There's no one trapped beneath it, but there are bloodied people around it, too shocked to cry.

James and Michelle lock eyes, both somewhat surprised that the other is still there. Real all along.

"Did it work?" Michelle whispers.

"I think?" James looks around, muscles still tense. He scratches his head. "I don't know. It's hard to tell." That's when he hears it. From the bookstore/café next door: music. Nothing particularly good. A generic singer-songwriter tune, coffee-house inoffensive. He can't help himself. He laughs.

Michelle feels the joy of his smile before she hears the music too. A beautiful smile that she'll miss seeing. Then the chords reach her ears, and her eyes widen, because the music sounds normal. "James, I think it worked." She takes two short steps to close the distance between them, and she holds him as close as she possibly can.

\\\\\\\\

Thirty minutes later Asiana flight 247 to Anchorage, Alaska, begins to board, the first plane at Hartsfield-Jackson Atlanta to be cleared for departure in over fifteen hours. A slew of PA announcements offer apologies on the airport's behalf and update travelers on typical airport protocol, reminding them to report any suspicious activity and not let strangers pack their bags for them. All gates with scheduled flights are staffed by their typical airline crews, unless some of them died during the last few hours, in which case they'll have to make do. Quickly, lines of unhappy customers form.

After clicking through the terms and conditions again, passengers are able to post on social media about the airport and the delays, though the specifics don't show up in their posts and never will. After a few days, most who were present stop trying. They move on. What the world learns about the events that transpired at the airport is from people speaking directly to each other, though the details get muddied by imperfect recollections, by the flimsy hold the human brain has on the past. The books, the movies, the articles—they capture the gist, the most harrowing details, the most heartening moments.

People call their family members and are strangely relieved to hear the sound of actual ringing on the other end. When they start crying at the sound of their loved ones' voices, they can't find the words to explain why. They look out in silence at the terminal, phones pressed to their ears, crying and smiling and not believing that it's all over. That their boarding zone has just been called.

The morning janitorial crew arrive for work. Their jaws drop at the sight of so much glass, at the garbage, the puddles, the blood. Then they shake their heads and promise to themselves that they will look for other jobs when they get home.

Three vans from the Atlanta coroner's office arrive to carry away bodies, the drivers quickly realizing that they are nowhere near enough. In an office somewhere, a public official starts making calls about refrigerated trucks, her stomach dropping as she says the words, disbelieving. The TSA and Homeland Security issue a small statement about the long delay at the airport on their websites, which exactly fifty-four people read. News vans come with their cameras, but almost everyone who could serve as a witness is gone: boarded on flights, clocked out from their shifts, or simply having fled from the building as soon as they could. The relatives of the dead do not want to speak. The reporters stammer on as the bodies and rubble are carried out, adding commentary despite not knowing a thing about what has transpired.

James stands at gate B36, and he feels like running. He watches his family get in line to board flight 1138 to Chicago. His dad gives him a little wave, which prompts Ava to roll her eyes. James scratches the back of his neck and turns to Michelle. She's biting her bottom lip, smiling.

"I can't believe I'm getting on a flight home right now," he says softly.

"Yeah," Michelle says. "I thought we'd never leave."

"I'd almost be okay with it, if I could keep talking to you."

She rolls her eyes again and lays a hand on his chest. "I'm not a good enough conversationalist to justify that."

James runs his hand over his head. The gate attendant announces they are now boarding all zones, all passengers. "Is this really it? I'm not gonna see you anymore?"

Michelle keeps her hand on his chest and steps closer. She rests her head in the nook between his neck and shoulder, breathing him in. "I don't know. I never told you about my grandparents, and I feel I owe you that. Plus, I have a newfound appreciation of what's possible in this life." She plants a kiss on his jawline and takes a single step away. They look at each other for a long time. The line at the gate gets shorter. The sun rises higher in the sky. Rosa Velarde leaves the airport. Roger

Sterlinger tucks his pant leg into his sock. Ulf Pshyk goes into a bathroom and uses paper towels to dry off the icy water clinging to him. In Savannah, a man with Taha's name written on a piece of paper waits at baggage claim for a man who will never show.

"Yeah, me too," James says softly. They kiss, maybe for the last time.

Then the gate attendant announces the final boarding call, in a way that makes it clear she's addressing James Herrera specifically. He steps away from Michelle, though it's the last thing he wants to do. He walks onto the plane and takes his seat next to his sister. He slips his hand in his pocket, remembering the flower from his game with Michelle. It's still there, stripped of its petals. Without his headphones, he can't shut out the sounds of the airplane: the baby wailing a few rows behind, the chatter of two strangers becoming acquainted, the flight attendants asking people to prepare for takeoff. He rests his head back and shuts his eyes gently, his breathing calm and measured.

ACKNOWLEDGMENTS

This book is a reminder that rejection still comes after success. I struggled for years to find a home for my weird trip of a book, as my agent calls it. I'm thankful to Pete Knapp for seeing something in it, and for sticking with the book through the years and a few rounds of "no"s. And I'm extremely thankful that it landed where it did: on Marisa DiNovis's desk so that she could say some incredibly nice things about it, then help me get it into its best possible shape.

After the luck of being consistently published for years, you learn that there are too many people involved in the making of a book to thank them all. Many are even unknown to me, making decisions about the way the book will look in your hands, and how it will come to be there. I'm thankful for every single one of those people on the editorial team at Knopf (the copy editors work such magic, so helpful in a book where the laws of the universe are wobbly), the artists and designers for the jacket (every iteration!), the marketing and sales teams, the book-sellers, librarians, and teachers who put books in kids' hands. And, of course, the readers. You make it so I can keep doing this, and I am immensely thankful for that.

To the readers of early drafts: Jay Coles, Cam Montgomery, Fred Aceves, Elizabeth Eulberg. Your enthusiasm and wisdom carried the book into existence.

To the travelers and employees at Atlanta Hartsfield-Jackson for the inspiration.

To my friends and family, who help me celebrate all my small victories and believe in me before they come.

Thanks to Laura, for being the best person to travel with and the best person to be holed up with and just the best (sorry about the superlatives, Michelle).